THE CLARET PALS

EVAN BALDOCK

The Book Guild Ltd

First published in Great Britain in 2024 by
The Book Guild Ltd
Unit E2 Airfield Business Park,
Harrison Road, Market Harborough,
Leicestershire. LE16 7UL
Tel: 0116 2792299
www.bookguild.co.uk
Email: info@bookguild.co.uk
Twitter: @bookguild

Copyright © 2024 Evan Baldock

The right of Evan Baldock to be identified as the author of this
work has been asserted by them in accordance with the
Copyright, Design and Patents Act 1988.

All rights reserved. No part of this publication may be
reproduced, transmitted, or stored in a retrieval system, in any form or by any means,
without permission in writing from the publisher, nor be otherwise circulated in
any form of binding or cover other than that in which it is published and without
a similar condition being imposed on the subsequent purchaser.

This work is entirely fictitious and bears no resemblance to any persons living or dead.

Typeset in 10.5pt Adobe Garamond Pro

Printed on FSC accredited paper
Printed and bound in Great Britain by 4edge Limited

ISBN 978 1835740 217

British Library Cataloguing in Publication Data.
A catalogue record for this book is available from the British Library.

*To the real Claret Pals, you know who you are.
Thanks for the inspiration.*

ONE

The first time Mario Spiteri saw Gail Grover, she was sitting alone at a table in the pub garden of the Hammer and Sickle, just outside the town centre in Rotherham. His shift as a waiter on that quiet Monday afternoon had been busy, bordering on hectic, but things were beginning to quieten down.

The tabletop where Gail sat was scattered with empty bottles and glasses left by the previous occupants. She seemed oblivious to the mess, her eyes closed and her head tilting up towards the warming rays of the dazzling early August sunshine.

Mario approached her carrying a tray which already contained three empty glasses, neatly balanced on the splayed fingers of his left hand. "Hello, can I clear your table?"

Smiling warmly, she eyed his handsome features and flicked her long, brown hair back. "Sure."

He saw her greedily drinking in his good looks. He was tall, tanned and had thick, shoulder-length, jet-black hair. His slim body and bright-red Hammer and Sickle uniform T-shirt sat atop a pair of tight black trousers. As he leant across to remove the empties, she breathed in the pleasant scent of his aftershave and gently placed a hand on his arm.

That's how it all started, that's how they met, as simple as that. They met twice more that week: a lunchtime coffee in a retro café in the centre of town (just the type of place Mario loved), and an evening meal at a small village pub a couple of miles outside town.

From that first meeting, Mario was utterly beguiled by her: she was attractive, with gorgeous long brunette hair, an athletic body, tight blue jeans, pixie boots and a loose-fitting, lemon-coloured cheesecloth shirt. He adored the classy way she dressed. They'd kissed passionately and enjoyed a quick fumble on their first date, and by their second date, he detected the lingering promise that further delights might be happening soon, very soon… and he couldn't wait.

Mario had always been comfortable around women, but he had never previously experienced such tight excitability deep in his gut, or the pounding chest and light-headed sensations now engulfing him. There had been an instant spark of attraction, a sense that, for once, this relationship might just go somewhere. There was something special between them, something tangible, and they were falling for each other in a big way.

Volunteering for all the shifts going in a bid to earn much-needed money, Mario had been disappointed to be told by Derek, the pub's owner, that he'd already arranged sufficient staff for the Saturday lunchtime shift. It was going to be a busy day for the pub: Rotherham were at home to Burnley in a championship league football match, and there would be large numbers of fans from both clubs in attendance. The place was guaranteed to be packed out, so Derek had arranged staff numbers well in advance, so, sadly, with his late arrival as a staff member, there was no place for Mario.

His disappointment vanished in a heartbeat when Gail called and asked to see him that Saturday. She lived over eighty miles away, close to Blackburn in Lancashire, and had travelled over to Rotherham twice already, so he offered to catch a train over to visit her. After all, it was his turn to make the effort. Surprisingly, she firmly refused, insisting she would drive over to him once again. This left Mario perplexed, but Gail was determined. Not wishing to reject her, he didn't push the matter any further.

He suggested places nearby where they could go out for the day – local beauty spots, or maybe an attractive village in the Dales with a lovely café or pub. He even offered to drive over to Whitby, on the coast. But whatever he thought of, she wasn't interested, asking instead if she could be sneaked into his room above the Hammer and Sickle.

"Every member of staff will be rushed off their feet dealing with customers, nobody will be paying attention to what's going on upstairs, so we'll have the chance to be alone in your room," she said, suggestively.

"I can't risk it. Only staff are allowed upstairs – I'd lose my job if we were found out."

Gail playfully turned on a whiny voice. "Aren't I attractive enough for you?"

"Of course you are."

"Well then?"

Mario smiled, sensing what she was suggesting. "Well then what?"

"Wouldn't you like to see me naked?"

Despite his very real reservations about putting his new-found employment at risk, the throbbing in Mario's groin won the day, and he relented.

When Saturday came, he waited just inside the pub's side door at 12.30 with bated breath, listening out for the five knocks they'd agreed on. When he heard them, he quickly opened the door and looked up and down the alley in both directions. The coast was clear, so he ushered her inside and closed the door.

They kissed passionately and he found her scent utterly intoxicating; then he held her at arm's length, drinking in her beauty. He loved the trendy combat trousers and tight navy-blue T-shirt she was wearing. Her long, brunette, wavy hair tumbled over her shoulders, and the hint of a sultry smile played constantly on her lips. The straps of the tiny rucksack she was carrying stretched over each shoulder and under her arms, perfectly pulling the T-shirt a little tighter over her breasts.

Gail was ten years older than Mario, but he couldn't have cared less. In his eyes, she had the most gorgeously pretty face, a great body, and to cap it all, a lovely personality. She was perfect. *Fuck, she looks good!* he thought.

They skipped upstairs, the possibility of being caught by another member of staff had raised Mario's ardour to previously unexperienced levels. He'd heard tales of how the risk of getting caught increased sexual sensation, but he'd never personally experienced it.

Reaching the top of the stairs, they heard voices around the corner of the landing and Mario's heart sank – his room was around that corner, up another small flight of sticky-carpeted steps. At that very moment, the sounds of a busy bar wafted up the stairs – the door from the bar area had been opened, meaning someone might come up. They couldn't go downstairs, but if they continued around the corner of the landing, they would be discovered… they were trapped.

TWO

Mario desperately didn't want to lose his job, yet here they were, about to be caught. Thinking quickly, he opened the door closest to the top of the stairs and, pulling Gail with him, stepped inside. Closing the door quietly, he pressed his ear to the wood, his heart beating hard, his breathing laboured.

Unintentionally, he'd dragged her into one of the pub's stockrooms, a room containing boxes of crisps, peanuts, soft drinks, spare bedding and a single rickety chair. They were both panting heavily with excitement, falling into each other's arms and giggling like naughty children, each one holding a raised finger to their lips, urging the other to keep quiet. Hearing the voices on the landing getting nearer, Mario recognised they belonged to Derek and his wife, Daisy. They were arguing heatedly about something. This wasn't unusual, they were always arguing, but right at that moment, he couldn't make out what the disagreement was about.

Their footsteps were suddenly right outside the stockroom door, where they stopped and continued shouting at each other about the amount of money he spent on gambling. Then, when he thought all was lost, and Derek would enter the stockroom for supplies, Mario heard their voices receding. They were going back downstairs, and it didn't sound like anybody else was around. He blew out a controlled breath of relief.

Gail stepped forward and grabbed Mario's crotch, pushing him back against the shelving and kissing him heatedly, her passion and intent obvious.

"I want you, right here, right now!"

He shook his head. "We can't, not in here."

He tried breaking away, pulling her towards the door. "Come on, my bedroom's just around the corner."

But Gail wasn't moving; she squeezed his crotch again, growling in a shouted whisper, "No. Right here, right now!"

He tried resisting but could feel himself weakening. He really, really wanted her.

"But someone might come in. If we're caught, I'll be sacked and thrown out – I'll lose my job and my home. It's too risky."

Completely ignoring his concerns and unzipping his shorts, Gail said in a voice dripping with sexual tension, "Exactly... and that's what makes it fun!"

She pushed him down onto the wooden chair and whispered into his ear while flicking a tongue inside and sucking his earlobe, "I'm going to do something to you I'll bet you've never experienced before."

His eyes met hers and he knew he was beaten; slowly nodding his head, he capitulated. Offering no further resistance to her advances, Mario submitted to the blood pumping through his groin and the desperate longing to enjoy whatever pleasures Gail had in mind. They kissed warmly, tongues eagerly exploring. When their lips parted, she stepped behind him and began rubbing his shoulders. The anticipation was driving him insane.

Suddenly Gail grabbed a handful of his shoulder-length jet-black hair, pulled his handsome, tanned head back and ran her tongue over his lips. Her eyes were fixed on his, her breath warm on his face, their foreheads only a few centimetres apart. "Are you ready for your surprise?"

Mario nodded urgently; he'd only met her a week ago, yet already true love flashed in his eyes. Suddenly, he wasn't in the slightest bit worried about getting caught – all he could think about was how much he wanted this wonderful woman.

"Yes, I'm ready."

He ran his fingers through her dangling locks, moving them aside to better see her gorgeous face. "Gail, I want you so much."

Reaching across Mario's neck with her right hand, Gail pressed the brand-new pruning saw hard into his flesh and dragged the blade firmly across his throat, tearing through skin, flesh, muscle and tendons, causing firstly small spurts, then a torrent of blood to pour from the horribly messy wound.

Standing behind him, she avoided the blood as it gushed from his neck. Which was just as well, because very shortly she would be back out in the busy streets, and she didn't want to be covered in a red, sticky mess.

Seconds earlier, when Mario had spoken his words of longing, he'd been looking up into Gail's face, his eyes were fixed on hers, so misted with lust that he didn't see the small pruning saw she had pulled from the long pocket of her combat trousers. He didn't see her unfolding it against her leg and gripping the handle tightly as she'd pulled his head back, but he certainly felt it as she pressed it into his flesh and ripped his throat apart.

In the two or three seconds it had taken her to slice his neck open, Mario experienced an explosion of agony, followed by a surge of panic. A panic that became utter terror as he tried to breathe and felt himself unable to draw a lungful of air, the horrific sound of bubbling, gurgling and popping sounds only heightening his fear. As he felt warm liquid filling his lungs, he wanted to cough and choke. But try as he might, he simply couldn't. His hands moved involuntarily to his neck in an utterly futile attempt to stem the tsunami of blood.

Mario slipped from the chair, gurgling in wide-eyed horror. His vision had become erratic: one second it was clear, the next blurring wildly. Yet, despite his sight going in and out of focus, he gained the vaguest image of Gail reaching down and dropping something onto him, before she walked out of the room and closed the door, leaving him to struggle alone.

He could sense his life force rapidly deserting his body, and his fear reached new heights. He began thrashing in his panic, his body contorting as he struggled for the breath that might just save him. He was trying desperately to find a position that would allow him to breathe again, but there was no chance. As he writhed, lying on his side in a growing pool of his own blood, Mario slipped into the inky darkness, which reached out and grasped him tightly, before enveloping him completely.

Opening her rucksack on the landing, Gail quickly removed the red hoodie with 'Rotherham FC' on the back and put it on, pulling the hood up and forward, concealing her face as much as possible. She'd worn it on her way to the pub to ensure she couldn't be identified by CCTV, only removing it once she was safely in the alleyway and before knocking on the door. Not only that, but she'd used the name Gail throughout her time with Mario – he never knew her real name was Gretchen.

As she exited the pub through its side door and moved from the alley back onto the roadway, Gretchen's heart was hammering, and she felt sick with fear.

THREE

"Ginny, Jack, over here!" Ian Calvert waved his arm to attract their attention, while making certain he spilled none of his full pint of beer. Ian was sporting a pair of black Nike trainers, knee-length, light-blue shorts and an old-fashioned Burnley FC football shirt with the number 10 on the back. Now in his mid-fifies, his once thick, brown hair had turned to grey, but his ready smile and bubbly personality made him appear younger than his years, endearing him to anyone he met.

It was approaching 1.00 when Ginny and Jack heard Ian's calls above the noise of about one hundred chattering football fans and the gradually increasing sound of approaching police sirens. Spotting him through the throng, they made their way through the crowded rear garden of the Hammer and Sickle, joining him standing at the end of a bench table.

"Good to see you!" said a delighted Jack, walking up and shaking Ian's hand vigorously.

"You too, it's been a long time," said Ian, before giving Ginny a hug and a peck on the cheek. "Have you had a good summer?"

"Yes thanks," said Ginny. "We spent a wonderful month on a narrowboat." She leant forward and muttered into Ian's ear, "I'm glad the footy season's here again, though."

As they exchanged the usual pleasantries of friends who hadn't seen each other for a while, Jack could see something in Ian's demeanour wasn't quite right. He wasn't his usual laid-back, full-of-fun self. In fact, he looked distracted. "Are you alright, mate?"

"Yeah, yeah, it's nothing," said Ian, forcing a smile.

"It must be something."

Ian scratched his head firmly with his right hand. "It's just that, outside the pub, I thought…" He stopped himself and gave a dismissive wave with his left hand. "Honestly, it's nothing. Just me being daft. Let's talk about something else. How have you both been?"

Moments later, they were joined by the rest of their colleagues in the 'Claret Pals' – a small bunch of Burnley football fans who regularly met up before matches… especially away matches.

Burnley Football Club are nicknamed the Clarets, and during the First World War, many 'Pals' regiments were formed in Lancashire. Most famously the Accrington Pals, a quarter of which came from Burnley and were known separately as the Burnley Pals. Fans within The Claret Pals were friends who followed Burnley all over the country, hence their group's name.

Every one of them was super excited to be at this game. It was the first away match of a new season; they would be getting their first sightings of three new signings purchased during the summer transfer window; and today was a reasonably easy trip to make… away at Rotherham, only seventy miles from Burnley!

One of the group, Ryan Pryce, was a tall, stocky, powerfully built man, with short, dark-brown hair. His round face rarely gave away what he was feeling inside, which meant his viewpoint was often sought by others, because his opinion was not easily swung by emotion.

Stepping forward, he shook hands with Jack, his large right hand squeezing Jack's almost painfully. He was about to greet Ginny, when his mobile phone sounded its barking dog ringtone. Ryan paused as he looked at the screen, and his face reddened. Instead of hugging Ginny, he simply waved a hand at her in greeting and held his phone up for all to see. "Sorry, I need to take this."

He swiped the screen upwards theatrically with a forefinger to answer the call, indicating he was answering a video call. This was confirmed as he smiled at the screen and moved well away from the group, standing in a far corner of the garden, where he would be able to speak privately.

Those Ryan had left behind cast puzzled glances in his direction. His matching navy-blue shorts, T-shirt and trainers perfectly suited his usual calm and unruffled manner, but this secretive behaviour seemed completely out of character.

"What's up with him?" asked Ian, jutting his chin in Ryan's direction over the top of his pint.

"Never seen him answer a call like that before. I reckon he's got himself a bird," laughed Simon, another of the group, who travelled down from the Scottish borders to most games.

FOUR

Ryan was delighted to see Gretchen's pretty features filling the screen and smiling back at him, although he was confused as to why she was calling him.

"Hi, how's things?" he asked. She grinned broadly, moving her face closer to the screen. "I'm good. What's all that noise in the background? Where are you?"

"I'm in Rotherham with the Pals – we're in the garden of a pub called the Hammer and Sickle."

He smiled as she stretched out on her bed, stroking her duvet absent-mindedly.

"Have you just got up, you lazy cow?" he joked. "It's lunchtime!"

"No, I've been up for hours. I had a late night out with a couple of girlfriends. It's left me with a hangover. I've just had a nap and I'm feeling better now."

Ryan playfully turned his bottom lip over. "Gretchen, can I ask you something?"

She nodded.

"I understand why you split up with John, but why have you stopped coming to matches? I miss you… it's not the same."

She smiled, her face reddening.

"I only ever went to games to keep John happy. I've never been a big football fan, and to be honest I couldn't face turning up at matches with him there."

She could see the disappointment on Ryan's face and a few seconds passed in silence.

"I hope you're not too upset… you're still my friend, aren't you?"

His heart leapt. Ryan loved Gretchen; he'd loved her from the moment they met three years ago.

"Of course I am."

Ginny and Jack were chatting enthusiastically with more members of the Pals: Stuart, Becki, Joe and Val. As new members arrived, they greeted them all with nods, raised glasses or waved hands.

To celebrate everyone being back together, one of their number leant back and shouted into the air, "E-I-E-I-E-I-O, up the football league we go!"

Every Burnley fan in the pub garden joined in.

"When we win promotion, this is what we'll sing: we are Burnley, we are Burnley, Stevie G is King!"

The weather was overcast but warm, and fans from both teams were happily mingling, red-and-white mixed with claret-and-blue football shirts in the pub garden. Each of them excitedly, but nervously, anticipating the first match of a new campaign after twelve long weeks of the close season.

Another of the Pals was John Horsfall. Like Ian, he was in his mid-fifties, and hailed from Barley, a pretty hillside village that rests in stunning countryside at the foot of Pendle Hill – a flat-topped mini mountain towering over the town of Burnley.

He welcomed Jack and Ginny with a firm shake of the hand for Jack and a kiss on the cheek and hug for Ginny.

Holding up his glass enquiringly, he said in his deep Lancashire drawl, "Can I get you both a drink?"

"I'd love a pint of bitter please," replied Ginny. She looked around but couldn't see John's girlfriend. This was unusual – she was normally standing alongside him at most games. "Where's Gretchen?"

John pursed his lips. "We've split up – she dumped me a couple of weeks ago. We had an almighty row, and that was that." He looked wistful for a few seconds, but then he brightened. "To be honest, I don't blame her; I'm probably a nightmare to be with."

He mustered a forced grin, although everyone could see the sadness in his eyes.

"That's a shame," said Jack. "I liked Gretchen. She was a laugh."

"Me too," said John, his expression quickly becoming thoughtful. "I thought we had something special." He shrugged. "Wasn't to be though."

Ginny's face was a mask of concern; she could feel John's hurt but wanted to know more. "But you were together for years – what on earth caused you to break up?"

Looking down at his feet, John gave the merest of shrugs. "I think she was fed up with how I treated her. You know, coming second best to Burnley all the time!"

Ginny's concerned face swiftly transformed into a wide grin. "Yep, that would have done it for most women!" Then she qualified her statement. "I wouldn't have minded though, because any man in my life would come second to Burnley too!" She wrapped an arm around Jack's waist and playfully pulled him close. "Isn't that right?"

Moving the conversation back to what he considered a hugely more important topic, John lifted his glass. "Now then, this beer, which one do you fancy?"

"I don't mind – you choose – I'm quite shallow, so anything will do. I normally go for the one with the silliest name," said Ginny.

John laughed. "That's easy in this pub, a pint of Hopfart for you!"

Ginny giggled. "Hopfart? That's brilliant! I want a pint of that!"

"What about you, Jack?"

"Diet Coke please, no ice or lemon."

"Righto, back in a mo." Downing the last few drops of his pint, he headed off through the throng of supporters towards the pub's rear door.

As John disappeared, Becki sidled up to Ian, linking her arm with his, a mischievous smile playing on her face as she looked at Ginny. "I've got something to tell you about Gretchen, haven't I, Ian?"

Raising his eyes to the heavens, Ian shook his head, his face turning scarlet.

Ginny noticed his discomfort, a reaction which piqued her interest. "Ooh, do tell."

Releasing her link with Ian's arm, Becki smiled at Ginny. "Long before you and Jack joined the Pals, and shortly before Gretchen went out with John, Ian had a thing going with her for a while, didn't you?"

She prodded him playfully, demanding a response.

Ian rolled his eyes, his features reddening even more. "It was nothing," he said, dismissively. "We were only together a few weeks – John's been with her for six years!"

"That's true, but she wasn't happy when you dumped her after you argued about you going to matches, was she? She was like a bear with a sore head for a while!"

Ian swept his hands flamboyantly down over his face and body. "Come on, Becks! What woman would be happy to lose all this? She's only human. She reacted just like any other woman would have – devastated!" He grinned for a moment, then became serious. "Joking apart, she started seeing John less than a fortnight after we broke up, so she couldn't have been too upset, could she?"

The laughter at Ian's vanity slowly subsided, and as it did so, Ryan finished his call and returned to the group, walking straight into a barrage of ribbing and questions.

"Who was the bird on the phone?"

"Are you shagging at last?"

"What's her name?"

His face turning beetroot red, Ryan stared at his pint, saying nothing and shaking his head ruefully, fighting to restore his usual calm exterior.

The ribbing subsided quickly though, and conversation returned once again to the subject of the upcoming match.

FIVE

The call from Gretchen meant more to Ryan than he could ever reveal to his friends. She might have believed he was just a friend, the Pals might have believed they were just friends, but to Ryan, their relationship meant something entirely different – he was completely and utterly besotted with her.

He'd been a member of The Claret Pals for three years, having been introduced by the mother hen of the group, Becki Murton. The instant he was introduced to Gretchen, he wanted her, despite how happy she appeared to be with John. To Ryan, she was the perfect woman: attractive, friendly, full of fun and a great listener.

But she was devoted to John, and John was a man Ryan thought the world of, so he'd just had to swallow down his pain… and wait.

Slowly but surely, Ryan whittled his way into Gretchen's affections. She was John's girlfriend, he understood that, and he had no intention of interfering in their happiness; he just wanted to place himself in prime position should that situation ever change.

Throughout the call, he'd wanted to ask her so many questions. Why won't she come to matches anymore? After all, she could go with him, and he'd keep her well away from John.

Why was she calling *him* and not one of the others? Would she like to go out for a drink sometime? Ryan knew those questions must wait; all he wanted was to get closer to Gretchen, much closer. But he didn't want to drive her away by seeming too keen.

There would be perfectly reasonable explanations why she was behaving like she was, he was sure of that. He'd bide his time and ask her in person when he got the chance. One thing he knew for certain – too many questions would push her away, and he'd waited far too long for this moment to allow that to happen. So, for the time being, he said nothing.

It would all be worth it in the long run; Gretchen was the woman he was destined to be with, he was convinced of that, and he would do whatever was necessary to ensure she realised that.

And that meant, for now, he couldn't mention to the rest of the Pals that it was Gretchen who'd called.

SIX

Heading through the garden to get Jack and Ginny's drinks, John made his way past the throng of fans and into the pub's rear entrance. But, within seconds, he was backing quickly out of the door, being ushered out by three police officers and two PCSOs sporting bright-yellow jackets, their faces set with grim determination.

"Right, listen up," bellowed the largest and oldest officer, his commanding voice instantly drawing silence from fans in the garden. "There has been a serious incident inside, which has now been cordoned off as a crime scene. The pub is closed, so can you all leave quickly and quietly through the rear gate. Officers are waiting outside to take down your contact details."

Confused looks on faces urged the officer to clarify the necessity for details being taken. "Some of you may unknowingly have vital information."

Holding out an arm, he indicated a gate being held open by a distressed-looking woman in the pub's uniform Hammer and Sickle T-shirt. The gate led out into an alley along one side of the pub.

A chorus of boos and loud groans erupted from the fans, who up until then had been thoroughly enjoying their day out. A small group of Rotherham supporters began singing

'We shall Not Be Moved', which made some of the Pals chuckle.

Nevertheless, they quickly finished their drinks and headed for the gate. The garden was clearing slowly, and more officers emerged from the pub to assist their colleagues in collecting details from the disgruntled punters.

"What the fuck's happened in there?" mused Becki, pushing her glasses back up her nose, her usually jolly face sporting a rare frown.

Becki Murton was popular with everyone in the group – a vibrant character with a huge personality, she was nearly always cheerful and bubbly. It was often Becki who brought the group together at matches, posting which pubs to meet up at on The Claret Pals WhatsApp group. And it was always Becki who suggested a tray of shots before they headed off to the stadium.

Ryan was the only one to reply. "I've no idea. I was in the pub twenty minutes ago and it was a great atmosphere. Plenty of singing and banter, but no trouble."

"Then what's going on?" asked Ian.

Ryan shrugged, his face a customary mask of calm. "Whatever's happened, it must be serious if they're closing the place."

"Come on, we'd better give them our details," said Ginny, nodding in the direction of the approaching officers. "This lot look like they mean business."

Jack held back from the group, his eyes eagerly assessing the situation. He had been an officer in the Metropolitan Police for thirty years and could smell something more than just a run-of-the-mill crime had occurred.

Allowing the rest of the Pals to exit the gate before him, he stepped over to the barmaid who'd held it open. She was just out of view of officers outside the gate, so Jack moved to stand alongside her. He opened with a white lie.

"Hello, I'm a detective from down south. Off duty. What's happened here? It looks serious."

The young woman studied the slightly overweight, late middle-aged Jack through reddened eyes; his Burnley football shirt pulled tight over his belly looked, as it did on most middle-aged football fans, rather ridiculous and almost comical.

"Sorry," her voice fractured with emotion, "the police have told us not to speak with anyone."

"Really?"

She nodded. "Yes."

Jack pursed his lips, his eyes fixing the woman's tearful face with a piercing gaze; he gave her a reassuring smile.

"That's okay," he said, shrugging his shoulders. "I understand. You're following orders; I'd have given the same advice if I'd been in charge. I just wondered what has happened to cause all this activity."

The woman stared down at the bunch of keys in her hands, seeming to inspect firstly one key, then another – anything to avoid Jack's stare. "I suppose it would be okay to tell a detective what's happened," she muttered.

She paused, unsure whether to continue, one eye watching the pub's customers as they continued to exit the garden.

Jack had to think quickly. What could he say to persuade her to release the information? His policing experience told him that this poor woman probably needed to unburden herself; she would be desperate to tell someone what had happened. If it was as bad as he thought, the knowledge would be weighing heavily on her. He reached into his back pocket.

"I'll show you my warrant card if you'd like?"

It was a bold ploy, because he didn't have one, and it was probably his last throw of the dice. If she was still unsure about telling him, he'd have to give up and leave her alone. Jack hadn't held a warrant card for twelve years, but at that moment, he couldn't think what else to say which might prise the information out of her.

"It's okay," she said after a few seconds, her head vigorously shaking from side to side, her blonde ponytail swishing. "No need, it's fine. I'm just being cautious."

Jack thought his chance to find out more had slipped away, but she leant over and whispered quickly into his ear. "A member of staff has been murdered in an upstairs stockroom. He had his throat ripped open. There's blood everywhere."

SEVEN

Jack's jaw dropped open in astonishment and he placed a reassuring hand on the woman's shoulder. "Jesus, I'm so sorry. Was he a friend of yours?"

She shook her head, her voice filled with sorrow. "No, he only started two weeks ago."

Jack could feel her shoulders juddering as she sobbed, tears flowing freely down both cheeks.

"He was a really lovely guy." She wiped away the tears with the back of her forearm, then juddered again as another wave of sadness hit her. "He was only twenty-eight."

A female officer spotted Jack speaking to the sobbing barmaid and glowered angrily at him. Not wishing to explain himself, Jack thanked the woman and beat a hasty retreat, giving his contact details quickly and quietly to the waiting officers, before heading off to join the others.

Shuffling along the thronged alleyway, Jack didn't feel like joining in with the rousing chorus of, "Amir, Amir Shanami runs down the wing for me!" He eventually reached the relative calm of the roadway, where two ambulances, three police cars and a police van had been hurriedly parked on the road.

Officers were stringing cordon tape for the emergency services directly in front of the pub, while others were encouraging fans to move away from the area.

Seeing the Pals gathered on the opposite side of the street, Jack strode through the crowd to join them.

"Where have you been?" asked Ginny. "I looked around and couldn't see you. We thought we'd lost you!"

Jack smiled and held his arms out wide. "Just thought I'd use my natural charm and charisma to find out what happened."

"Charm and charisma? You?" joked Ginny, raising her eyes to the heavens. "That wouldn't have got you very far!"

Ian widened his eyes and held out his hands pleadingly, desperate to know what Jack had learned. Ian lived in Tunbridge Wells, in Kent, but he was Burnley through and through; his strong Lancashire accent and loud voice demanded a swift reply. "Well? Come on then, don't leave us hanging!"

Putting on his best Detective Taggart Scottish accent, Jack said, "There's been a murrdah!"

Becki, who was always prone towards the more excitable side of any conversation, said loudly, "Fuck me, a murder!"

Ryan, generally the calmest and most rational of the group, simply murmured, "Thought it had to be something serious."

"Was it a Burnley fan?" asked Ian.

Jack turned to face him. "No, a member of staff."

"How was he killed?" asked John, who had somehow held on to his pint and was finishing the last dregs, before placing the empty glass on a low garden wall.

Jack chewed his top lip gently. "Had his throat cut in an upstairs storeroom," he said. "The barmaid described it as 'ripped open'. Apparently, there was a lot of blood. The poor bastard was only twenty-eight."

Ginny shook her head. "Oh my God, that's awful, who told you all this?"

"I chatted up the lady holding the gate open."

"What do you mean 'chatted her up'?" asked Ginny, looking annoyed.

"I told her I was a member of the Clowns in Disguise."

Most of the Pals stared at Jack uncomprehendingly.

But Ginny had heard the phrase endlessly over the years, so she translated for them. "CID, he means CID."

Jack grinned mischievously. "Clowns in Disguise was the polite acronym used by us uniformed officers for the CID, but most of the time we weren't so polite; we normally called them Cun—"

"That's enough!" snapped Ginny.

At Ginny's admonishment, a small ripple of laughter rose from the group, but it soon subsided. Deep down everyone knew this wasn't a laughing matter.

Ian seemed genuinely upset. Standing with hands on hips, he stared down at the ground shaking his head. Ian could occasionally let his emotions get the better of him, and this was one of those times. Seeing his distress, Ginny put her arm around him and pulled him tightly to her.

"Come on," she said. "Chin up."

He forced a broken smile, his features creased with sadness. "Poor lad. Twenty-eight. It doesn't seem fair!"

The group mumbled their agreement.

Her role as mother hen of the Pals coming to the fore, Becki looked at her watch. It was already 1.25, just over an hour and a half before kick-off, and despite the desperate sadness of the situation, they were first and foremost Burnley fans, and they were losing valuable drinking time!

"I'm not sure we've time to search for another pub that allows away fans."

"There's only one other away pub," said Joe, standing alongside Becki. Joe Pyle, known by the other Pals as 'Fat Joe' was one of the younger members and liked nothing more than having a good drink and starting songs.

He pulled gently at his short, neatly trimmed beard, as he

thought about it. "The Craven Heifer allows away fans, but it's right across the other side of town; we'll be even further from the ground than we are now."

Becki quickly took charge. "Let's skip that then; we could get a few more drinks inside the stadium. I've heard they sell decent beer and pies at Rotherham's ground."

Her suggestion was met with nods and general acceptance that this was the best result they could hope for in the circumstances. They moved off in three small groups, each exploring the same topic of conversation. Any thoughts of singing songs and cracking jokes had been silenced.

EIGHT

Detective Chief Inspector Wilf Marsh was decidedly unimpressed at being called into work at 1.30 on a Saturday afternoon. It was his day off and he'd been about to go cycling with his wife and two young daughters when the phone rang. However, he was the on-call CID senior officer and there had been a gruesome killing on his patch, so here he was.

At thirty-three years old, he was young to hold such a senior rank in the Criminal Investigation Department, but he'd worked hard to get where he was, was well respected by those under his command and had earned a reputation as a bloody good detective.

Arriving at the scene just after 2.00, Wilf ducked underneath the cordon tape being held open by a young police constable. He stared up at the large brick façade of the pub, with its huge rectangular sign above the main door naming it as the 'Hammer and Sickle'. The white letters on a red background were so big he thought they must be visible for quite some distance.

Judith 'Jude' Sparks, an experienced detective sergeant in her late forties, with over twenty-five years' service in the South Yorkshire Police, smiled warmly as he approached. Jude was an uncompromising officer and known by fellow officers as a detective who took no shit.

Using his fingers to sweep back his thick, dark-brown hair, he greeted her. "Jude, good to see you. What have we got?"

Jude moved close to him, ensuring she would be heard above the surrounding commotion.

"Hi, boss. The victim is male, IC2, twenty-eight years old. He arrived here three weeks ago on a working holiday from Malta." She referred to her notes. "His name is Mario Spiteri and he's been living in staff accommodation over the pub since getting the job here two weeks ago."

"Injuries?"

"His throat has been ripped open from arsehole to breakfast time. It's a right fucking mess."

Wilf lowered his forehead and raised his eyebrows at her. He knew what she'd meant but, just in case, thought he'd better confirm it. "You mean ear to ear?"

She nodded. "Yes, but it's not quite ear to ear. It's a diagonal tear, just underneath the left ear down to his right collar bone. It's ripped his throat wide open." She shook her head recalling the image. "It must have been a horrible way to die."

Wilf swept his hair back again. "What do you mean by tear?" he asked.

"Sorry?"

"You said tear, not cut… tear. What did you mean by that?"

She lowered her chin. "You'll see in a minute. Let's just say it's not a normal knife wound with neat edges."

Closing his eyes and pinching the bridge of his nose between thumb and forefinger, Wilf thought for a moment. "Where was he found, in his room?"

"No, in a stockroom used for storing crisps, snacks, soft drinks and bedding."

"Bedding? What's bedding doing in a pub stockroom?"

She raised her shoulders and held her palms upwards. "How should I know?"

Wilf raised his eyebrows and dropped the corners of his mouth. "Sorry, silly question. So, was he collecting snacks when he was attacked?"

"That's the strange thing, according to the other members of staff, he wasn't working today, so nobody knows what he was doing in there. According to the pub's owner…" she checked her notes, "…Derek Coles, members of staff are strictly banned from stockrooms when off duty."

Wilf rubbed the back of his neck, a thoughtful frown on his face. He stared up at the side wall of the pub. "What was he playing at, then?"

Jude shrugged. "I don't know, but it cost him his life."

"Any family in the UK?"

"None. We've sent a message to the police in Malta with his details. They'll pass on the death message and give the incident room's contact number to his next of kin."

"That's great. Thanks, Jude."

Jude looked up as a flock of ducks flew overhead in perfect formation. Then she returned her gaze to Wilf. "Bloody awful for his parents to hear that news. One minute their life is rolling along as normal, the next, they hear about this happening to their son."

Wilf guessed she might be thinking of her own twenty-four-year-old son, doing well in his first proper job, slowly making his way in the world.

Snapping them both back to the moment, Wilf indicated the pub's front entrance. "Okay, lead the way, I'd better take a look."

Jude took him into the pub and led him through the hallway, turning right through a heavy wooden door into the cavernous bar area.

Inside the main bar, the Hammer and Sickle's staff were gathered, each of them having initial statements taken by officers. Jude raised her eyebrows and inclined her head towards them, asking her boss a question that didn't need words.

But Wilf wasn't ready to address the staff just yet. "No. I'll speak to them once they've done their statements." He held Jude by the elbow and ushered her back into the hallway. "I want to see the scene first."

The hallway was large, dark and sparsely decorated, with a brown linoleum floor and cream-painted walls. At the bottom of the stairs were two uniform officers.

"Hi, boss," said one, whom Wilf had gone through training school with twelve years previously.

"Hi, Suzie." He smiled. "How are the kids?"

"They're great thanks. Yours?"

"All good." They looked at each other for a moment. "Right, what can you tell me?"

"It's a horrible mess up there. Blood everywhere. We've got your forensic suits here."

"Thanks."

Suzie's colleague reached into a bag and handed them a protective white suit each, with a hood to cover their hair. He also gave them blue nitrile gloves and a pair of disposable blue shoe covers. They quickly put everything on, then headed upstairs.

They passed a young detective constable halfway up the flight. He'd been posted there to keep the crime scene log, and he dutifully made a note of their names and the time they entered the scene.

Wilf's senses were on high alert; he'd been the same since completing his CID training and gaining his first posting as a young detective. His eyes looked all around quickly, busily scanning for anything other officers may have missed.

Arriving at the door of the stockroom, he saw two female scenes of crime officers (SOCOs) who were also in white forensic suits. They were standing just inside the door but, on seeing Wilf and Jude, stepped out onto the landing to let them in.

The elder SOCO said, "Nothing to tell you yet, we've only just arrived ourselves." She fixed him with a solemn stare. "It's one hell of a mess in there, one of the most horrific scenes I've ever seen."

Raising his eyebrows in surprise at such an experienced SOCO making a comment like that, Wilf forced a smile and muttered a quiet, "Thanks for the warning – that's what everyone keeps telling me. Is the pathologist on the way?"

"He is, but he's delayed. A jumper threw themselves in front of an inter-city just outside Sheffield. Once he's finished there, he'll be straight over."

"No others available?"

"Not on a weekend apparently."

"Oh joy! It's a wonderful world, isn't it?"

He held out an arm to politely allow Jude into the stockroom first. She gingerly stepped across the threshold, being very careful where she placed her feet. Wilf sucked in a long a breath to prepare himself, blew out slowly, then followed her in.

NINE

The stockroom was larger than he'd anticipated, about four metres by three metres. It had shelving around three sides containing boxes of Walkers crisps, Nobby's nuts, Mr Tubs pork scratchings and numerous crates and boxes containing soft drinks. There were also shelves of blankets, sheets and pillows. Hanging from a ceiling with flaking and peeling paint was a single bare light bulb.

A single wooden chair, so old and in such poor condition it looked on the point of collapse, sat on the dark, wooden floor in the centre of the room, facing the boxes of Apple and Raspberry J2O drinks on the shelf directly opposite.

Spreadeagled on the floor in front of the chair, his head hanging down and tilted backwards towards his left shoulder, was the lifeless and horribly contorted body of Mario Spiteri. He was lying on his left side, left arm extended forward with its palm facing upwards, right arm twisted forward and hanging limp from the shoulder, resting in a pool of dark-red blood. Mario's thighs and knees were together, but his lower legs and bare feet had splayed apart. His unseeing eyes, devoid of life, were half closed.

Despite all his experience, Wilf was stunned into silence. As the two detectives slowly drank in every detail of the horrific scene, no words were necessary, and none were spoken.

Mario was wearing only a pair of dark-green tailored shorts and a plain sage-green T-shirt. Well, it had been sage green once, but most of it was now soaked in deep, dark-red, almost purple, blood. The soles of his bare feet had collected a layer of dirt and grime from the stockroom's unswept floor.

Wilf had seen many dead bodies during his career, numerous victims of murder, killed by many different methods, but he had never seen so much blood loss from one human being. It had pooled around Mario's upper body, spread down to his hips and soaked into the hair hanging down from his head. The pool had spread across the floor, almost to the door, creating a sinister red mass that had once contained the life force of Mario Spiteri.

Wilf could sense the familiar metallic tang of blood assailing his nostrils. It was an aroma he'd smelled many times before, and for some strange reason he'd never truly fathomed, it always calmed him, making him feel relaxed and in control. It reminded him of the seriousness of the situation he was dealing with and the importance of his job, a job he excelled at, a job he loved doing… and right now, a job he needed to give his very best effort.

Whoever had carried out this murder was obviously unhinged, the level of violence alone made them a danger to society, and he would move heaven and earth to bring them to justice.

TEN

The huge pool of blood covering the dark, wooden floor emanated from an untidy and deep gash. It started close to the bottom of Mario's left ear and ran diagonally down across his throat, severing both the left carotid artery and windpipe, before finishing at his right collar bone, which was partially visible through the torn flesh and gore.

The depth and raggedness of the wound was something Wilf had not seen on previous stabbing or slashing victims. Knife victims' wounds were gruesome sights, but their injuries nearly always had clear and sharp edges. This certainly wasn't the case with Mario Spiteri – the edges of his wound were frayed, fragmented, shredded, like he'd been crudely butchered in a way likely to cause extreme suffering.

"Fuck me, what did the killer use, a blunt saw?" Wilf's voice was angry. Mario had suffered a truly horrific and painful death, and the sight of his mutilated body left Wilf steaming with anger.

Jude's eyes swept across the scene over and over. She relayed her thoughts out loud, giving her impression of the killer's actions as she did so. Carefully avoiding standing in the huge pool of blood, she stood behind the chair and made a slashing movement with her right hand as she said, "I reckon his throat was cut from behind while he was sitting on the chair. Then he slid off and ended up where he's lying now." She turned to Wilf, looking at him enquiringly. "What do you think?"

Wilf nodded. "That sounds about right. Everything else in the room is as it should be, no mess, no signs of a struggle." He stepped carefully around the edges of the blood. "All this horror, yet there's nothing much in the way of clues."

"It makes no sense," said Jude, thoughtfully. "Surely you'd be fighting for your life?"

Wilf turned his bottom lip over, looked up at the bare light bulb, then back down to Jude. "Unless the attack took you completely by surprise." He leant forward with his hands on his knees, peering intently at the body. "What's that?" He pointed at a small scrap of yellow paper, lying just above the crook of Mario's elbow on his right arm. Blood had stained one side of the paper, but he could still see something written on it.

After checking with the SOCOs that all the necessary crime scene photographs had been taken, Jude reached down and pinched one corner of the paper between thumb and forefinger of a gloved hand, lifting it clear. It was a small yellow Post-it note, which she inspected closely. "The blood on it has dried." She looked closer still. "There's the letters TCP written on it in maroon capitals." She held it up for Wilf to see. "Do you think it could be some sort of message from the killer?"

He shrugged. "I doubt it, probably just something that's fallen from a shelf. But we'd better bag it up, just in case."

Jude pulled a small evidence bag from her pocket, carefully placed the Post-it note inside, made a note of the time it was discovered on the bag's side, then folded it and pushed it into a back pocket. She rested a hand on Wilf's forearm and pointed at the wound. "I think there's real rage in that wound – whoever did this wasn't going to be satisfied with just killing him. They wanted to cause a great deal of pain and suffering. Killing someone is one thing, but savaging them like this is on another level; it shows something deeper to me, like they're unhinged."

Raising his eyebrows and opening his eyes wide, Wilf turned to his subordinate. "You're quite the Miss Marple, aren't you? I hadn't spotted any of that, but you could be right." He pondered for a moment. "I wonder if revenge was the motive."

Wilf then did what he always did in these situations – he closed his eyes lightly shut and went through the likely timeline of events in his mind's eye, before deciding on which course of action to take next. Jude had seen him perform this ritual on more occasions than she cared to remember and knew not to disturb him, remaining silent while he concentrated. After twenty seconds, his eyes sprang open. "What's the score with CCTV?"

"Inside the building it's only in the bar areas."

He smiled and nodded. "That's standard for pubs around here – they'll do anything to save money, including installing crap CCTV systems. Is there anything in the hallway and corridor leading to the door at the bottom of the stairs?"

"Nope," she scratched her forehead, "and that causes us a problem."

"Why?"

"Because the killer didn't necessarily go through the bar; they might have entered through the side door."

Wilf frowned. "How do you mean? The side door is locked, surely, otherwise anyone could walk in?" Realisation dawned, and his eyes sparkled with understanding. "Unless Mario knew them! That's what you're thinking, isn't it? He could have let the killer in?"

Jude shrugged, her face impassive, then she nodded gently. "It's a possibility, especially as it looks like he trusted whoever it was enough to let them stand behind him while he sat on the chair."

"So, you're thinking it was someone he knew?"

"Certainly looks that way."

ELEVEN

For a while, not a word was spoken, as Wilf's mind raced with what to do next. After what seemed like an eternity, he'd come to a decision.

"Right, move that DC with the crime scene log off the stairs and position him just outside the side door. I'm now including the staircase, the downstairs hallway and corridor in the crime scene, and I want an officer posted at the door from the bar area to the hallway."

"Why make the scene so big?"

Wilf swept his hair back again. "There must have been huge sprays of blood when the killer did this, and they might well have copped some of it, so there's a chance he left some traces when he fled down the stairs."

"Okay." Jude eyed him for a few seconds. "Why are you so certain the killer is a he?"

Wilf's head span around to face her, his face momentarily flared red, irritated at his train of thought being interrupted. "What?"

"You keep saying he, but the killer might be a she!"

Wilf bristled for a moment, then visibly calmed as he realised the sense in her words.

"Sorry, figure of speech, or course it might be a woman,

although she'd have to be either pretty furious, or immensely strong, to have done that." He pointed at the gaping wound. "That would take some serious downwards pressure. You're right though – we mustn't discount anyone."

Jude disappeared from the room, leaving Wilf to absorb the horror of the scene around him until she returned.

"I've repositioned the DC, posted an officer on the door to the bar and informed the uniform outside. The SOCOs are asking when they can get back in?"

"We'll be done in a second. Do we know yet how many staff were here when this happened?"

Jude checked her notes. "Apart from the owner and his wife, nineteen. Four kitchen staff, six bar staff, six waiters and three table clearers. All their statements should be finished by now."

"Do they all have access to the private areas upstairs?"

"Yes."

"Including the kitchen staff?"

"Yes."

He scratched his nose, a small vein in his temple visibly throbbing. "I want PNC checks done on all of them. For the moment we need to concentrate our efforts on the pub staff, until evidence to the contrary comes to light; our killer is likely to be someone within that group."

"I've already made arrangements for the PNC checks, and they've all been given a cursory once-over by forensics with the ultra-violet. No sign of blood spatters on any of them."

"I'm not surprised – they're not going to be daft enough to go back to the bar with blood all over them, are they? Just in case, we'll need to check the rooms upstairs. If any refuse permission, don't let them back in and tell them we'll get warrants."

Jude nodded. "When would you like to speak to them?"

"Let's do it now. If the killer is amongst them, they'll be shitting themselves, so let's strike while the iron's hot. If we put them under pressure, they might slip up."

He crouched on his haunches, taking one last look at the piteous sight of Mario Spiteri's prostrate body. He was about to stand up again, when he narrowed his eyes and pushed his neck forward. Mario's groin area was angled towards the ground and blood had soaked into the left side of his shorts, but there was a small gap between the pool of blood and Mario's crotch.

Wilf pointed. "His flies are undone."

Jude crouched alongside. "Oh yeah, good spot." She glanced sideways at him, puzzled.

Wilf turned to meet her gaze. "Why on earth would his flies be undone?"

She shrugged. "Sexual encounter that went wrong?"

Tilting his head to one side as he slowly stood up, Wilf said, "Fucking hell, Jude, I've been with some bad women in my time, but I've never had a sexual encounter this bad!"

They both chuckled, the mood lightening for a moment. Standing up straight, Wilf scratched the top of his head through the plastic hood covering. "Maybe he just forgot to zip up following his last piss?"

"Could be."

"Although we can't discount it being sexually motivated."

Five minutes later, Wilf Marsh stood on a raised floor area inside one of the pub's huge bay windows. The staff were spread out randomly throughout the bar, their grim faces staring at him expectantly, all eager to hear what would happen next. He urged them to move closer, then started to speak.

TWELVE

"We are the Longside, Burnley, we are the Longside, Burnley!" The chant rang out loud and clear through the Mears Stand, where away fans are housed in the New York Stadium – the home of Rotherham United FC. The same refrain had sounded throughout much of the second half, leaving some fans almost hoarse.

The match had been filled with end-to-end entertainment, which had thrilled both sets of supporters. Rotherham took an early lead, before Burnley equalised late in the game, then snatched an added time winner, sending the 2,500 travelling supporters into a state of near delirium. They thanked the players for their efforts by giving them a great ovation at the final whistle, cheering them to the rafters as they walked over and clapped the fans. One player took his shirt off and handed it to an eager young fan, a gesture copied by three other players, as they lapped up the adulation.

"We're gonna win the league, we're gonna win the league, and now you've gotta believe us, and now you've gotta believe us, and now you've gotta believe us! We're gonna win the league!" The Burnley fans' elation resounded around the stand, with The Claret Pals in their element. As usual, they were front and centre of the celebrations.

Exiting the ground, a group of the Pals assembled across the road from the stand to say their goodbyes.

"Do you think the police will contact everyone?" asked Ginny.

"Probably," said John. "Let's face it, we'd all been inside the pub at some stage." He shrugged. "So what if they do question us, we've nowt to hide, have we?"

Everyone sounded their agreement, and soon enough the group dispersed, mingling with the thousands of fans departing the stadium, rival supporters mingling happily together and heading back to their homes.

Half of the Pals heralded, naturally enough, from the Burnley area, but Jack and Ginny came from Newbury in Berkshire, Becki from Wimbledon, Val from Southampton, Ryan from Kew in South West London, Stuart from Ardingly in Sussex and Ian from Tunbridge Wells in Kent. All but Jack once had links to Burnley and had moved down south for varying reasons but were now proud 'Southern Clarets'. Indeed, at many of the away games down south, it seemed like around half of Burnley fans in attendance were Southern Clarets.

Jack and Ginny took their seats as the train pulled out of Rotherham station on its short hop to Doncaster, where they would change for the journey to London. Jack stared vacantly at the town's outskirts, as the houses whizzed by faster and faster outside the window. He felt increasingly uneasy, shifting uncomfortably on his seat.

"What's up?" Ginny asked.

"Huh?"

"What's the matter? We've just seen Burnley win, but you were practically silent on the walk back to the station, and since we've boarded the train, you've hardly said a word."

Jack eyed her thoughtfully. "I'm sorry... it's nothing."

Ginny shrugged, but her expression couldn't conceal the

fact that she was miffed. "Okay, if you don't want to tell me, that's fine."

Jack sucked in a lungful of air; he had been with Ginny for eighteen years, and he knew she would be in a mood for hours if he didn't say something. Reluctantly, he blew out a long breath. "It's just that..." He paused, unsure whether to continue.

"Go on," she urged.

"...I saw something when we arrived at the pub."

"What?"

"Well, remember after we got there, we walked through the bar to get to the garden?"

"Yes, what of it?"

"Well... I saw someone coming into the bar through a doorway." He rubbed both hands up over his face and across his hair.

"So?"

He shuffled uncomfortably. "Well, when the door closed, I saw a sign on the door... it said 'Private'."

She gasped, suddenly comprehending why he was so ill at ease. "So they might have been upstairs?"

"Possibly, yes."

Ginny reached up to rub her forehead. She was wide-eyed, her head shaking. "God, Jack, why didn't you say something sooner?"

He shook his head. "It's only just come back to me," he muttered, his voice barely audible. "I can't believe I didn't make the link earlier. I used to be a copper for fuck's sake, it just completely went out of my head!"

Leaning across the table, Ginny gripped Jack's hands. "You realise you can't keep this to yourself, don't you? You must report it to the police."

Jack snapped back angrily, "Of course I do." He glared at her. "I've got no intention of keeping it to myself!"

Ginny softened her voice. "Sorry, bad choice of words, I didn't mean it like that."

He looked down at their entwined hands without replying.

She gently pulled her hand away, reached forward across the table and lifted his chin to look at her. "This person, did you recognise them?"

He nodded, his bottom lip quivering.

"Who was it?"

"Fat Joe."

THIRTEEN

"Boss, you need to see this."

Wilf Marsh looked up from his computer screen to see one of his favourite detectives standing in front of him. She was holding a piece of paper.

"Hi, Minnie, what's up?"

DC Hana James was born in Samoa, the product of an English father and Samoan mother. She was always smiling, very attractive, and her bubbly personality was infectious. Wilf thought the world of her. She was known to her colleagues as Minnie, because of a striking resemblance to the actress Minnie Driver.

With her usual happy countenance, she handed him an information report phoned in to the incident room by someone called Jack Simpson. He slowly read though the report, his interest increasing with every line.

"Did we take details from anyone called Joe Pyle at the Hammer and Sickle?"

"Yes, boss, someone gave exactly those details. Joe Pyle, a Burnley fan, lives in Clitheroe, Lancashire."

Wilf leant back in his chair, balancing on the rear legs on the point of tipping over. "Clitheroe, eh?"

"That's right. What would you like done next?"

He bit his top lip thoughtfully, working out the best plan of action in his head. "Where does Jack Simpson live?"

"Newbury, in Berkshire."

Letting his chair drop back onto all four legs with a bang, Wilf smiled warmly at Hana.

"Great work, Minnie. Get a local officer to take a full witness statement from him and have them email it to us as soon as possible. Also, check CCTV in the bar and see if they've got a camera with a view of that door. Whether we've got footage or not, let's bring Joe Pyle in. I think he's got some explaining to do."

"Do you want him arrested?"

He thought for a moment. "See if he'll come in voluntarily first."

"Will do, boss." She turned to leave.

"Oh, and Minnie."

She looked back over her shoulder. "Yes?"

"This could be just the breakthrough we've been looking for."

"Thanks, boss." Smiling broadly, she tossed her brunette ponytail as she turned and left the room.

FOURTEEN

Joe Pyle downed a long draught from his can as he sprawled out on his settee watching the Community Shield match between Manchester City and Chelsea at Wembley. It was 4.20 on Sunday afternoon and he had already finished three cans of lager, as had his best friend Steve, an eighteen-stone redhead who was slouched in an armchair with one leg over the arm. "Can't believe Chelsea are winning this game, they've been shite," said Steve, swallowing a glug of his fourth can.

Joe replied through a mouthful of Doritos, liberally spraying crumbs over his thighs as he spoke. "Lucky Southern bastards, City should be out of sight by now."

Their conversation was interrupted by the ringing of the doorbell, swiftly followed by three loud raps on the knocker.

"That'll be Aaron," said Joe, leaping to his feet and walking to the door. "He said he might pop round."

On opening the door however, he was surprised to be greeted not by Aaron, but by two plain-clothed officers holding up warrant cards. Not only that, but on the roadway directly outside his house, he could see a uniformed officer sitting on the wing of a marked car, with two further uniformed officers inside a police van parked behind the car.

Joe forced a smile and politely enquired, "Hello, can I help you?"

"Joe Pyle?" The question was asked by the younger of the two male detectives, a fair-haired man in his late twenties. The tone of his voice was decidedly unfriendly, bordering on aggressive.

"Guilty!" said Joe loudly, making a joke of the situation and holding out his wrists to be handcuffed. In truth though, he was more than a little confused as to why they could possibly want to speak with him.

The younger officer wore a blank expression, his voice remaining a robust monotone. "We're detectives from the incident room at Rotherham Police Station."

"Okay," said Joe, still puzzled.

"We're investigating the murder of Mario Spiteri at the Hammer and Sickle public house in Rotherham last Saturday."

Joe nodded. "Yes, I heard about it – we were drinking at the pub when it happened. Terrible business." He stood to one side and held an arm out. "Would you like to come in?"

The older of the two officers stepped forward and took control. A rotund man of around forty years, he was blessed with thinning salt-and-pepper hair. He fixed Joe with a steely gaze. "Yes. We were coming in anyway. We have a warrant to search these premises." He held up the warrant for Joe to inspect. "After that, we'd like you to come with us to Rotherham Police Station – there are a few questions you need to answer."

Joe stared in disbelief. "But… I… are you arresting me?"

The younger officer took the lead again. "We'd rather you came in voluntarily at this stage. But, if necessary, we *will* arrest you."

"But Rotherham? That's miles away! How long will I be there for?"

"You'll be there as long as it takes, Mr Pyle."

Twenty minutes later, the search of Joe's property was complete; Steve had made his way home; and Joe was in the back of the police car on his way to Rotherham.

*

"Shit, shit, shit!" Wilf Marsh banged his desk in frustration. "You're sure this is right?"

DC Minnie James confirmed what she'd just told him. "Yes, boss, the door leading to the private areas is only covered by one of the cameras in the bar, and it wasn't working last Saturday. Sorry."

"But we've got Pyle on other cameras moving towards that area?"

"Yes, he enters that part of the bar and reappears three minutes later, when he makes his way back outside to the garden." She drew another breath to continue, but Wilf cut her off.

"Okay, thanks, Minnie." He turned his swivel chair away from her to face out of the window overlooking the station yard, indicating in no uncertain terms that this conversation was at an end. He often enjoyed banter with Minnie, but this was not the news he wanted to hear, and right now, he wasn't in the mood for small talk!

FIFTEEN

The long, buzzing noise prior to the interview commencing seemed to last much longer than Joe had anticipated. He'd watched loads of crime dramas, but it never lasted that long on the telly… did it? He'd been offered the aid of a duty solicitor but declined. He figured he'd done nothing wrong, so what was the point?

Wilf Marsh and Judith Sparks sat across the table in the spartan interview room, Wilf absent-mindedly tapping the middle finger of his left hand on the tabletop, while Jude ran a finger over the list of questions on the page before her.

When the buzzing stopped, all three of them identified themselves for 'the benefit of the tape', and Jude opened the questioning. "Where are you from, Joe?"

"Clitheroe."

"In Lancashire?"

"Yes."

He rested his hands on the tabletop and linked his fingers, staring at the woman sitting opposite him. He saw her eyeing his claret T-shirt with a circular logo written in light blue stating, 'Burnley FC Keep the Faith'. The logo sat above the words, 'No Nay Never No More' and inside the circle was a light-blue clenched fist.

"Can you please tell me what you were doing at the Hammer and Sickle public house in Rotherham last Saturday?" she asked.

Joe was a little unnerved by the aggressive tone of her question, and he took a deep breath to calm himself before answering. "I was there with friends; we were enjoying a few drinks and a bite to eat before going to watch Burnley. It was the first game of the season."

"You say you were meeting friends?"

"Yes."

"How many friends?"

"I'm not sure, about a dozen, maybe fifteen. We meet up before every away match. We've got our own WhatsApp group."

"Where exactly were you in the pub?"

"We were only inside the pub when we first arrived. Long enough to get our drinks. We spent most of our time in the garden."

"I see. I assume you re-entered the pub to order your drinks and food?"

"Yes, why?" He started biting the inside of his cheek, a nervous habit of his.

Jude looked at Wilf, who gave her the merest of nods. She leant further forward, resting her forearms on the tabletop and laying her palms flat.

"I'll get straight to it, Joe. Just after 1.30, you were seen returning to the bar through a door marked 'Private'."

Joe's mouth dropped open in shock. He wanted to speak but couldn't find the words.

"What were you doing in a private area of the pub?" Jude continued.

Joe was staggered. He fully understood what she was suggesting, and it was several seconds before he finally managed to find the words. "That's bollocks – I was never in a private area of the pub – check the CCTV if you like."

Wilf and Jude exchanged another glance.

"That's not true though, is it, Joe? You were seen coming through a door marked 'Private', making your way back into the bar. So, I'll ask again, what were you doing in a private area of the pub?"

His voice cracking with stress and emotion, Joe banged his hand down onto the tabletop. "I've already told you, that's bollocks! I wasn't in a private area!"

Jude removed her hands from the table and held up three sheets of A4 paper.

"Well, we've got a statement here from a witness who says he saw…"

Her question was interrupted by loud and urgent banging on the interview room door. Everyone in the room turned to the door in surprise. This was highly unusual. Real-life interviews are not like those in TV dramas, when they are interrupted all the time, with officers swanning in and out without an apology. In real life police interviews, interruptions are vanishingly rare, and officers would only interrupt if something was very urgent indeed.

A clearly irritated Wilf stood up and pulled the heavy interview room door open. Standing before him was the custody sergeant, Dean Alexander. "I need a quick word before you continue, boss."

Wilf looked around at Jude and Joe. "Apologies, I'll be back shortly." He stepped outside and the soundproofed door swung closed with its customary sucking sound. "This had better be good, Dean. That bastard is on the ropes; we might have a confession shortly."

"Minnie's just phoned. She says they've discovered a camera behind the bar that's aimed at the tills…"

"So?" snapped Wilf. "You're interrupting an interview to tell me that?"

The sergeant glared at the DCI. He was an experienced custody officer approaching the end of his service and didn't take kindly to being berated by an officer in his early thirties, no matter what rank he was. Blowing out a long, impatient breath, Dean continued. "...As I was saying, it's aimed at the tills, but it also has a long view of the door you're interested in. It's in the top right corner of the screen and it's a bit grainy, but Minnie says it's good enough."

Wilf's mood was transformed in an instant. "That's excellent, just what we're looking for!"

Dean Alexander shook his head, holding Wilf's stare. "Not really."

Wilf stepped towards the sergeant and growled quietly. "What do you mean?"

"You're not going to like this… Joe Pyle's hand never lets go of that door."

Wilf shook his head, unable to believe what he was hearing. "But… it must have done."

The custody sergeant shook his head. "Apparently not. He steps into the corridor, then back into the bar within a few seconds. The important thing is that the door never quite closes… his hand is always clearly visible holding onto its edge."

*

Just after 10.00 that evening, Joe left Rotherham Police Station with the profuse apologies of the detectives ringing in his ears. Once Wilf Marsh re-entered the interview room after speaking with the custody sergeant, Joe only faced a few further questions – all from Wilf, who had taken over as sole interviewer. Joe reaffirmed he'd known nothing about the murder of Mario

Spiteri while in the pub garden and explained how he'd first heard rumours about the killing when they'd gathered in the street outside.

Soon enough, Joe's ordeal was over, and shortly afterwards a car was provided to take him home.

On the journey back to Clitheroe, it was fully explained why he had been taken in for questioning and why a warrant had been obtained to search his house.

"It's okay," he assured the officers. "You've got a hard enough job without people like me making it more difficult. Don't worry, I won't be submitting a complaint."

"That's good of you, Joe, thanks."

"Why can't you tell me who gave a statement saying I'd been through that door?"

The officer driving the car smiled at Joe, eyeing him in the rear-view mirror. "Because it was another Burnley fan, and we don't want you going looking for them."

SIXTEEN

A dozen officers waiting in the incident room of Rotherham Police Station looked up as the door opened, and a flustered-looking DCI Wilf Marsh strode in. He swung the door closed with a bang and turned to face them, carrying four blue manilla folders tightly between forearm and chest.

He addressed the gathering in his usual measured tone. "It's one week since the murder of Mario Spiteri, and despite a couple of promising leads, we're no nearer closing in on whoever gouged his throat open." He turned to Jude Sparks and lifted his chin, indicating for her to take the stage. As she stood up, he moved to the chair she'd vacated and sat down.

Jude walked quickly to the front and turned to face her colleagues with a grim expression. "This is proving to be a very difficult inquiry, so the DCI and I have set goals to progress matters." She pointed at a large map pinned to a side wall. Moving alongside the map, she used a pen to indicate the areas she was talking about, pointing to each one in turn. "Comprehensive searches inside and immediately outside the Hammer and Sickle proved negative, so we extended our search to the surrounding area. Despite this, to date, we have failed to find the murder weapon."

She walked to the table where she'd been sitting and

exchanged a glance with Wilf as she sipped a drink from a bottle of water. "As you already know, the killer used what the pathologist described as a jagged-toothed blade. A weapon with a line of staggered teeth of various sizes." She held up a small pruning saw. "Something like this." She handed the item to the nearest officer. "Please pass it around; I want everyone to take a good look at it. The actual murder weapon might be a different design to this one, or made by a different manufacturer, but this is almost certainly the type of blade that was used."

A detective raised his hand.

She pointed at him. "Yes, Bill?"

"How do we know it's this size, couldn't it have been something bigger?"

Jude raised her eyebrows and nodded to acknowledge the point Bill had made. "The truth is, we don't know, but it's a reasonable bet the killer was carrying the weapon concealed somewhere on their person. I'm not sure I'd have gone into that storeroom with someone carrying a big fuck-off saw for no apparent reason."

Her reply brought a smattering of laughter from the room, before she revealed the first goal. "Whatever its size, we want every place locally that sells this type of implement visited, and we want details of every tool like this sold in the two weeks prior to the killing. You never know, if it is a new one, we might be able to obtain an image from the shop's CCTV of the killer purchasing it.

"Secondly, door-to-doors have returned nothing of interest, so we want the houses directly opposite the pub's entrance, together with the houses opposite either end of the alleyway visited again. Someone may have unwittingly seen the killer leaving, and it's possible people with vital information may have been out when officers called. There are at least three houses to my knowledge where we've had no response thus far, so we'll keep trying."

She rapped hard on the table and glared at an officer whose attention seemed to be on his mobile phone screen rather than her. He sheepishly returned the phone to his trouser pocket and raised a hand in apology.

"Thirdly, the pub only has CCTV in the bars, the rear car park, about half the garden and the front entrance. It's not the most comprehensive coverage, but it's better than some pubs in the area, so we'll have to make do." She wagged a finger. "We want every frame gone over again; it's just possible we've missed something."

Jude looked enquiringly at Wilf, ready to hand back control to him, but he urged her to continue.

"Sadly, there is no CCTV covering the side alley linking Smith Road and Goldhawk Road." She sat on the edge of a desk. "Slightly more understandable, because who would want cameras in their private living space? There is none covering the downstairs hallway, or the staircase leading upstairs." She tapped the map. "Although the alleyway itself is not covered, people exiting onto Goldhawk Road are captured by the camera at the front."

She took in a breath and nodded to a female detective, who clicked a button, illuminating a screen above her. Displayed on the screen was a slideshow showing the crime scene, the horrific images enough to disturb even the most hardened of detectives. "We're assuming that if the killer isn't a member of staff, they will have left the scene immediately. We've managed to narrow down the timeframe for people using the alleyway, concentrating only on those seen exiting either end between 12.25 and 12.50, which allows five minutes either side of the pathologist's new best guess for time of death, between 12.30 and 12.45. However, it's a busy conduit on match days, and even with that narrow window for the time of death, it leaves us with at least a hundred potential suspects.

"Lastly, the victim's flies were undone, which begs the question, was he meeting someone for a sexual encounter? If he was, we urgently need to discover who that person was. A couple of the pub's staff think he may have been seeing someone, but he tended to keep himself to himself."

Another detective raised her hand. "Has CCTV in and around the pub been checked going back to when Mario started working there?"

Jude nodded and grinned at the questioner. "It has, and at no time does he meet up with anyone who he seemed romantically involved with." She returned her gaze to the rest of the room. "We know from family members and friends that he was bisexual, so we might be looking for a man or woman… who knows?"

The room fell silent for a few seconds as Jude allowed her remarks to sink in. "Officers on team one please stay behind for taskings. Everybody else, thank you for your attendance – you can get back to work."

Wilf, who had been leaning back in his chair, stood up and stepped forward, holding out a hand indicating for her to take a seat once more. "Thanks, Jude." He tapped the tabletop nervously with the middle finger of his right hand. His narrow, but chiselled and stubbly, chin pushed forward. "Ladies and gents, I know how hard you've all been working, but we now need to redouble our efforts, because the bosses are piling on the pressure." He cleared his throat with a cough. "We're all going to have to work harder, because at the moment there's a vicious, nasty killer wandering around out there as free as a bird, and right now, despite all our efforts to find them… we've got the square root of nothing."

He handed out the four blue manilla folders to four separate detective constables. "I've been through the statements from members of staff, and I've identified these four as possibly having further information if they had been pushed just a little harder." He opened one of the folders and pointed. "I've given hints at the line of questioning I want on Post-it notes. Any questions?"

"No, boss," came the replies.

"Okay then." He paced slowly across the room. "I'm fairly certain we're looking at a member of staff being the killer, but I'm not discounting the possibility it might have been a random maniac from the street, or even an angry lover." He paused for a moment. "The fact is, this is a real puzzle, but there's no such thing as the perfect crime. The killer will have slipped up and left a clue somewhere, and it's our job to find out where!"

SEVENTEEN

Gretchen had endured a week of sleepless nights since murdering Mario Spiteri. She couldn't rid the thought from her head that the police would see her somewhere on CCTV, or one of their forensic officers would find a clue pointing to her. Despite her efforts not to touch anything inside the pub with a bare hand, she was terrified she'd left a clue somewhere. She was a great fan of crime dramas and fully understood there was no such thing as the perfect crime, and she had been fearing a knock on her door ever since she'd arrived home.

One matter she could control was her relationship with Ryan Pryce, which she fully intended to take advantage of from hereon in. He doted on her, he had done since they'd first met, but she held not the slightest interest in him romantically. However, his devotion was such that she could use him to gain information about the Pals, allowing her access to knowledge that would help her achieve her aims. She had huge plans for him going forward. Ryan would ultimately be the instrument she would use to break the Pals' hearts.

At 10.30 on Wednesday evening, Gretchen spoke to Ryan by phone. She wrongly thought he would have been at Burnley's home ground, Turf Moor, that night, for the first home game of the season against Sunderland. But he was still in Kew, having been unable to get the time off work.

Despite suffering terrible anxiety attacks between the murder and the phone call, Gretchen tried to sound as happy and upbeat as usual, but she detected a change in Ryan's tone. He was unusually distant and cool, as though something was troubling him. She knew it couldn't have been the result – she'd seen on the local news that the Clarets had won 1-0.

At one point, the conversation moved onto the killing in Rotherham. "I'm so pleased I didn't go to the game," she said.

Ryan became silent, a silence that hung like a brooding cloud between them. Unable to stand it any longer, Gretchen broke the silence. "Are you okay?"

"I'm fine. Look, I've got to go. I'll call you in a few days." With that, Ryan abruptly ended the call. They'd only been chatting for five minutes, which was way shorter than she'd anticipated. She knew from experience that once Ryan was talking, he would happily keep jabbering on for half an hour, given the chance.

A continuous stream of questions turned over and over in her head. *Why was he being like that? Doesn't he like me anymore?* But one question worried her far more than the others. *Does he know something?*

*

Back home in his flat in Kew, South West London, Ryan had been moping since ending the call with Gretchen. He was desperately trying to figure out what to say to show he was interested in a relationship, but unable to express his feelings during the call, he found the best way to manage his emotions was to end it. He understood she was hurting over John, but now she was available, and each day without her seemed like an eternity.

He loved her so much it hurt, but if he wanted to have any chance of a long-term relationship, he had to accept it might take her a while to fully recover from her break-up with John. He could only hope that her reasons for keeping in touch with him, rather than any of the others, was because she trusted and cared for him more than them.

In the meantime, he'd simply have to wait. He was confident she'd reveal all to him in good time, once they were a couple.

EIGHTEEN

Three days later

"Hi, Ryan. Are you going on the Turf today?" Gretchen's voice was happy and upbeat.

Delighted at hearing her sounding so full of beans, despite the way he'd ended their call on Wednesday evening, he moved quickly to repair the damage. "Hey. Great to hear from you. Yes, it's my first home game of the season. I'm meeting everyone in the Royal Dyche before the game."

"Sounds good. Where are you staying?"

"The Premier Inn."

"Good choice, I love it there."

"Look, I'm sorry I was off during the week, I've had a shit time of it lately."

"I was worried it was something I'd said."

He laughed to reassure her. "Don't be daft. I'd had a bad argument with my sister. I couldn't think straight, that's all."

Gretchen quietly blew out a breath of relief. "I'm sorry to hear that. Is everything okay now?"

"Yep, all sorted. It's lovely to hear your voice again. Match days aren't the same without you."

"Ahh, that's so sweet. Thank you."

"I mean it." *Oh well, in for a penny, in for a pound.* "I'd love to see you sometime, you know, maybe go out somewhere?"

For a few seconds, Gretchen said nothing. Just as Ryan was beginning to worry he'd pushed her too far, she replied. "Okay, let's meet up. What are you doing after the match tonight?"

Her offer took Ryan by surprise. "I would love to, I really would, but I've been invited out for a meal at the Pendle Inn this evening by John and Joe. It's the first time they've ever asked me to join them – it wouldn't look good if I blew them out."

He knew as soon as he mentioned John's name it was a mistake. Gretchen spat her words out. "Well, if you'd rather go out with that bastard than spend an evening with me, there's nothing much I can say, is there?"

Hearing the hurt and anger in her voice swiftly made Ryan's mind up for him. "Don't be silly. Of course I'd rather spend time with you. Where would you like to meet?"

"How about The Crooked Billet at Worsthorne? It's a lovely pub with a great atmosphere; the beer's good; and they do the best pies for miles!"

Ryan's heart swelled with happiness. He was going out for the evening with the woman he adored! Not only that, but she loved beer and pies every bit as much as he did!

"That sounds great. I'll grab a taxi and see you there. 7.30 okay?"

"Perfect. I'll take a taxi too. I fancy a good drink."

NINETEEN

The home game against Hull City had been a cracker. Three times Burnley took the lead, only to be pegged back each time by Hull, who refused to lie down. The final five minutes left the home fans with their nerves in shreds, as Hull camped in the Burnley half and bombarded their goal, hitting the post with the last kick of the match.

Having held on against the sustained assault, the Burnley crowd exploded with relief at the final whistle, happy to see their team hang on for a point.

Meeting up with John and Joe in the cricket club after the game, Ryan sheepishly insisted on buying them both a pint to soften them up before letting them down.

"I'm sorry, lads, I won't be coming tonight. Something's come up and I need to be elsewhere."

Surprisingly, he saw John and Joe exchange a smile.

"Why are you so happy I can't come?"

John downed a mouthful of his pint. "We met a couple of birds on the concourse in the Jimmy Mac Upper at half-time."

"A couple of birds?" Ryan furrowed his brow.

"Yeah. One looked in her forties; the other was in her fifties."

"They were fit as fuck though," grinned Joe. "Proper MILFs."

"They chatted us up and looked well up for it, so we asked them to join us at the Pendle Inn!" said John.

Ryan's mouth fell open in disbelief. "So, if I hadn't cancelled, you would have blown me out anyway?"

Joe chuckled and nodded. "Sorry, mate, you'd have been playing gooseberry. Anyway, what have you got planned?"

Ryan could feel his face flushing. "Oh, it's just a friend I haven't seen for ages who asked to meet up."

Relieved at being off the hook and annoyed at being shunned so readily in equal measure, he forced a smile and all three chinked glasses.

"Here's to us all having a great evening!"

TWENTY

The evening at the Crooked Billet was a complete success, filled with beer, great food, free-flowing conversation and laughter. Sitting across from each other at a small table for two, they both made a conscious effort to keep the conversation light, never mentioning the events in Rotherham.

The only time the mood was broken was when Gretchen briefly explained how poorly John had treated her, and how she came to the sad realisation the relationship was going nowhere after six years. As her voice fractured with sadness, Ryan reached across and squeezed her hand. She looked up in surprise and their eyes locked; he fully expected her to pull away, but quite the opposite happened. Squeezing his hand back, she interlinked her fingers with his.

Almost quaking with excitement, Ryan made his move. "He didn't deserve you. I'd have never treated you like that. I love watching Burnley, but I can't imagine why anyone would choose a game of football over being with you."

Her face slowly split into a smile, but her eyes remained filled with sadness. "I know you wouldn't."

"I mean it, I love spending time with you." He stared at her through misty, love-filled eyes. *How could any man prefer football to you?*

She narrowed her eyes slightly, as her gaze burned into him. He felt her grip become a little more urgent. *Right then, Ryan, let's see what you're made of.*

"Are you asking me out?" she asked.

He gulped and his cheeks reddened. "Yes, I am."

Her grip tightened further, and she placed her free hand on top of their entwined fingers. "I'd love to, but not just yet, I'm still hurting too much. It wouldn't be fair on you cos I'm carrying too much baggage. Maybe in a couple of months?"

The sensation of his heart hammering on the inside of his ribcage was the best feeling Ryan had ever experienced. In a few weeks' time he would be going out with the most gorgeous woman in the world!

"I'll wait however long it takes."

Leaning across the table, he planted a lingering kiss on her cheek. His world was complete.

*

They shared a taxi back to their respective destinations, holding hands in the back seat throughout the journey.

As the car pulled up outside the Premier Inn, Gretchen embraced Ryan with a warm hug. She released her hold and stared deeply into his eyes. "This has all taken me by surprise, and I've got a nightmare time at work coming up. Could you give me some space this week? I promise I'll call next weekend."

He forced a smile, sad that he wouldn't be speaking to her for a whole week but happy the evening had gone so well. "Of course."

She pulled him close again and whispered, "Thank you," in his ear, accompanied by a kiss on his neck.

*

With the Premier Inn receding in the distance, Gretchen relaxed back into the taxi's rear seat. Her plan was going perfectly. Ryan was a nice enough man, but he wasn't her type at all. She didn't fancy him in the slightest. He was, however, perfectly positioned for her to make use of his puppy-dog devotion, and she fully intended to.

TWENTY-ONE

Gretchen suffered from severe mental health issues that, in the main, she managed to keep hidden from the rest of the world, including those closest to her. From a very young age she had been unable to process and handle episodes of abandonment, and her habit of reacting each time with extreme violence against those who rejected her had meant years of psychiatric treatment, most of which had been paid for by her concerned parents.

When she was only six, her best friend was her next-door neighbour, Emily Spicer. And in Gretchen's mind they weren't just ordinary best friends – they had linked little fingers and made a 'pinky promise' to each other. Then came the terrible day when Emily suddenly told her that Sarah Shortland was now her best friend, and she didn't like her anymore. Gretchen was completely and utterly devastated, but instead of reacting by crying in her bedroom like most young girls, she experienced no shedding of tears, just an overwhelming rage, coupled with a desire for revenge. She was gripped by an all-encompassing urge to make Emily pay for ditching her, without hurting her physically.

That evening, just before bedtime, while her mother and father were engrossed watching one of their favourite TV programmes, she walked calmly out of the back door, across the lawn, and through a small gate in the fence. The gate linking the two gardens had been installed by Emily's parents twelve months previously, to allow the children easy access to each other, so they could play together whenever they fancied it.

Once in Emily's garden, she walked the few steps to the hutch containing her former friend's pride and joy: her pet rabbit, Lucy. Sliding the bolt to open the hutch door, she smiled as Lucy, who loved being picked up and stroked, poked her nose out to greet her.

Reaching out, Gretchen grabbed Lucy and lifted her up by her ears, making the rabbit kick her legs frantically. Then she lifted the pencil she'd removed from her school pencil case and stabbed Lucy in the eye, penetrating right through to the brain.

Leaving the pencil embedded in Lucy's head, she dropped the still twitching rabbit to the ground. After wiping a small amount of blood from her hand onto her nightie, she turned to head back through the gate.

Throughout the whole episode, she'd experienced an almost trance-like state of mind, a trance which was shattered into wakefulness only when she heard Emily's mum Susan, who had witnessed the whole event through the kitchen window. Running out of the back door, she shouted, "Gretchen! What have you done?"

From her bedroom window above the kitchen, Emily had also seen the whole thing. She'd been playing with her dolls on the windowsill and could only stare in disbelief at what her former best friend had done. She had witnessed an event she would never forget and suffered an ordeal so traumatic, it would affect her for the rest of her life.

Up until the age of fifteen, that event had resulted in Gretchen's only contact with psychologists, psychiatrists and doctors. She had undergone treatment with three separate specialists for just over two years after butchering Lucy, and all three agreed it was a one-off loss of control brought on by an incident of severe emotional trauma. Her parents were assured their little girl was not suffering from any long-term condition; she wasn't in need of medication; and she would go on to live a normal life.

Then came the incident that changed everything. She was fifteen years old, teenage hormones were crashing through her system, and she'd fallen head-over-heels in love with a young boy in her class called Cornel. He was tall, slim, black and gorgeous! He was the boy that every girl in the school wished she could be with, and he was all Gretchen's. They'd been going steady for just over three months, and although they were still young, they'd recently enjoyed intercourse for the first time.

Cornel was a wonderful boyfriend: thoughtful, kind, considerate and caring. Gretchen loved him so much. She thought it was cute how he doted on his six-year-old twin sisters – they meant so much to him, and because of that, they meant so much to her too.

One Friday evening in winter, Cornel's parents decided to go out for a meal, leaving Cornel and Gretchen in charge of the girls for a couple of hours. Like all parents of young children, they fretted about leaving their teenage son and his girlfriend in charge.

"Call us if there's a problem and make sure they go to bed on time. We won't be long. We'll be back soon."

Cornel shook his head and sighed. "I will, Mum, now go! Enjoy yourselves!"

Almost as soon as their parents had left, the girls started playing up, trying to delay bedtime as long as possible. "Can we stay up late, Corny?"

"No, you can't."

"Can we have a bath?"

"No. You had one last night," said Cornel, an unusual hint of irritability in his voice.

"Oh, please, Corny. Please, please, please!"

Gretchen squeezed his hand. "It's okay, babe, I'll bath them. You look stressed – go and watch some TV and chill; we'll be done soon enough, then they can go to bed, and we can have a cuddle." She raised her eyebrows slowly and seductively at him.

He nodded and pulled his hand from hers without changing expression. "Okay. Sorry, I've got to make a call – there's something I need to sort. I'll be in the lounge."

Ten minutes later, bath time was going well. The girls were pouring water over each other and splashing Gretchen, who was joining in by splashing them back, which made them shriek with delight. They loved Gretchen so much, and she loved them.

Soon enough, the children were clean, happy and ready for bed. "Right, you can have two more minutes, then it's time for sleep."

The girls groaned but accepted they'd done well, and this was how it would have to be. Gretchen decided to use the two minutes to nip downstairs and give Cornel a kiss, before returning to the bathroom and drying the girls off.

As she reached the bottom of the staircase, she heard him speaking on the phone; it didn't sound a bit like Cornel's usual tone – he was speaking in a shouted whisper and sounded agitated. She tiptoed along the hallway without making a sound, eager to listen outside the lounge door.

"Okay, okay, I get it… look, I'll speak to Gretchen tomorrow." He then went quiet, listening to the person at the other end, before speaking once more. "I will, I promise you I will…" There was a long pause. "Of course I want to be with you… look, just be patient for one more day. I'll dump her tomorrow, then we can be together."

Gretchen felt her legs buckle under her and she had to fight hard to remain on her feet. Her thoughts began to run riot... *He's dumping me? He's fucking dumping me? But I love him. I'll never love anyone again like I love him!*

She didn't scream out, didn't burst into the lounge, didn't swear at him and hit him like any normal person would have done; she simply stared into space, and not one tear appeared in her eyes. That wasn't Gretchen's way. She walked calmly into the kitchen, half-filled the kettle and switched it on. Three minutes later, she stomped loudly along the hallway, intending that he should hear her footsteps. She heard him trying hard to keep his voice down, but she managed to catch the words, "She's coming, gotta go, love you."

Having slowly and calmly climbed the stairs, she placed the kettle on the landing, then lifted the children from the bath and dried them.

"Right, one quick game, then bed."

The girls jumped up and down in excitement, totally naked.

"Lay down here," said Gretchen, pointing at the landing carpet. The girls happily complied. She then took a large bath towel and laid it over the top half of the girls' bodies, covering their heads and torsos down to their upper thighs.

"Are you going to tickle us?" squealed one of them.

"Sort of," said Gretchen. "Ready?"

"Yes, yes!" came the gleefully shouted replies.

Reaching down and lifting the kettle, Gretchen said, "Here you go then," and poured boiling water over the girls' legs, an action that produced ear-piercing screams of agony.

Within seconds, Cornel had raced up the stairs. "What's happening?" he screamed. Seeing what Gretchen was doing and his sisters writhing in agony, he shouted, "What the fuck are you doing?"

Gretchen, who was still standing over the girls holding the kettle, simply stared at him without answering. She had done what she needed to do; she'd taken her revenge by hurting the things he loved most in the world.

TWENTY-TWO

When she appeared in court, the judge accepted reports submitted by numerous medical experts that Gretchen was of unsound mind and unfit to plead. He sentenced her to be detained for an indeterminate period undergoing psychiatric treatment, until she was considered fit for release.

At the age of twenty-one, Gretchen was released from the secure unit where she'd been housed undergoing treatment for borderline personality disorder for the past six years. She'd been a model inmate, and the small team of psychiatrists in charge of her care persuaded the assessment board that, with correct ongoing medication, she no longer posed a risk to society.

In the modern way of doing things, Cornel's parents' views were considered, but their heartfelt assertions that Gretchen hadn't yet received sufficient punishment were insufficient to sway enough members to vote against her release. So, despite there being a huge amount of disagreement within the assessment board, by a majority of four to three they decided to release her under supervision.

So it was that, despite giving two innocent young girls disfiguring and life-changing injuries, let alone the damage to their mental well-being, Gretchen Grover walked out of the unit that had been her home for the past six years and back into the world.

Five years later, with no further incidents occurring, supervision was ended, and Gretchen was once more regarded as a normal member of society.

TWENTY-THREE

Alighting the taxi, Gretchen cast her gaze across the surrounding area. A run-down housing estate sat along the opposite side of the road, and it looked perfectly suited for her purposes. Looking carefully all around a particular tower block, and not seeing CCTV cameras anywhere in the vicinity, she'd made her mind up: this was the place she'd been looking for.

It had been two weeks since she'd brutally killed Mario Spiteri in Rotherham, and despite suffering crippling anxiety during the first week, she'd felt much better during the second week. Having literally got away with murder, she was now buzzing with excitement at the memory. Paying the driver through the front passenger window, she smiled warmly.

"Thank you. Keep the change."

"No, thank *you*, darling," he leered. "Always a pleasure to drive for someone as gorgeous as you."

She leant seductively through the passenger window, rested her forearms on the door and peered at him sexily over the rims of a pair of red-framed spectacles. Her low-cut top partly exposed the curve of her breasts and her long, blonde, and remarkably realistic, wig tumbled over her shoulders.

"Perhaps you could help me?"

The taxi driver's eyes sparkled with delight and anticipation. "Now that would be a pleasure!"

Gretchen chuckled and pretended to be embarrassed. *God, getting men to do what I want is so easy!* She nodded towards the nearby estate. "I'm looking to rent a flat somewhere around here, so I thought I'd check out the area before going to an estate agent."

"Very wise."

"Problem is, I can't afford much. What's that estate like?"

"How do you mean?"

"Well, it looks a bit rough."

"Rough?"

Oh shit, have I offended him? "Don't get me wrong, I don't mind that, but is it safe?"

The driver narrowed his eyes without speaking. Was he annoyed with her?

She moved to recover the situation. "Sorry, I didn't mean to offend you. The area surrounding the estate looks lovely, it's just the estate itself."

The driver lifted a finger and pointed up through the windscreen. "See that block there?"

Gretchen followed his finger all the way to the tallest block on the estate, less than fifty metres away.

"Yes."

"One of my mates lives in a flat on the eleventh floor. He's disabled and doesn't get out much, but he's been there for years."

She shrugged her shoulders. "So?"

"He's never had an issue in all the time he's lived there. It might look dingy, but there's very little crime around here compared to parts of St Annes. And he's had no problems with the neighbours either."

She lifted her eyebrows in genuine surprise.

"That's good to know, maybe I'll have a quick walk around."

She leant lower into the car window, exposing her cleavage even more. "Look, I don't usually do this, but I like you. Do you fancy going out for a drink sometime?"

He shook his head, holding up his left hand to show the wedding band on his ring finger.

"Sorry, love, I'm happily married."

She sighed. "Shame, you seem really nice. It's true what they say – the best ones are always taken."

He sucked in a deep breath. "Look, I need to get off to my next job, but I'm free this evening. If you like, I'll take you up to my friend's flat – you could ask him about the rent and the neighbourhood – it might give you some idea?"

She shook her head. "Sorry, I'm booked on the 4.00 train from Temple Meads to Stafford. I'll be back at Saturday lunchtime though."

He tapped his fingers nervously on the steering wheel, mentally shifting his life around inside his head. "Okay, I'll meet you at the bottom of the block on Saturday. What time would suit you?"

"Around 12.30?"

He nodded. "Sounds good. I'll be here."

She pulled away from the door and held a hand up. "Thank you so much – you've been a great help. By the way, what's your name?"

"Gavin. What's yours?"

"Adrienne."

The radio crackled a message which Gretchen found indecipherable but Gavin seemed to have no trouble understanding. Picking up the radio mic, he held it to his mouth and pressed the transmit button. "Yep, send my apologies. On my way now." He winked at her. "See you on Saturday, gorgeous." He gunned the accelerator and drove quickly away.

TWENTY-FOUR

The August sunshine was pleasantly warm as Gretchen waited anxiously for Gavin's arrival; he was a few minutes late and she was starting to get edgy. For her plan to work, she was reliant on tight timing.

Luckily, her fears proved groundless, and she heaved a sigh of relief as Gavin's taxi appeared round the corner of a nearby Sainsbury's local, at the far side of the housing estate. Moments later, his grinning face greeted her as he pulled into a parking space alongside the bottom of the tower block. A large black plaque above the door proclaimed it to be 'Roberts House' in white writing.

"Hello, gorgeous, you look amazing."

She preened at the compliment and smiled with satisfaction. She had made a real effort for this meeting. Apart from wearing the same glasses, she had slicked down her own brown hair tightly to her scalp, so the long, blonde locks of the wig once again looked totally convincing and natural. She had applied just the right amount of make-up and lipstick to look attractive, but not tarty, and dressed in skin-tight blue jeans and a light-blue T-shirt.

Hmm, not bad for thirty-nine, she'd thought to herself as she looked in the mirror that morning.

Locking the car with a press of the fob, Gavin walked up to Gretchen. This was the first time she'd seen him standing, and he was much taller than she'd imagined, somewhere around 6'2" she guessed. "Wow, you're a big boy, aren't you?"

"You have no idea," he replied, lifting his eyebrows suggestively.

She smiled politely and reddened at the obvious joke.

"Come on," he said. "I'll take you up to meet Keth."

"Keth? That's a strange name."

"His real name is Keith." Gavin chuckled. "But he's got an eye missing, so everyone calls him Keth."

Shaking her head in disbelief, Gretchen said, "That is so cruel!"

"It's not really, even he calls himself Keth now. He's a great bloke, and very aware of his condition."

"His condition?"

"Yes, he's got an extremely rare wasting disease; I can't remember the name of it right now, but his body is basically rotting – that's why he had to have an eye removed." He nodded in the direction of a communal entrance door to the block and Gretchen walked alongside him.

"That sounds awful."

"It is. He can't walk because his spine has crumbled. He's going deaf; only one kidney works; he's lost an eye; and he relies on his motorised wheelchair to get about."

Gavin punched in a code on a panel and the door opened. They walked a few yards into a corridor, where the doors to two lifts stood side by side; he pressed the call button and the left-hand pair of doors opened. Holding out an arm, he allowed Gretchen to enter first.

"How does he fill his time?" she asked.

"He loves music and likes listening to the radio mostly; the sight in his good eye isn't great, so he can't really make out what's happening on the telly."

This was music to Gretchen's ears, but she continued to play her part to perfection. "The poor man, I'll give him a big hug when we get up there."

"He'll love that!" laughed Gavin, pressing the button for floor eleven.

Shortly after a soft pinging sound heralded the arrival of the lift on the eleventh floor, the doors opened, and they stepped into a poorly lit corridor. An unpleasant, musty smell assailed Gretchen's nostrils, and she could feel the carpet was tacky under her feet.

The doorway to flat forty-three was only three metres to their left, and Gavin moved swiftly to the door and pressed the bell, which sounded a traditional *bing-bong*.

Twenty seconds passed in absolute silence, until Gavin quietly muttered, "Takes him a while to lift himself from the armchair onto his wheelchair; he'll be here in a minute."

The soft hum of an electric motor slowly grew in volume, followed by the sound of locks being released. Finally, the door handle turned, and the dark-green door was opened wide.

TWENTY-FIVE

"Blimey! I can't see your face, love, but I can see your shape. I see what you mean, Gav, she's a corker!"

Gavin reddened and sheepishly said, "Sorry about that, Adrienne."

She laughed out loud, putting an arm around Gavin. She placed a hand on the top of his backside and patted his bottom, her hand lingering there far longer than was necessary. "Don't be silly, I'm flattered!"

Keth was smiling up from a very substantial motorised wheelchair. He was a painfully thin man, wearing spectacles with one very thick lens and one that was clouded, presumably to obscure his missing eye. His thinning grey hair, gaunt expression and hollow cheeks made him appear in his sixties, although he was probably more like forty. He skilfully reversed the wheelchair to allow them access.

On entering the flat, she noted how clean and tidy everywhere was. There was no musty smell in here; the carpets and furniture looked in good condition; and every surface was dust free. She walked down the narrow corridor, passing doorways into the bedroom, bathroom and kitchen.

"Lovely place you've got here," she commented, leaning down to give Keth the hug she'd promised Gavin.

She could see that he loved being squeezed by such an attractive woman; she guessed it was something he'd not experienced for a very long time.

"Thank you, I like it."

At the end of the hallway was the lounge, with its beige corner unit, glass-topped coffee table and huge TV screen resting snugly against the opposite wall. The walls were adorned with action-shot illustrations of Bristol City football matches, the irony of which brought the merest hint of a cruel smile to Gretchen's mouth. Just like the other rooms, everything was clean and tidy, although she did detect cigarette smoke, something she detested.

Glancing through the patio doors, she saw chest-high railings surrounding a good-sized balcony; it was certainly much larger than it appeared from ground level. At even intervals over the height of the railings were four rails, the gaps filled by diamond-shaped wire netting, which was surprisingly attractive.

Keth wheeled his chair alongside Gretchen. "Gav says you're thinking of moving into the area?"

"Yes, I've been offered a promotion to Assistant Manager, which would mean transferring to our depot here in Bristol. But before I accept, I wanted to see if I could find anywhere suitable to live."

Keth nodded. "Very wise. Look, I know it doesn't look great around here, but the people are nice and there's not much crime. On top of that, you won't find many areas this close to Bristol city centre where the rents are so reasonable. You've only got to move a few streets away and the rents are fifty per cent more."

She smiled. "Well, if your flat's anything to go by, I'm very impressed." She walked over to the closed patio doors and looked downwards. "Amazing view. What's that place with all the table and chairs over there?" She pointed downwards, knowing full well what the answer to her question would be.

"That's the Five-Pointed Star," said Gavin. "It's a shithole pub but popular with football fans before City home games." He opened the patio doors and stepped outside, allowing a waft of warm air into the flat.

Gretchen needed Keth out of the way. Turning to him she said, "Sorry, could I trouble you for a glass of water? I'm parched."

"I'm so sorry, I should have offered you a drink sooner. I don't have many visitors, so I'm probably not the best host. Would you like a tea or coffee rather than water?"

She smiled warmly. "A coffee would be lovely, no sugar thanks. I'll tell you what, you relax, and I'll make it." She made the offer confident in the knowledge that he'd refuse, which he duly did.

"You won't," he insisted. "You're a guest in my house... I'll make it. Gavlar!" he shouted, mimicking Smithy from the TV show *Gavin and Stacey*. "What do you fancy?"

"I'm fine thanks, mate, nothing for me."

Keth expertly span the wheelchair around, guided it into the hallway, then turned left and disappeared into the kitchen.

Joining Gavin on the balcony, Gretchen fawned over the vista.

"Wow! That's an amazing view – I can't believe how far you can see!"

As she did this, she carefully checked that the surrounding balconies were all unoccupied.

He agreed with her. "Yes, it's wonderful on a beautiful day like this, isn't it?"

Leaning over the top rail and peering down, Gretchen placed her right foot on the bottom rail, about a foot off the balcony floor, and hoisted herself up, bringing her waist level with the top rail. Removing a handkerchief from her handbag, she gripped the handrail with the handkerchief, leant forward and pointed straight down. "Oh no, what's happening down there?"

Gavin grabbed her left arm and pulled her back to safety. "What the fuck are you doing, Adrienne? That's so dangerous – one slip and you're gone!"

Feigning contriteness, Gretchen said, "But there's a man down there trying to break into your car!"

In a flash, Gavin had released her arm and placed his left foot on the first rail, swapping places with her, hoisting himself up and leaning over to get a view straight down to his car, which was almost directly below them. His right leg was jutting backwards, almost horizontal, as he strained to get a good view of his vehicle. Gretchen quickly stepped behind him, firmly grabbed his flailing right leg and lifted hard, pushing him forward.

"What are you... wait... no, no, no!" The final 'no' was prolonged, as he lost his grip on the handrail and plummeted through the air.

Not wasting any time, Gretchen wiped the rail clean where she'd gripped it with the handkerchief, making doubly certain she hadn't left any trace of her being there, then she walked silently into the kitchen.

Using the handkerchief to pick up the carving knife with the sharpest point from a knife block resting on a worktop just inside the door, she crept up behind Keth, who was spooning coffee into a cup.

Her need for a silent approach was greatly helped by the noisy kettle coming to the boil. Lifting the knife high, she plunged it into the back of Keth's neck, severing his spinal cord and killing him almost instantly. He slumped forward in his wheelchair, his nose and cheekbone smashing into the edge of the worktop, the knife's handle protruding from the wound.

Grabbing a smaller knife from the block with the handkerchief, she carved the letters TCP into the wooden chopping board, leaving the knife embedded in the centre of the letter C, before opening the door with the handkerchief and walking out.

Moving quickly away from the flat, she skipped down the stairs rather than taking the lift, passing nobody on her way down. The crowd, which had quickly gathered around Gavin's wrecked body, didn't take much notice of the attractive blonde lady exiting the block. People were screaming and shouting, and some were dialling 999 on their mobile phones, but no one appeared to notice as she calmly left the bedlam outside Roberts House behind her.

Ten minutes later, she was well away from the area, walking quickly towards the city centre. Her whole body quivered with a mixture of fear and excitement, but she allowed herself a contented smile. Now all she had to do was contact Ryan, and once again he would unwittingly provide her with the perfect alibi.

TWENTY-SIX

On her way to the city centre, Gretchen followed her plan to the letter and called Ryan.

"Hi, how are you?"

"Good thanks, you?"

"I'm fine. Thanks for giving me space; I've got my head sorted now."

"That's good." Ryan was running late and about to enter the Five-Pointed Star when the call came in, so he leant on a wall outside the front of the pub to chat in private before joining the Pals inside.

"I loved our date last week. Do you fancy coming out for another drink sometime soon?"

Her words had testosterone pumping through Ryan's groin in seconds. This was a chance he didn't want to turn down.

"I'd love to, but I live in Kew – you live in Blackburn, and I'm only up there two or three times a year."

"I live in Darwen, not Blackburn," she corrected. "You Burnley fans are obsessed with Blackburn! The distance is a nuisance, but I'm sure we can work something out."

"Are you coming down to London anytime soon?"

"No." She feigned a pleading voice. "Couldn't you make another trip up here... for me?"

Ryan's lust quickly took control of all reasoning. "Okay, I will. I'm busy for the next home game, but we've got Birmingham at the Turf next month. I'll book a B&B."

"Great, I'll look forward to it." A noisy group of teenage girls passed close by her, which worked perfectly. "Sorry, Ryan, I've got to go, I'm with my mates at the Trafford Centre."

He laughed. "They sound like a noisy bunch. Have a great time. I'll call you during the week."

"Great, I'll look forward to it. Bye."

Hanging up the call, Gretchen experienced a warm glow of satisfaction that her plans were coming together perfectly. Despite having just killed two men, she smiled to herself and strode out for Bristol Temple Meads train station.

TWENTY-SEVEN

"Here's to you, Stevie Grimberly, Burnley loves you more than you will know, woah-ooh!"

Every Burnley fan in the pub garden responded by singing the song on repeat. "Here's to you, Stevie Grimberly, Burnley loves you more than you will know, woah-ooh! Here's to you, Stevie Grimberly, Burnley loves you more than you will know, woah-ooh!"

Fifteen Pals had pulled two bench tables together in the rear garden of the Five-Pointed Star, a large pub just under a mile away from Ashton Gate Stadium – the home of Bristol City FC.

The two large umbrellas fitted snugly through the centre of each table and met in the middle, forming a half-decent cover for them, providing at least a modicum of protection from the constant light drizzle.

"Can't we go back inside," moaned Val. "It's pissing down out here, and those sirens are really annoying."

It was true – the drizzle was coming down steadily, and there had been police and ambulance sirens wailing since they'd arrived, although their frequency was now diminishing.

"Nah, we're better off out here," said Stuart. "It's packed solid in there."

As usual, most of the group had arrived around 12.30. They'd spent the first half an hour inside the pub, then moved into the garden when it got too crowded. They were already in high spirits. Burnley were playing well – they'd beaten Millwall 4-1 away in a league cup tie during the week, won one and drawn one league game since the Rotherham game and were sitting fourth in the Championship table.

Only four of the Pals – John, Joe, Ian and Stuart – had attended the Millwall game, but they were still raving about how good the team's performance had been.

"Bristol City haven't won a game yet. I reckon we'll turn them over no problem." John Horsfall was in particularly ebullient mood, helped in large part by the five pints of bitter he'd consumed.

"They're not playing badly," said Ian. "They've had three draws against good sides and look decent to me. It'll be a tough game. I'd be happy with a draw."

"How are you feeling, Joe?" asked Becki, wrapping a motherly arm around his shoulder.

Joe frowned, not because of the question, but because her actions had caused a tiny amount of his beer to spill. "I'm fine, why? Shouldn't I be?"

She took her arm away and played hurt at his sharp response. "I was just trying to be caring after the police nicked you!"

"What's that about you being nicked?" asked Jack.

Becki said, "Joe saw a man coming out of a door into the bar and assumed it was the toilet, so he stepped in and took hold of the door, but the man shouted, 'It's staff only through there,' so he stepped back into the bar again, closed the door, then spotted the actual toilet a couple of metres away."

"What's wrong with that?" asked Jack.

"Some wanker told the police they'd seen him coming out of a door marked 'Private'."

"That's right," said Ryan. "And the thick coppers didn't do their job properly. They could see Joe's hand never left the door, so he couldn't possibly have gone upstairs and killed that man."

"Some bastard's made a statement telling them about me," added Joe. "Fucking Burnley fan too, according to the cops. I've got no idea who though."

Jack was cringing with embarrassment but fought hard to act as naturally as possible.

The mood was changed by Becki shouting, "Group photo, group photo!"

She held her phone aloft and began herding the group tightly together. It was something she often did at away games. She liked to post the images onto various social media sites so that members of the Pals unable to make the trip could still feel part of the day.

She climbed up onto one of the bench seats to enable her to fit everyone in, found the best angle and clicked off a few shots.

Memories of the dramatic events at their trip to Rotherham two weeks ago were fading fast, and even Joe was only speaking of it very occasionally, despite being dragged off to Rotherham Police Station. Burnley FC was once again the main topic of conversation, interspersed with the usual chat among friends regarding everyday trials and tribulations.

Twenty minutes later, the drizzle had stopped. Ginny and Jack were in the middle of regaling everyone with a funny story about Jack falling into the canal during a recent narrowboat holiday, when Stuart returned from the bar with a tray of drinks.

"One or two people inside the pub are badly shaken up – they are saying they saw a man fall from that building." He indicated a nearby residential block of flats, the first two floors of which were obscured by the pub garden's two-metre-high panel fencing.

"Shit," said Val. "When did that happen?"

"Half an hour ago, apparently."

"Fucking hell, we must have just missed it," said Val.

"Is he dead?" asked Ginny.

Stuart nodded. "He fell from a balcony on one of the upper floors; they're saying he was screaming all the way down. Did anyone hear anything?"

They all shook their heads.

Jack looked over to the block. "It looks about fifteen stories; if he fell from near the top, he'd have been almost pureed when he hit the ground. I'm surprised we didn't hear him."

"We were probably inside," said Simon.

"That explains all those sirens!" said Becki.

Ian placed his beer on the table and stood with hands on hips, staring blankly at the ground. John knew that stance well and was fully aware how easily upset Ian could get when bad things happened. He walked over and placed a reassuring arm around his friend's shoulders.

"You okay, mate?"

Ian's eyes moistened. "What a horrible way to die. Can you imagine how terrified he was as he fell?"

"No, I can't, but maybe he'd had enough of life, maybe he wanted to die?"

Shaking his head vigorously, Ian said, "Didn't you hear what Stuart said? He was screaming as he fell! Doesn't sound much like someone who wanted to kill themselves!"

John had to concede the point. "Yes, you're right. The only way to look at it is… he's at peace now."

Ian pulled away from his friend's embrace.

"I hate that attitude. He was somebody's son for fuck's sake!" Moving away from the group, Ian found a relatively quiet spot near the fence. Nobody followed him, recognising that he needed to be alone for a while.

"Fucking hell," said Becki. "That bloke had his throat cut at Rotherham, now some poor bastard has thrown himself off a tower block!"

Ryan downed a draft of beer and pursed his lips.

"None of us know what happened up there – maybe he did kill himself, but have you considered the alternative… maybe he was pushed?"

TWENTY-EIGHT

The group were shaken to have another violent death taking place so close by, but they remained true Burnley football fans and continued drinking as if nothing had happened. Simon insisted on buying everyone another round of drinks and the conversation returned to the subjects of team selection, the upcoming match and how big Burnley's away following would be.

As it turned out, there were just under two thousand Burnley fans in the Atyeo Stand – the away section of Ashton Gate Stadium. They made a tremendous amount of noise throughout the match, a small group constantly singing their latest song in support of the chairman, "Ian Grace, Ian Grace, Ian Ian Grace. He's got grey hair, but we don't care, Ian Ian Grace!"

They were enjoying a good performance from their team, but without the end result of a goal. However, they were silenced by a dubious penalty awarded to the home side two-thirds through the second half, clinically despatched by their French striker, Lechange. Nothing more really happened, despite intense pressure on the City goal, and the game ended with Burnley's first defeat of the season.

"Well, that was shite," said John, washing his hands alongside Jack in the concourse toilets, shortly after the final whistle. "The performance was okay, no end product though."

Jack didn't reply but just grunted, staring hard at his reflection in the large mirror, turmoil in his eyes.

"You okay?" John asked, looking at him.

The question snapped Jack back into the moment. "To be honest, mate, all match I couldn't stop thinking about that guy falling from the tower block."

John patted him firmly on the back, and they moved away from the basins to allow others to access them.

"Is that the policeman coming out in you?"

"Probably."

"Come on," said John. "It's not like there was anything we could have done to stop it."

Jack walked alongside John towards the exit, wiping his hands dry on his jeans. "That's not what's worrying me."

Frowning, John asked, "Worrying you, why should anything be worrying you?"

Standing still and turning to face John, Jack pursed his lips. "I'm probably being stupid, but my copper's instinct is telling me something's not right."

"What do you mean?"

"Three men dying in suspicious circumstances at two separate locations, each time close to where we were gathered."

John laughed. "It's just a coincidence, mate."

But Jack wasn't convinced. "The one in Rotherham was murdered for certain, and this bloke was screaming all the way down. What if they're not just a coincidence? What if they're linked somehow?"

Suppressing a snort of laughter, John smiled. "Sorry, mate, you're talking daft. Now come on, they'll be wondering where we are."

He tugged Jack by the arm, and they stepped back onto

the concourse. The crowds of fans departing the stadium had thinned out, but Ginny and Ian were still waiting patiently for them.

Looking up and down the concourse, Jack was perplexed. "Where are the others?"

Ginny said. "A few headed off looking for a pub, but Becki needed to get home in a hurry because she's out with friends tonight, and she was giving Ryan a lift, so they said they'd see us at West Brom."

The four of them strode away from the stadium, refusing to react to taunts and jeers about the result from a large group of mouthy Bristol City teenagers.

"Silly little tossers," snapped Jack. "They're only brave in a crowd."

Soon enough it was time for Ian and John to head for the station, while Jack and Ginny returned to their car.

Pointing at Jack, John chuckled. "Jack thinks there's something sinister going on with the two blokes who've died at Rotherham and here – he thinks they might be linked!"

Ian looked at his friend. "Don't laugh – innocent men have died. Jack might be right; stranger things have happened."

TWENTY-NINE

Sunday morning dawned wet and windy, and the incident room hurriedly set up at Broadbury Road Police Station was humming with conversation. Six detectives from the Avon and Somerset Major Incident Team were gathered in the briefing room, their numbers supplemented by two local CID officers. The room was filled with the buzz of excited chattering, awaiting the arrival of the man in charge, DCI Stan Jarvis.

The double doors leading into the incident room burst open, and DCI Jarvis paced confidently in. "Good afternoon," he barked. "For the two local officers assisting us, my name is DCI Jarvis…" he threw a deep pile of papers onto the table at the head of the room with a thud, then turned to face everyone, "…and I don't suffer fools gladly. So, work hard, don't piss me off and we'll all get on famously!"

The local officers exchanged an uncertain glance – this was not the type of senior officer they were used to, and it was certainly not the welcome they'd anticipated.

Stan Jarvis was very much an old-school detective. A man who was liked and loathed in equal measure by the more senior officers in the Avon and Somerset Constabulary. Liked, because he was the best detective in the force by some distance – a man who solved difficult cases where others had failed. Loathed, because he refused to move with the times – he detested modern methods of policing, and that included how briefings were conducted.

Jarvis was not a physically imposing man, small of stature at 5'7" and slim build. At fifty-two years of age, and no longer worried about keeping fit, he had developed a small pot belly and flabby, hanging jowls.

As usual, he was wearing a dark-blue suit with white shirt and blue tie. His hair had remained remarkably dark brown, with only a few specks of grey creeping through here and there. It was not his appearance that was imposing but his supremely confident manner and, surprisingly for such a small man, a deep, booming voice that demanded attention.

Instantly making a point about how he liked things done in the old-fashioned way, Stan removed an A4-sized photograph from the pile of papers he'd dropped onto the table and stuck it onto a board using a drawing pin. He tapped the horrific picture noisily with the back of the middle finger on his right hand.

"Gavin Stoneman. Forty-one years of age. From the St Annes area of Bristol." He cast his gaze around the assembled officers. "Pushed from the balcony of his friend's flat on the eleventh floor of Roberts House, Queen Anne's Walk, on the Meadows estate."

Another A4 photograph was lifted from the pile and placed alongside the picture of Gavin's smashed body, lying on the paving slabs where he'd landed. Once again, he tapped the new photo.

"And this is Keith Clarkson, the man who had rented the flat at number 43 Roberts House, where he'd lived for the past seven years. He was almost blind, severely disabled and spent most of each day in a wheelchair."

There was an audible gasp from a couple of officers at the

sight of a defenceless disabled man in a wheelchair with a large knife protruding from his neck.

"Some sick bastard wasn't satisfied with throwing Gavin Stoneman from the balcony; they then stabbed Keith Clarkson in the neck from behind, the gutless coward."

Pulling back a chair, Stan stood on the chair seat and rested his bottom on the back support, a habit the MIT officers had witnessed many times before, but his unusual behaviour caught the two local officers unaware. One of them turned to the other and raised his eyebrows in surprise.

"Is there a problem?" barked Jarvis.

The officer thought quickly and deflected Jarvis's question with one of his own. "Couldn't Stoneman have stabbed Clarkson in the neck, then thrown himself off the balcony?"

Jarvis fixed the officer with an icy stare, before his expression slowly mellowed, one corner of his mouth curling upwards.

"Good question." He cast his gaze around the room. "I'm surprised one of the MIT failed to ask that." The hint of a smile grew, and he grinned wickedly at his own officers, before turning serious once more. "Two of the neighbours heard Stoneman shouting at someone to get back from the railing. Moments later, they heard him screaming, 'No, no, no,' before falling. So, I don't think he committed suicide, do you?"

"No, sir," replied both local officers in unison.

"Good. Correct answer."

This brought a ripple of laughter from the MIT officers, and once more a corner of Jarvis's mouth curled. He reached into an inside jacket pocket and produced a small, clear plastic police evidence bag; he held the bag up for everyone to see.

"This is a Clarets Foundation members card from Burnley Football Club." He turned the bag around to reveal a signature on the back. "It's an untidy signature, but we believe it's been signed S. Quigley."

Stepping down from the chair, Jarvis handed the evidence bag to an officer, who scrutinised it, then passed it on.

"The card was found in the rear trouser pocket of Gavin Stoneman," Jarvis scratched the side of his face, "which set me wondering… why would a Bristol taxi driver have a membership card belonging to a Burnley football fan in his trouser pocket?"

A female detective from the MIT raised a hand. "It could have been left in his cab that morning, sir, Burnley were playing at City yesterday; things get left in cabs all the time."

Jarvis gave the merest of nods. "Usually, I'd agree with you, but I've contacted the company he works for, Custom Cabs. He wasn't due to start work until 1.00, so he wouldn't have taken any fares by the time he died."

"Maybe he was doing a bit of moonlighting before he started his shift?"

Jarvis shook his head. "We've checked with his wife. He didn't leave home until just after 12.20. He'd told her he needed to leave early for work because he was popping to see a friend. He fell from the balcony around twenty minutes later, so he didn't have time to take any fares."

"Perhaps he was lying to his wife. Men have been known to do that," said the female detective sarcastically. A comment which filled the room with laughter.

"CCTV of his vehicle has been found showing him just after he left home, and we've managed to hop from camera to camera all the way to Roberts House. Unfortunately, there are no close-up images available near Roberts House, but a single camera does capture a long view of his car approaching the block. The fact is, he didn't pick any fares up; he drove there alone."

The room fell silent, with only the shuffling of bums on seats audible.

Sucking in a breath, then blowing out hard, Jarvis said, "As we've nothing else to go on, I've contacted the Clarets Foundation at Burnley Football Club, and they've given us the address of a Stuart Quigley. Who, by the way, they supplied a ticket to for the match here on Saturday, so we know he was here. Not only that, but he is also the only Quigley on their books, so to my mind that makes him worth speaking to." He paused for a moment. "Guess where he lives?"

"Burnley?" Three MIT officers called in unison.

"Nope, Ardingly in Sussex. I've contacted Sussex Police, and officers are on their way to arrest him as we speak. I've also despatched a car to collect him and bring him back here."

A low murmur of surprise swept the room.

"Dan and Kelvin."

"Yes, guv," responded two MIT detectives.

"You will be interviewing Mr Quigley. The remaining MIT officers will conduct door-to-door enquiries around the area and check for any CCTV that may have been missed."

"Have we found anything else of interest yet, guv?" asked one of the local officers.

"Yes, witnesses say about a dozen people exited the block in the minutes following Stoneman's fall. Most were probably wanting to see what all the fuss was about, but one of them might be our killer." Lifting a water bottle to his lips, he drank greedily and wiped his mouth. "I want every person who exited that block identified and statements taken."

He pointed at the local CID officers. "Your job will be to take statements from those identified as leaving the block after Stoneman fell, and if there are any other witnesses who have come forward overnight, take statements from them too."

The local officers acknowledged their duties.

Jarvis paced up and down like a caged tiger for a few seconds, then turned to face the team once more.

"Anyone here know what the letters TCP stand for?"

His question was met with blank faces, shaking heads and silence.

"I'm asking, because it looks like the killer carved the letters TCP into the chopping board before making off."

"What, like a clue?" asked an officer.

Jarvis shrugged. "Who knows? Cocky bastard if so." A determined expression filled his features. "And I don't like cocky villains."

The detectives murmured their agreement.

"Anyone got anything else to add?"

The room remained silent.

"Any questions or anything you're uncertain of?"

Once again, silence.

"Good, let's get to work."

THIRTY

Stuart had just returned from his regular Sunday morning cycle ride. Riding into his driveway, he was more than a little surprised to see two marked police vehicles parked on his drive. Already partially dismounted, he glided onto the paved driveway balanced on one pedal, finally stopping alongside the police vehicles. Seeing him arrive, two uniformed officers climbed out of each vehicle.

Dripping in sweat following his forty-two-mile ride, Stuart greeted the officers with trepidation, fearing something terrible may have happened to a family member.

"Good morning, is there a problem?"

A chubby-faced male constable wasted no time in coming straight to the point. "Stuart Quigley?"

"Yes."

"I'm arresting you on suspicion of the murders of Gavin Stoneman and Keith Clarkson yesterday morning at Roberts House, Queen Anne's Walk, Bristol."

He firmly gripped Stuart's left arm while a colleague gripped his right arm.

"What the fuck are you on about? I've never heard of these people! I was with friends all day yesterday – you can check!"

Roughly turned around to face the van, Stuart was secured in handcuffs behind his back.

"You do not have to say anything, but it may harm your defence if you fail to mention when questioned something that you later rely on in court. Anything you do say may be given in evidence. Do you understand?"

Throughout the caution, Stuart shouted continually, protesting his innocence and struggling to release himself.

"This is bullshit – I've done nothing wrong! Let me go!"

The officer turned Stuart to face him. "Please calm down, Mr Quigley. If you're innocent, then you've got nothing to worry about, have you? But we have evidence which shows you had contact with one of the victims yesterday. Now, would you like us to take you indoors for a shower and a change of clothes? You might be quite a while."

Racking his brains trying to recall the events of yesterday, he couldn't think of a single time when he'd been alone with anyone, let alone had the opportunity to commit murder. Fighting to control his overwhelming anger, Stuart slowly began to calm down and accepted the offer to clean himself up.

Ten minutes later, the rear door of the police car slammed closed, leaving him handcuffed to an officer on the back seat. He secured his seatbelt and settled down to steel himself for the long journey to Bristol.

THIRTY-ONE

Shortly after being booked in at the Broadbury Road custody suite, Stuart was taken to have his fingerprints, photographs and DNA taken. Once that was complete, a detective signed him out on the custody record and took him to interview room two.

"How did you arrive in Bristol yesterday, Mr Quigley?" Detective Constable Kelvin Cross posed the first question, asking it as soon as introductions for the tape had been completed.

Leaning back on his chair and blowing out hard, Stuart said, "By train."

"And why did you travel to Bristol?"

"I'm a Burnley fan; I came here for the match."

DC Cross jotted something down. "What were your movements before arriving at the stadium?"

"I went to the Five-Pointed Star and met some friends. The place was filled with people talking about a man falling from a tower block."

"The Five-Pointed Star is a long way from the train station. How did you get there?"

"By taxi."

DC Dan Frost slowly wrote the word TAXI in block capitals. Kelvin glanced down at the word.

"Who was the driver?"

Stuart looked bemused by the question and glanced at the female duty solicitor alongside him. She shrugged and inclined her head, urging him – as she'd advised him before they started – to answer, "No comment." But Stuart had already dismissed this idea shortly after he met her.

"I've no idea, just some guy."

"Did he say his name?"

"No, why should he? He hardly said a word throughout the journey."

"Can you describe him?"

"I dunno, Asian, about thirty, olive-green T-shirt... oh, and he had a beard but no moustache."

Kelvin narrowed his eyes. "Asian, you're certain about that?"

"Indian or Pakistani I reckon. When he asked for the fare, I noticed he had a really strong accent. Oh, and his English wasn't too clever."

"So, he wasn't a white man, aged around forty?"

Stuart screwed his face up in bewilderment. "No."

Dan Frost took over the questioning. "Did you visit anywhere other than the Five-Pointed Star before the match, around 12.30 to 12.45?"

"No, why?"

Dan leant forward. "Because I think you did. You're lying, aren't you, Mr Quigley?"

Stuart shook his head. "I don't know what you're talking about."

The tone of their questioning had him feeling decidedly uncomfortable. He'd been advised by his solicitor regarding the strength of the police evidence and advised to answer 'no comment' to every question, but he'd scoffed at the advice, certain he would quickly prove his innocence and be released. But now he wasn't so sure.

"I stepped out of the taxi and into the pub. As soon as I walked in, I was with my pals all the way through until after the game, so I couldn't have thrown that man off the roof. If you don't believe I travelled from the train station straight to the pub, why don't you check with the taxi firm?"

"Oh, don't worry, Stuart, we will." Scanning through the notes in front of him, Dan sighed heavily. "Tell me about these friends you met up with?"

"I meet the same crowd at every away match, sometimes there's only a few of us, sometimes as many as twenty. We arrange which pub to meet at through our WhatsApp group, The Claret Pals."

This time it was Kelvin taking down notes, and when he'd finished writing down The Claret Pals, he tapped Dan on the arm and pointed at the words. The detectives exchanged a glance, both excited by the relevance of what they were seeing. It was a glance that Stuart spotted.

"What's so odd about being called The Claret Pals?"

Kelvin opened his briefcase and removed a batch of photographs and a plastic bag with the words 'police evidence' on the top and side. He slid the bag over to Stuart. "Do you recognise this?"

Lifting the bag from the table, Stuart's heart sank as he recognised his signature on the back of his old Claret's Foundation membership card. *How the fuck have they got hold of this?*

"Yes, it's mine."

Sitting back in his chair, Kelvin was being deliberately casual. "Remember you telling us about the fuss at the pub, when customers said they'd seen a man fall from a tower block?"

"Of course," said Stuart, angrily.

Kelvin picked up the bag and held it up in front of Stuart's face. "The man falling to his death was called Gavin Stoneham."

Stuart was confused. "What's that got to do with my Foundation card?"

A wickedly knowing smile creased Kelvin's face. "Officers found this in Mr Stoneham's rear right-hand trouser pocket."

His mouth falling open in shock, Stuart looked aghast at the self-satisfied expressions on the detectives faces. For a few seconds his mind was struggling to make sense of it all, and he found himself unable to speak. When he did eventually pull himself together, all he could come up with was, "I… I don't understand… that's not possible."

Dan rested his forearms on the table and leant heavily on them, fixing Stuart with an icy stare. "It would be possible if you'd been in his taxi earlier, and if you'd gone with him up to Keith Clarkson's flat!"

"But why would I give him my Foundation card? Why would he keep hold of it? And why on earth would I have gone with someone I'd never met before up to his friend's flat?"

Dan shrugged. "I don't know, but I'm putting to you that this is what happened. You pushed Gavin Stoneham over the balcony rail to his death, then stabbed Keith Clarkson in the back of the neck, severing his spinal cord and killing him…"

"I didn't. I told you. I've never met either of them. I—"

"…and you carved the letters TCP into the wooden chopping board before you left!"

"TCP? What the fuck does that mean?"

"It's the initials of your group of friends – The Claret Pals."

His head hurting with the barrage of accusations, Stuart fought back. "That must be a coincidence. It could stand for any number of things!"

"Well, I think it refers to The Claret Pals! Let's face it, your membership card in a victim's pocket and the initial letters of your group left at the scene… it doesn't look good for you, does it?"

Stuart stared wide-eyed, as the possible link to the Pals became clearer. He was becoming distressed; his eyes grew heavy with moisture, leaving him close to tears.

"I didn't... I wouldn't... you've got to believe me!"

"Well, I don't believe you, Mr Quigley. I think you're lying!"

Suddenly, a light bulb illuminated in Stuart's brain, and he reached out for the bag. "May I?"

Dan allowed him to take it. Stuart examined it closely.

"Wait a minute, this card was discontinued at the end of last season! They had some sort of problem with them, so they reissued new cards for all members at the start of this season." He sat forward excitedly. "If you check my things, you'll find my current Clarets Foundation card in my wallet."

"Doesn't prove anything – you could have kept the old card."

"No, no," Stuart jabbered excitedly. "I've got OCD. I keep everything neat and tidy. I'd have thrown this card away as soon as it expired. And that was a couple of months ago. Check in my wallet – you'll find everything is neatly arranged, there's no way I'd have left the old one in there."

Five minutes later, the officers were satisfied that what Stuart had told them was at least partially true. His new card was indeed in his wallet, which had all the signs of someone with OCD, immaculately neat and tidy, with everything properly arranged and in its place. The detectives called a break in the interview, and after a short consultation with his solicitor, Stuart was returned to his cell while the officers checked his story so far.

CCTV showed that Stuart had arrived at the Five-Pointed Star in a taxi driven by an Asian driver. Further images of both inside the pub and its garden, supported his story that he was in the company of others the whole time. The taxi company was contacted, and the driver confirmed he'd taken Stuart from the train station directly to the Five-Pointed Star. At no time did they stop at Roberts House.

Although the detectives were now satisfied Stuart had not committed the actual murders, further inquiries still needed to be made regarding how his expired Clarets Foundation membership card came to be in Stoneham's possession, and why the initial letters of the group he'd met with had been carved in the bread board. They demanded contact details for every member of the group, which Stuart managed to supply from the WhatsApp section on his phone.

At 8.30 he was released on bail for four weeks pending further inquiries. The friendly female detective who escorted him out of the station smiled warmly as he left.

"See you in four weeks. Sounds like you've done nothing wrong, so try not to worry."

THIRTY-TWO

Living in a terraced house in the small Lancashire town of Darwen, Gretchen's home was around fifteen miles from Turf Moor, the home of Burnley Football Club. She had been raised by parents who supported Burnley's bitter rivals, but she'd never been interested in football herself, despite her relationships with firstly Ian, and then John.

She had never truly enjoyed going to the matches and was envious of the pleasure both Ian and John got from meeting up with the Pals at Burnley away fixtures. She couldn't comprehend how they allowed their relationship with the Pals to supersede everything else in their lives – including her. She certainly wouldn't have let meeting a few football friends get in the way of a loving and caring relationship, which is exactly what John had done.

So far, things had gone much better than Gretchen could possibly have imagined. Her blossoming, though completely fake, relationship with Ryan was already paying dividends. It was him who'd told her about Joe being questioned, and him who'd phoned her the instant he'd learned about Stuart being arrested and interviewed. Usefully, he'd also told her that the police had linked the letters TCP to The Claret Pals.

Once upon a time, Gretchen had genuinely liked Ryan.

Other than John, he really was her favourite member of the Pals. But things had changed, so making use of his obsession with her seemed the sensible thing to do in the circumstances. Her overwhelming urge for revenge meant she needed to make use of him. So far, she had successfully deceived him into thinking she was interested in him romantically, and she had even bigger plans for him later.

On Sunday evening, a report on a local radio station confirmed that a male Burnley fan had been arrested and taken from his home in Sussex to Bristol for questioning. The report stated he was taken in on suspicion of a double murder at Burnley's away match at Bristol City, the previous day. The report finished by saying the man had been released on bail. Turning the radio off, Gretchen blew out a long breath, then poured herself a glass of red wine.

Although she was pleased the Pals were being disrupted, matters weren't progressing anywhere near fast enough.

Lying on her settee and downing the last mouthful of wine, Gretchen could feel herself sinking back into the welcoming warmth of the upholstery. Stage one and two had gone better than she'd hoped, but now it was time to move onto stage three, and if everything went to plan, stage three would disrupt Ian and John, in ways they couldn't possibly have imagined!

THIRTY-THREE

Four weeks earlier, Gretchen had been sent a friend request by someone called Cindy Pauser on Facebook. The timing was perfect, arriving just when she needed a friend. It happened the day after she'd broken up with John, when she was at her lowest ebb, when she badly needed someone to talk to.

Her two main friends – Claire and Evie – both flitted from one relationship to the next without seemingly suffering too much upset. Gretchen knew they simply wouldn't understand the pain and hurt she was experiencing. So, she responded to Cindy by accepting the friend request. Within minutes they were exchanging messages, sharing details about their lives and slowly learning about each other.

Following their first few sessions, as trust began to build, they began to dig more deeply into each other's lives, especially their love lives. And now, just after Gretchen had carried out a double murder in Bristol, Cindy, who lived near Phoenix, Arizona, in the USA, revealed something astounding.

Cindy told of recently being dumped by a man named Kent, whom she'd been with for three years. She'd believed he was her soulmate, a man she would be spending the rest of her life with, but sadly he was a man she was now struggling to live life without. Her story resonated strongly with Gretchen; it sounded very much like Cindy was suffering every bit as much as her, and she was keen to learn more.

Gretchen responded by offering sympathy and telling her own story, pouring out her emotions through the keyboard. Once she'd finished, they both sent profanities about how utterly vile men were. A few seconds passed with neither of them messaging, then they simultaneously sent emojis of crying with laughter.

Moments later, Cindy sent: *Do you ever feel like getting revenge on Ian and John for what they've done?*

Gretchen's reply was immediate: *Every minute of every day.*

There was a brief lull, with nothing coming back from Cindy, then she replied: *I've already gained my revenge on Kent.*

Gretchen's eyes widened. She needed to hear more. Excitedly, she leant closer to the screen, wishing she could leap through it into Cindy's world.

What do you mean? What have you done?

Cindy's next message made Gretchen's mouth drop open, her eyes widen even further and her heart beat faster. She sat up straight, staring in disbelief at the words on the screen.

I've punished him so badly, Gretchen… I've made certain he won't ever hurt another woman again.

Quivering with anticipation, Gretchen asked the same question again.

What have you done, Cindy?

There was no response. Nothing. Just a small cursor flashing on the screen. She waited for a couple of minutes, the tension unbearable.

Cindy, are you still there?

Thirty seconds later, Cindy responded with: *Okay, I'll tell you, but you must promise me you won't tell anyone… I could end up in prison.*

Gretchen felt a thrill of excitement coursing through her.

Of course, I promise. You can trust me.

Nothing came back for two minutes, and Gretchen was about to check again that Cindy was still there, when her reply came back.

Kent lives with his sister in a house on the edge of a small town just outside Phoenix, about thirty minutes from where I live. His sister has never liked me and I'm sure she was poisoning him against me. Eventually, she got her way, and he dumped me. I was so angry with her for ruining the best relationship I'd ever had, and furious with him for being weak. I went to their house in the early hours of the morning, poured petrol over the front door and threw a lit match at it. By the time I'd run one hundred yards away, the hallway and part of the lounge were engulfed in flames.

The message ended abruptly, leaving Gretchen breathless with what she'd just read. Uncertain how to respond, her breathing became ragged and fast, as she slowly absorbed the enormity of what Cindy had revealed. Her heart was hammering hard in her ribcage; her eyes scanned the message again and again before she slowly started to type a reply.

You're not alone, Cindy, I know exactly why you reacted like you did... and I think I want to do something similar. Then she asked: *What happened to them?*

Another couple of minutes passed before the reply came. *His sister was woken by the sound of neighbours shouting. She sleeps on the ground floor and managed to get out of a window, but Kent was trapped upstairs by the flames; he was badly burned before he jumped from his bedroom window. The fall shattered his lower spine and pelvis – he'll be badly disfigured and in a wheelchair for the rest of his life.*

Far from feeling shocked, Gretchen was full of admiration for Cindy. She'd been so engrossed with reading her messages that she hadn't noticed her mouth had dried up. She swallowed a drink of water and licked her lips several times to moisten them. This woman she was now in contact with had suffered just as badly as herself, and just like her, she'd had the strength of character to brutally punish those who'd hurt her.

Over the following week, they were in contact daily, exchanging deeply held feelings they had shared with nobody else throughout their lives. It was proving to be hugely cathartic for Gretchen – at last she'd found someone who truly understood her.

Eventually, she confided in Cindy that her favoured method of punishing those who betrayed her was to destroy something, or someone, they loved. She couldn't explain why, but it came from an overwhelming need somewhere deep inside. And then she told Cindy about the murders she'd already carried out.

Far from being shocked, Cindy appeared to completely understand, and before Gretchen knew it, they were making plans for how she would continue to destroy The Claret Pals. It was truly wonderful to have someone to confide in who fully understood where she was coming from, someone who had done things equally as dastardly and criminal as those she was planning and, more importantly, someone who wouldn't judge her.

THIRTY-FOUR

Three men were dead, and two of The Claret Pals had been taken in for questioning. Despite her initial thrill at Stuart's arrest – meaning that her placing his Foundation card in Gavin Stoneham's back pocket had worked perfectly – she'd been annoyed that he'd been released on bail so quickly.

Gretchen needed to step things up a little – it was time to really hurt them. She'd spent time online discussing her successes so far with Cindy, then a further hour planning for the next match. Gretchen was delighted with their latest idea, which she would fully research, then implement a week on Saturday.

Thank you for everything, Cindy, I'm so excited about Saturday. I'll let you know how it goes. Take care.

Take care yourself. You're a very brave lady. We'll speak soon.

Cindy sat back in her lounge, which was not actually in Arizona but in Skipton, Yorkshire. Her name wasn't Cindy, either – it was Emily, Emily Spicer, and she watched with hate-filled eyes as the link with Gretchen disappeared from her computer. Staring in fury at the blank screen, she seethed with a burning rage that stretched back over thirty years.

Emily had suffered throughout her life with severe mental health problems and crippling depression, conditions that doctors agreed were caused by the trauma of watching her pet rabbit Lucy being stabbed in the eye when she was only six. An event which all the experts agreed had left her mind unbalanced. She'd struggled at school, struggled at work, had always struggled to make friends and still lived with her parents at the age of thirty-nine.

She was a woman consumed not only by hatred, but also an all-encompassing lust for revenge. Her fake persona of Cindy Pauser from Arizona had worked perfectly up to now, slowly sucking Gretchen into her web of deceit. A web she would use to ensnare the bitch and ensure she spent the remainder of her life in prison. Innocent people would suffer terribly through Gretchen's actions, but for Emily, it was a necessary evil to see the woman she hated so much properly punished.

Gretchen believed she was in control and that she was the hunter. Little did she know that Emily Spicer had made her the prey.

THIRTY-FIVE

The following week passed with heated discussions between the Pals. They'd all been contacted by detectives from the murder team, and short statements had been taken over the phone. Their stories were basically the same, and the police, by and large, seemed satisfied; they were unlikely to be wanting to speak with them again.

The Southern Claret members of the Pals rarely travelled all the way to Lancashire for Burnley home games – it was a long journey for them and something they all did sparingly. But they all wanted to be at Turf Moor the following Saturday for the visit of Blackburn Rovers, known universally among the Burnley faithful as 'Bastard Rovers'. It was the biggest of local derbies in Lancashire and, for both sets of fans, one of the two most important games of the season. It was quite simply a fixture nobody wanted to miss.

Recent events urgently needed to be discussed, so plans were made via the WhatsApp group to meet at 1.00 at Burnley Cricket Club, which just happens to adjoin Turf Moor Stadium. The cricket club was usually recommended as a friendly venue for away fans, but Blackburn fans knew to stay away from drinking establishments in the town to prevent disorder and violence, so the Pals were unlikely to be disturbed.

The first weekend in September produced overcast weather, with an almost uniform grey sky, but it was warm and muggy, one might almost say sticky, with many fans in shorts and T-shirts. In a way, this was excellent news for the group, and they moved outside onto the banked seating area, which swept around one corner of the cricket ground below the clubhouse and bar.

After meeting in the bar, where they purchased drinks and takeaway food, fourteen Claret Pals walked outside and moved left on the walkway towards Turf Moor Stadium, before dropping down into the seating area, well away from other fans. They needed somewhere they could speak privately without whispering and without worrying about being overheard.

Joe and Stuart described their experiences of being taken to their respective police stations and the questions they faced, experiences that turned out to be wildly different. Unlike Stuart, Joe didn't go through the indignity of being arrested, handcuffed, then having his fingerprints, photograph and DNA taken before being interviewed. But the pressure they felt during questioning was very much the same.

Stuart, who was still angry and emotional about the indignity of being hauled away in front of his neighbours, mentioned the letters TCP being found in the flat, the initials of The Claret Pals.

"I was set up by whoever did this, I'm convinced of it! Someone is using us as a cover. They're diverting police attention away from themselves and pointing them at us!"

Ryan gave a dismissive snort. "Don't talk shit. How could anyone manage to pull off something like that?"

Becki nodded. "Sounds far-fetched to me."

Finishing a swig of his beer, John asked, "How the fuck did your Foundation card end up in that man's pocket?"

Stuart shrugged. "I've no idea; it was an old one. I must have chucked it out."

John rubbed his chin thoughtfully. "It's bizarre that it ended up in a Bristol taxi driver's pocket. Can you remember when you threw it away?"

"Not really. But I would have done it as soon as the new one arrived." He screwed his face up and rubbed his forehead, thinking hard, then his face brightened. He turned to John. "Hang on a minute, remember your birthday barbecue?"

John nodded. "I remember some of it, but I was too pissed to remember it all!"

Laughter swept the group, but Stuart wasn't laughing, his voice and demeanour deadly serious. "I saw that card at the barbecue. I remember it clearly – the new one had arrived earlier that day and I'd forgotten to bin the old one – I binned it at the barbecue."

"Hang on a minute," said Ian, turning to John, his face set with a steely gaze. "The barbecue at Gretchen's house?"

John nodded. "Yeah, brilliant day, wasn't it?"

"I remember now – I threw it into the wastepaper basket in the lounge."

Ian was sitting with his bottom on one seat and his feet rested on the adjoining seat; his knees were folded tightly, and he was cuddling his legs with his arms. "I don't know how to say this; you'll probably think I'm crazy."

Ginny, sitting in the row above him, put a hand on Ian's shoulder. "No, we won't; we're all here to listen to each other's viewpoints."

"That's right," said Val. "Go on, we're listening."

Shifting his feet off the seat, releasing his legs and sitting up straight, he sucked in a deep breath.

"When I arrived at the pub in Rotherham, I saw this woman in a Rotherham hoodie hurrying away from the area.

She was looking down at the ground and didn't see me." He began to look distressed, whispering silently under his breath, "Fucking hell…" He put his head in his hands.

"Alright, mate, calm down," said Jack. "What's wrong?"

Ian raised his eyes, scanning the group. "I almost ran over to her at the time, but then I thought I was being stupid. I was sure I had to be mistaken. So, I gave myself a talking to, walked into the pub and found you lot in the back garden. I forced myself to forget all about it."

"For fuck's sake, Ian," said Becki. "What was so important about this woman?"

He drew in a breath and said forcefully, "It looked like Gretchen."

"Gretchen, in a Rotherham hoodie?" Becki's voice raised to a shrill pitch. "Fuck off!"

Ian climbed to his feet, speaking quickly and excitedly, pointing at a vacant space, still seeing her in his mind's eye. "Maybe she was dressed in a Rotherham hoodie because she didn't want to be recognised!"

"Are you suggesting she killed that man?" asked an astonished Ginny.

"I don't know… maybe?"

"You're talking shit!" said John. A comment which garnered unanimous support.

"Don't be daft," added Jack. "Gretchen is lovely; I don't think I've ever met a gentler soul."

Comments rubbishing Ian's suggestion poured from the Pals.

"Is that why you seemed distracted when we arrived?" asked Jack.

Ian nodded. "Yes. I only got a glimpse of the face from side on, but it could have been her. Right size, right shape. Even the way she walked!"

Simon was the only person to offer Ian even a smidgen of support. "I think it's highly unlikely, but we shouldn't discount what he says out of hand."

John reddened as he turned to face Simon. "You can fuck off too!"

Fired up by John's reaction, Simon snapped back, "Think about it for a moment. Ian dumped her after only going out for a few weeks, then she started seeing you. Six years later, she felt she had no choice but to dump you because you preferred going to watch Burnley over spending time with her."

Jack was bemused. "What's that got to do with anything? She'd have to be suffering from some severe mental health shit for that to turn her into a killer. And Gretchen seemed perfectly level-headed to me."

Simon shrugged. "I know, but someone is the killer. And whoever it is, they're deliberately framing us. Why couldn't it be her?" He downed a gulp of beer. "Three murders, all near where we've been drinking on match days, and the letters TCP are written at one of the murder scenes. Makes you think, doesn't it?"

"For fuck's sake," said Becki. "This is bollocks! Nobody's trying to implicate us – it's coincidence!"

The group was fracturing, opinions were put forward on both sides, with things beginning to get heated. Eventually, the raised voices were stopped by Ryan. "Stop, stop, everyone stop!"

This was amazingly out of character – he was normally the calm, considered, gentleman of the group – so with this outburst, everyone fell silent as he'd commanded. The group turned to him, uncertain what was coming next.

"Remember when I took that phone call and moved away from you all at Rotherham? The one where you all gave me shit about having a secret girlfriend?"

Some nodded; others remained silent. John said, "Yes, we thought you might have a bird on the go."

Ryan rubbed his hands together in front of his chest; his fingers twiddling nervously.

"Well, you're kind of right… it was Gretchen."

John's eyes flamed. He pointed angrily at Ryan. "You're bang out of order; she's only just dumped me. You don't move in on a mate's woman that soon after he's been ditched."

Becki moved to Ryan's side. "Piss off!" she said. "You started seeing her within a fortnight of her and Ian splitting up!"

John stood up. "That was different. Ian dumped her! He finished with her; I would never have made a move that quickly if she'd dumped him! I'd have put my mate's feelings first!"

Ginny gestured for everybody to calm down. "Can we please stop arguing and let Ryan finish?"

Retaking his seat and lifting his pint with a shaky hand, John fought back the words he wanted to say.

"I'm not going out with Gretchen, John, and I haven't made a move on her," Ryan lied, partly to spare John's feelings. "But I'm not ashamed to admit I'd like to."

He stared at John, hoping for an acknowledgement, but got none. John rested his elbows on his knees and looked at his feet, denying Ryan any eye contact.

"The thing is," Ryan continued, "Gretchen called me on a video call, so I could see where she was… and it wasn't in Rotherham."

Ian glared at Ryan.

"Go on then, where was she?"

"In her bedroom."

Jack wore a doubtful expression. "Her bedroom? How can you be certain?"

Ryan turned his gaze onto Stuart. "Remember that day at the barbecue, Stu? When you said what a nice place it was, and Gretchen offered to show us around?"

"Yeah."

"What was unusual about her bedroom?"

Stuart screwed up his eyes and scratched the back of his neck. "Nothing that I can think of."

John interrupted, "You're talking about the duvet, aren't you?"

"Oh yes!" exclaimed Stuart. "It was the New York skyline, amazing. I've never seen one like it before or since."

"Exactly," said Ryan. "And she was lying on that duvet when she spoke to me."

John was getting angry again. "Why the fuck would she be speaking to you lying on her bed?"

Ryan sighed heavily. "She'd been out with mates the night before and had taken a nap, that's all."

Visibly calming himself down, John said, "Fair enough." He lifted his head to face Ryan. "Sorry, mate, don't know what came over me. Do you speak to her often?"

"Not a huge amount, maybe a couple of times a week. We're just friends, really. Truth be told, I think she misses her days out with the Pals."

"What makes you think that?" asked Val.

"Well, she called me from the Trafford Centre just before the Bristol game too. She was out shopping with a bunch of mates." He chuckled. "They sounded really noisy!"

Simon moved over to sit alongside Ian and placed an arm around his shoulder. "Sorry, looks like you were wrong, mate. You couldn't have seen her."

Leaning back over the seat with his hands behind his head, Ian stretched himself out and offered up an apology. "I'm sorry, guys, it really looked like her, must have been a doppelganger." He sat forward again. "But if we are being set up, we still need to find out how the killer got hold of Stuart's Foundation card, how it got into the victim's pocket and why the letters TCP were found at that flat in Bristol."

Stuart agreed. "Ian's right, TCP – what else could it stand for other than The Claret Pals, for fuck's sake? And if we're not being implicated, then what do they stand for?"

Their opinions remained divided, entrenched in two distinct camps – a few believed someone was trying to implicate the group, but the majority couldn't bring themselves to accept it, preferring to believe the letters must refer to something else. Being the initial letters of The Claret Pals was, in their minds, nothing more than an unfortunate coincidence.

An hour later, the group dispersed and made their way into the stadium, agreeing to meet a week later at the Wolfe Inn, close to The Hawthorns, West Bromwich Albion's football ground.

The game turned out to be one-way traffic, with Burnley battering Blackburn throughout the match. The scoreline may have read only 2-0, but supporters from both sides knew it could easily have been much more.

THIRTY-SIX

John and Ian had collected fish and chips for the Pals, carrying them through to the pub garden in four flimsy white carrier bags.

"About time," groaned Becki. "I'm starving!"

They handed out the food, and soon enough everyone was happily munching through their portions. While they ate, the discussion that had started the previous Saturday at Burnley Cricket Club was continued in earnest.

Becki was the first to return to the subject. "So, any more news?"

Everyone said they'd been contacted.

"But only poor old Stu was dragged in and given the third degree!" said Joe, liberally spraying his mouthful of crunchy batter onto everyone in range. He patted Stuart on the back. "I know what you went through, mate."

"To be fair to the police," laughed John, leaning over and pinching a piece of Joe's fish, "the only reason you and Stu were taken in for questioning is because you both look like villains!"

"You've got a cheek!" laughed Stuart. "If anyone looks like a villain, it's you!"

John playfully patted Joe on the shoulder, before adding

more seriously, "I still can't believe they hadn't picked up on the fact that CCTV proved you couldn't have killed that man."

Jack arrived back at the table in the rear garden of the Wolfe Inn – the designated away fans pub, and The Claret Pals' meeting place for Burnley's fixture at West Bromwich Albion. He was carrying a tray full of drinks for everyone and had missed the start of the discussion.

"What's that about CCTV?"

Ginny glared at him angrily, opening her eyes wide in seeming disbelief that he'd asked such a stupid question, the piece of fish about to enter her mouth going uneaten. Her apparent anger left Jack bemused, and despite racking his brains, he couldn't figure out what he had done wrong.

Then it dawned on him, and Jack suddenly understood her hostility. He felt hot, bothered and uncomfortable. He'd been feeling bad for wrongly snitching on his friend and still found himself unable to hold eye contact with Joe. He decided to change the subject.

"Sorry I took so long; it's mobbed in there." He held up the tray. "Come on, grab your drinks." His nervousness showed through in his voice, which had a distinct crack in it.

"You okay, Jack?" asked Ian.

Thinking quickly, Jack said, "Fine thanks, just a bit of a scratchy throat. I think I've got a cold coming."

He gave Ginny a broken smile and raised his eyebrows quickly up and down. They were both feeling more than a little uneasy, desperate their friends should never suspect it was Jack who wrongly reported one of them to the police.

The next few minutes passed happily, as they busily tucked into their food, which had been supplied by For Cod's Sake, the fish and chip shop next door to the pub. It just so happened that the chippy was owned by the landlady of the

Wolfe Inn, meaning she was more than happy for customers to consume food they'd purchased in the chippy on the premises.

"Isn't that the chippy where you got nicked last year?" Becki asked Ian, laughing out loud.

Ian reddened. "It is."

"Remind me, what was it for?"

Ian pursed his lips, considering his reply. "The wanker behind the counter short-changed me. I gave him a fifty, but he only gave me change for a twenty!"

"That's right," laughed John. "And when he wouldn't back down and hand over the other thirty, you threatened him and said you'd never eat his shit food again!"

He elbowed Ian playfully in the ribs and pointed at his food. "Yet here we are!"

Everyone laughed.

"I didn't threaten him," said Ian.

"Yes, you did," said Becki. "I was there! As the police were dragging you away, you said you'd get even with him if it was the last thing you ever did!"

John turned to Becki. "I think it was the same bloke who's just served us." He looked at Ian. "Good job he didn't recognise you, or you'd have been wearing those chips!"

Ian forced a strangled laugh as he shovelled in a mouthful of fish but said nothing.

Their reminiscing was broken by someone at a nearby table starting a song. "Oh my lads, you should have seen them running…" His efforts were quickly swelled in volume by just about everyone else in the pub garden… "Running down the Brunshaw Road, the Burnley boys are coming, all the lads and lasses, smiles upon their faces, running down the Brunshaw Road, to see the Burnley aces!"

This was quickly followed by a chorus of, "We love you

Burnley, we do. We love you Burnley, we do. We love you Burnley, we do. Oh, Burnley, we love you!"

Once the volume had subsided, Ryan, who was standing alongside Jack and Ginny, posed a question. "What score do you reckon today?"

"I never predict the score," said Ginny. "I'm no good at it and thinking about it makes me more nervous than I already am."

"Good side, West Brom," said Jack. "I'll be happy with a draw. 1-1, I think."

"Me too," said Ryan. "I thought we played well to beat the bastards last weekend, but we were crap at Bristol. Tactics were all wrong."

"Nah, we'll be reet," said John. "2-0 Clarets."

The drinking, singing and footy conversation carried on until 2.15, when the group left in dribs and drabs to make their way to The Hawthorns Stadium, the home of West Bromwich Albion. Memories of the events at Rotherham and Bristol were still very much in their thoughts, but for now, they would be consigned to the back of their minds, at least until after the match.

THIRTY-SEVEN

Two hours earlier, Gretchen Grover had been watching John Horsfall and Ian Calvert walking into the Wolfe Inn. She prickled at seeing their unbridled joy as they laughed and joked, with arms wrapped around each other's shoulders. It hurt; it really hurt. They were clearly having a great time, while she was suffering because of them.

She fought to remain calm but could feel the familiar rage burning inside her. How could they have put their passion for a fucking football team above their love for her? Her obsession made her hate them both so much, and she knew the pain wouldn't abate until she'd made them pay. She needed to punish them so, so badly. From past experience she knew that once she'd gained her revenge, she would feel much better.

Cindy was the only person who fully appreciated her, the only one who understood why she had to commit such terrible crimes. And it was Cindy with whom she'd shared her plan for this week's match.

It had been four weeks since Burnley's first away match and two weeks since the Bristol game. Four weeks since she'd sliced Mario Spiteri's throat open, and two weeks since she'd thrown Gavin Stoneman from the balcony and plunged a knife into the back of Keith Clarkson's neck.

She had enjoyed dropping huge hints about which group the killer moved around with, and by doing so she'd disrupted the Pals' enjoyment of matches... but only to an extent. Two of them had been taken in and questioned, but that wasn't enough. Nowhere near enough.

Gretchen knew the score whenever the Pals visited the Wolfe Inn. Over the years she'd been there four times – once as Ian's girlfriend, and three times as John's. Each time when Burnley had been in town playing West Brom. On two other occasions, John had travelled without her, choosing to attend the match over spending a day doing something together with her, and each time it had resulted in a blazing row.

She was confident they would follow the same routine. The group would meet at the pub, grab a table in the garden (they only ever stayed inside if the weather was poor) and order a round of drinks. An hour or so after arriving, a couple of them would collect fish and chips for the whole group from For Cod's Sake, the hugely popular chippy right next door to the pub.

This meant the chippy was the perfect place for her to strike. She remembered only too well Ian's dispute with the man serving the previous year, followed by his subsequent arrest. It provided her plans with the perfect backstory.

THIRTY-EIGHT

Gretchen scanned the pub's front entrance from a distance, knowing for certain that in a few minutes' time, two or three of the Pals would exit through the front door and wander around to the chippy. *Please let it be John and Ian!*

She had no time to lose. She was terrified of being spotted by someone she knew, so she'd come prepared, disguising herself to the extent that even people who knew her well couldn't possibly recognise her.

She was sporting a navy-blue peaked cap with the letters WBA in white writing on the front, a striped navy-blue and white West Bromwich Albion home football shirt and dark-green rimmed glasses. Her black leggings were tucked into Doc Marten-style boots.

Moving urgently and with real purpose in her stride, Gretchen covered the distance to For Cod's Sake quickly. Her nerves should have been doing cartwheels as she crossed the street, but she remained fully in control, experiencing only a cool and calm determination to complete her task. Just inside the door, she joined the rear of the queue, which hugged the left wall, then turned right in front of the glass-fronted display.

She quickly took in her surroundings, deciding how she would manage it. She had already selected her victim, but her condition meant she felt no sympathy for him. He would suffer a slow and agonising death because of her, but his pain was necessary to accomplish her goal. And this time the finger would point directly at Ian and John – they would be blamed for yet another murder at a Burnley away match. By achieving this, she was hopeful her plan would bring about not only their downfall but also the end of the Pals' gatherings on match days.

The queue moved surprisingly quickly, with most customers just buying for themselves, and before long, Gretchen was second in line.

The man ahead of her was placing his order, and she now had an excellent view of her target: the middle-aged man behind the counter. The same man Ian had clashed with one year ago. She eyed him like a lion crouched in the long grass of the Serengeti, as it prepared to pounce on a baby gazelle.

Her target was a jovial, slightly chubby man, aged around fifty. He spoke with a strong accent that sounded Mediterranean, possibly Italian? She remembered him speaking with the police after Ian had been carted away last year. Each time he finished serving a customer, he took a short swig from a can of Vimto, which rested on the countertop, close to where the customer now being served was standing.

Her research for this match commenced immediately after she'd successfully murdered Gavin Stoneman and Keith Clarkson. She'd told Cindy all about how the days had panned out at West Brom games in the past, including the proximity of the chip shop to the Wolfe Inn. Their main discussion point bore down to the urgent necessity of finding a new method to murder someone, a method unrelated to her previous killings.

Gretchen loved the idea of making the police work hard for a result. It gave her huge satisfaction to know that, as time went on and the cases inevitably became linked, their increasingly urgent inquiries would home in more and more on the likelihood that the killer was one of The Claret Pals. One thing was for certain: after today, they would be looking more closely at Ian and John.

Her severe personality disorder meant the overwhelming urge to inflict extreme violence on something, or someone close to those who had abandoned or betrayed her, never left her. It was an urge that was always there, a permanent presence in her life, an itch she simply had to scratch.

Planning for the trip to West Bromwich Albion didn't take too long, and Cindy had come up with the novel idea of poisoning someone's drink. Gretchen's problem was that poisoning someone's drink in a pub would run a high chance of her being seen by another customer or spotted on CCTV doing it. No, the pub wasn't the place; it had to be somewhere different, somewhere unexpected. Like the chippy.

Taking Cindy's advice, she had accessed the dark web, where she'd found an illicit website that advertised 'assistance for those wanting to commit suicide'. After only an hour of searching, she found exactly what she wanted and purchased a pack of three extraordinarily expensive tablets containing concentrated cyanide. If swallowed whole, death would come swiftly. More importantly, it claimed that if placed in liquid, the tablets were slow release and dissolvable, which was perfect, because it meant the victim would die more slowly as they sipped their drink, giving her plenty of time to be well clear of the venue before it fully took effect.

Moving up alongside the man being served, she leant forward across the counter, squinting as though she was struggling to read the menu, written in black marker pen on a white board behind the counter. Her hand felt for the open can of Vimto, which she located somewhere under her chest, hidden from the sight of other customers and, more importantly, hidden from cameras.

She'd come prepared and had already removed one of the tablets from its plastic wrapping. Locating the can's ring pull opening, she carefully dropped the small tablet inside.

Still leaning over the counter and pretending to read the menu, while innocently waiting her turn to be served, she surreptitiously wrote the letters TCP in marker pen under the lip of a side panel on the hot over-counter display. Standing up straight again, she patiently waited for her turn to be served.

Disappointingly, the man behind the counter didn't take a swig of Vimto after serving the customer in front, but she breathed a sigh of relief when he took a glug from the can immediately after serving her. As he handed over her food and before turning to his next customer, he smiled broadly at her, with a twinkle in his eye. He spoke in a strong accent. "There you go, pretty girl. You have a nice day."

"Thank you." She smiled. "You're very sweet."

Walking swiftly from the shop with her order of small haddock and chips clasped tightly to her side, she saw that she was only just in time. John and Ian passed close by as they headed into the chippy. Luckily, they didn't recognise her; in fact, she was thrilled when neither of them gave her a second glance; her disguise had worked perfectly!

Gretchen returned to her observation point, tucked in a small gap between two stalls selling football scarves, badges and other memorabilia. It had provided her with a clear view of people entering and leaving the pub, and, more importantly, kept her partially hidden from view.

Once Gretchen was certain John and Ian had gone into the chippy, she walked calmly away to the train station. There was nothing to be gained from waiting around to watch events unfold, no matter how much she wanted to. The longer she was there, the greater the risk. It simply wasn't worth it.

Little did Gretchen know, that on the opposite side of the street, standing in a queue for match-day programmes, had been Emily Spicer. She'd been boldly standing right in Gretchen's eyeline, hiding amongst the throng in plain sight, and she had carefully recorded Gretchen's movements. *I fucking hate you*, she'd thought. *You'll soon be spending the rest of your life behind bars, you evil bitch. Not long now, Gretchen... not long now.*

THIRTY-NINE

The streets were thick with supporters of both teams crowding the pavements as The Claret Pals walked towards the stadium. They turned a corner, bringing the stadium's floodlights into view, chatting excitedly about the upcoming fixture as they did so. Walking a little further, they noticed about twenty fans gathering around the tiny front garden of an end-of-terrace house; an ambulance parked nearby indicated that all was not well.

On the pavement, directly outside the house, the paramedics were lifting a Mediterranean-looking man onto a stretcher. A woman, presumably the man's wife or partner, was crying out and wailing in a mixture of Italian and English. "*Per favore Dio no!* He's never been ill before!"

John squeezed between two of the onlookers to get a better view. "Isn't that the guy from the chippy?"

Ian managed to sneak a glance through a gap in the throng. "I don't think so; he looks too old."

John shrugged. "Looks like him to me."

They pulled back from the gawping crowd and continued towards the stadium, but many fans remained where they were, transfixed by the dramatic turn of events, crowding around the scene and generally hampering the efforts of the ambulance crew.

"Come on," said Ginny. "Let's leave them to it; we'll only be in the way."

Stepping out, they strode away from the incident without stopping or casting a backwards glance.

FORTY

The game was a rather boring affair. A high point for the Burnley fans had been watching their new signing, German centre-half Heinrich Schmidt. He had played superbly, bullying the Albion strikers throughout the match. Not only did he have them in his pocket, but he also equalised for the Clarets with a header from a corner midway through the second half. The match ended in a hard-fought 1-1, just as Jack and Ryan had predicted.

After clapping the team off at the end, Burnley fans endlessly sang their new song as they exited the ground, "Six foot two, eyes of blue, Heinrich Schmidt is after you! La la la la, la la la, la la!"

Walking away from the stadium and heading back to their cars, Ian, Becki and Ryan – who had become detached from the others – saw a police notice up ahead; it was near the house where the man had been taken away in the ambulance. 'Incident here 2.15 today. Any information please contact the CID at Smethwick Police Station'. At the bottom of the board was a contact phone number.

Becki looked at Ian and Ryan. "Blimey, they got that information board out quickly!"

"They probably didn't want to lose any information fans leaving the ground might have," said Ian, thoughtfully.

"But why would the CID be interested in a man falling ill at his house?" asked Becki.

Ryan replied in his usual calm and understated fashion, "If the cops are interested, it obviously wasn't an illness. There must be more to it."

Becki's face turned ashen, and she shook her head.

"Oh God, please no, not another one."

As they passed the house, a woman who had been working at For Cod's Sake was leaving the front door; her stern countenance fitted perfectly with the apparent seriousness of the situation. She moved seamlessly into the flow of fans heading away from the stadium, only a couple of places in front of them.

Without mentioning anything to Becki and Ryan, Ian moved quickly forward, dodging around those in front of him until he was walking alongside the woman. "Hello, we had some of your fish and chips before the match – they were great!"

The woman, who was around sixty, with greying, greasy hair in a bun, gave him the briefest of glances. "You're welcome." She said nothing else, but her face was screaming, 'Go away, I don't want to talk to you!'

Ian wasn't fazed and persisted, "We saw the ambulance here on our way to the ground. Is he okay?"

She began walking a little faster, trying to leave Ian behind, but he increased his pace and matched her stride, step for step. After a few seconds, the woman slowed down to normal walking pace again and looked at Ian, sighing heavily. "He's dead, okay… dead." She fixed him with a penetrating glare. "He was poisoned."

"Poisoned?" exclaimed Ian in disbelief. "What? In his own house?"

"No, he was poisoned at the shop. He suddenly felt sick and asked to go home."

"Oh my God, that's awful!"

She nodded. "I couldn't really spare him, but he looked so ill, so I let him go. I watched him through the shop window, he looked really unsteady as he weaved through the crowds, then one of our regular customers came in and said he'd collapsed just before he reached his front gate."

Ian's mind was racing – four people killed in three unconnected incidents at three away matches? The odds against that happening by chance were astronomical... weren't they? If there was a killer on the loose, why were they targeting Burnley away games? It made no sense.

He decided against saying anything more to the grieving woman, leaving her with a simple, "I'm so sorry."

Moments later, he'd moved back in the crowd to rejoin Becki and Ryan.

"Why were you talking to her?" asked Becki.

Ian didn't respond; he just walked forward, staring into space.

"Are you okay?"

He moved closer to her and lowered his voice. "Remember that man being taken away by the ambulance earlier, the one John thought was the guy from the chippy."

Becki nodded. "What about him?"

"I think John was right – it was him, the bloke I threatened last year." He slowly shook his head. "He's dead, for fuck's sake, he was poisoned at the chip shop. And I was in there earlier." He was breathing fast, his eyes flashing with worry. "That doesn't look good for me, does it?"

"Don't worry, mate," said Ryan. "You've done nothing wrong; there's no need to worry."

"If he's been poisoned," said Becki, "was it deliberate, or could it have been something he ate?"

Ian was feeling decidedly panicky. His mind was bouncing

around with out-of-control thoughts, but he slowed his breathing down and managed to formulate a reply. "I don't know. I don't think there was a problem with the fish and chips if that's what you're saying. I'm sure she would have mentioned that. Anyway, loads of other people would be ill, wouldn't they?"

With all three exchanging worried glances, Becki said, "What the fuck is going on?"

Ryan's phone rang and he looked to see who the caller was.

"It's Gretchen, I'll call her back later." Pressing the red button, he declined the call but immediately sent her a WhatsApp message. *Sorry, can't talk right now. I'll call back when I'm free. x.*

Up ahead, Ian watched as the woman he'd been speaking to stood outside a police cordon surrounding For Cod's Sake. She was speaking to someone who he presumed to be a detective. Another police information board had been placed alongside the shop's entrance door, and the shop's interior was full of forensic officers in protective equipment.

FORTY-ONE

Monday morning at precisely 9.00, two days after the murder, officers assigned to the investigation team were gathered in the main CID office of Smethwick Police Station.

The first day of the investigation had been carried out by a mish-mash of officers cobbled together from Smethwick CID and local crime squads. The central major investigation team were overrun with work and unable to add to their workload, so responsibility for the investigation fell on the local CID office. By the end of Sunday, a team had been assembled.

"Settle down, please, settle down. I'm due to brief the senior leadership team in thirty minutes, so listen up." Detective Inspector Abbie Beard seemed agitated and nervous; this was her first murder inquiry as OIC (Officer In the Case), and she didn't want to mess up. The nine officers stopped their conversations and turned to face her.

Her smart grey suit, white blouse, shiny black shoes and brown hair, tied back neatly in a tight bun, may have given her the appearance of someone in charge, but nerves were overcoming her, leaving her feeling not the slightest bit confident.

Seeing she had their full attention, Abbie moved across the room and pointed at a photograph on the screen behind her.

"Our victim is Tommaso Romano. Fifty-four years of age. An Italian national. He moved from Italy to the UK with his wife Giana thirty years ago."

She lifted her gaze to the screen, displaying a smiling image of Tommaso Romano. "Death was due to cyanide poisoning. He suffered a slow and painful death after drinking from a can of Vimto while working at For Cod's Sake, the chippy next door to the Wolfe Inn on Brereton Street."

She clicked a remote control in her right hand and the screen's image changed, showing a toxicology report from the Midland Metropolitan Hospital. "A consultant at the hospital suspected cyanide poisoning as soon as Mr Romano arrived, but they were unable to save him. Apparently, it was something to do with crystals that had formed on his lips and in his nose."

She rubbed her own nose between thumb and forefinger at the thought of it. "So he arranged for urgent toxicology tests, and sure enough, he was right."

A young female officer in uniform knocked hard on the door and walked in without being invited to enter.

"Sorry, ma'am, there's—"

Abbie's cheeks flared at the interruption. "This had better be incredibly urgent, Bridgit… is it?"

"Well, I, er… no, not really, ma'am."

"Then please bugger off. I'll deal with it later."

Bridgit backed out of the room with her tail firmly between her legs. She offered a quiet, "Sorry, ma'am," as she pulled the door closed behind her. A couple of officers smirked at Bridgit's obvious discomfort.

Abbie took a breath and faced her audience once more, clicking the remote control and changing the image once again. "This is For Cod's Sake, the chippy on Brereton Street. It's where Mr Romano has worked for the past seven years." She paused for dramatic effect. "And also where he was murdered."

She was trying to hide her nerves from her fellow officers, but deep down inside she still felt a persistent trembling. She needn't have worried though – the detectives were captivated by her apparent strength of personality and gripped by her slick presentation skills. She may have been a young woman who'd been recently promoted to Detective Inspector, but right now, she was performing at the top of her game.

The image changed, and Abbie jabbed a finger at the screen. "That's an ordinary can of Vimto drink one might think, except the contents had enough cyanide to kill three men." Her eyes swept the room, making certain her words were sinking in. "Our victim died simply because he drank from that can, something he apparently did habitually… and our murderer must have known that."

A detective constable raised his hand. Abbie lifted her eyebrows at him. "Yes, Derek?"

"It's my favourite chippy, ma'am. Tommy was a great bloke – full of fun. He always had a can of Vimto on the go."

He looked around the room and three officers nodded, murmuring their agreement.

"Why would anyone do this to Tommy? And how the fuck did the cyanide get in there?"

Abbie held up an index finger. "Good questions. We've been through the CCTV, and initially a huge number of potential suspects were identified."

She clicked the remote again, and an image appeared showing seven screenshots taken from the chippy's CCTV of people waiting at the counter to be served: six men and one woman. "However, we have narrowed the suspects down to these seven."

She waited for the inevitable question, which was asked by Bill Striker – a grizzled old detective constable approaching retirement – but when the question came, it wasn't the one she was expecting. "It's down to their hands, isn't it, guv?"

Abbie liked Bill; he was a no-nonsense detective who often spotted something others had missed. "Spot on, Bill, I was anticipating something like, 'Why only these seven?'." She gave him a warm smile before addressing the room again. "The vast majority of customers had both hands visible at all times, so they couldn't possibly have dropped the poison into the can."

She pointed at Gretchen and two males wearing West Bromwich Albion colours. "These three are obviously Albion fans; I've no idea which team these two support; and..." she indicated two men wearing Burnley tops, "these two are obviously Burnley fans."

A female detective raised a hand.

"Yes, Jill?"

"Sorry, I'm probably being dim, but why are these seven our only suspects? Couldn't a member of staff be the killer?"

Abbie bit the inside of her lip and lifted a finger, directing attention back to the screen. "No, they couldn't. We have Tommaso opening the can on CCTV, and no other member of staff touches the can between him opening it, then falling ill and leaving the restaurant."

She looked at the suspects once again.

"Those seven are the only ones who lean across the counter with one of their arms tucked underneath their body, giving them the opportunity to drop something into the can. There's no doubt in my mind that one of those seven is our killer."

The female detective wrote something down. "Understood, thank you, ma'am."

"And there's one more thing," said Abbie. "One of these seven used a maroon permanent marker pen to scrawl the letters TCP on a side panel above the counter, just underneath the lip, right alongside the fryer."

"How do we know it wasn't there before?" asked Jill.

"Because the owner, who took over from Tommaso when he went home ill, spotted it. She was certain it hadn't been there an hour earlier, when she'd filled in to give him a ten-minute break."

Jill sat forward in her chair. "Do we know what TCP stands for?"

Abbie shrugged. "No idea, but it would be one hell of a coincidence that it appeared just as poison was being dropped into someone's drink."

Jill kept pressing. "Why not check before and after for each suspect on CCTV? That would be an easy way to find who'd written it."

Smiling and scratching behind an ear, Abbie said, "Yes, I'd thought of that. Unfortunately, the position of the camera is excellent for identifying customers being served, but a small section alongside the fryer is hidden from view by the top of the counter display. The bodies of those who leant over the counter obstructed the camera's view of that area."

A couple of officers shifted in their seats, and a low murmur of whispered comments filled the room.

Abbie decided it was time to stop further questions coming her way and move things along. "Jill and Colin."

"Guv," they chimed in unison.

"Get yourselves up to the divisional intelligence unit in Burnley. I've already had words with their DCI and sent up images of the two men wearing Burnley shirts. If they can identify either of them before you arrive, his team will be happy to give you all the assistance they can. You might be up there for a couple of days, so go home, get a change of clothes and get going."

Colin narrowed his eyes. "Do you want them arrested as a suspect if they're identified?"

"At this stage, I'd rather they voluntarily attended for an interview under caution. But if they refuse, then yes, nick 'em."

"When do you want us up there, guv?"

"Later on today. Go and speak to the garage hand – you can book out a pool car on my authority."

They nodded their understanding. All police officers enjoy a 'jolly' away from their normal working environment, and Colin and Jill were no exceptions, turning to each other to exchange excited thumbs up signals.

Abbie scowled at them. "Well, what are you waiting for? Off you go!"

Suitably chastened, Jill and Colin swiftly left the room.

Returning her gaze to the remaining officers, Abbie said sharply, "Lily and Derek."

They both raised a hand. "Yes, guv."

"You'll be working with our DIU. I want those Albion fans identified ASAP, and while you're at it, try to find the identities of the two not wearing team colours – they might be Burnley supporters, but the chances are they're Albion."

"Will do, guv."

"The images are good, so obtaining IDs for all of them shouldn't be too much of a stretch."

Lily and Derek lifted themselves from their seats. "On it, guv," said Derek, as they departed the office.

"Sam."

"Guv?"

"Speak to the family liaison officer and arrange to interview Tomasso's wife, Giana, and other members of his family as soon as possible. We need to ascertain whether he had any enemies, or whether anyone would want to cause him harm. Dig deep… find out about his friends, hobbies, anything which might give us a clue as to why anybody would want him dead."

"Yes, boss."

Abbie tapped the table with the knuckles of her right hand.

"But remember, go gently. They've had a terrible shock, so don't go steaming in."

Sam nodded. "Boss."

Pacing backwards and forwards across the room, hands on her hips, Abbie blew out a sigh. "I'd like the rest of you to concentrate on making certain we haven't missed anything obvious. We know what these seven did while they were in the chippy, but I want to know their movements before and after they entered. That will mean extensive checks on all CCTV in the area surrounding the shop."

Her words elicited a low groaning sound.

Abbie rolled her eyes. "I realise it's boring and laborious work, but it might be that one of you spots something vital, so please be professional and give it your best efforts."

"Yes, guv," came the staggered replies.

"Thank you. As soon as suspects are identified, we'll bring them in, and I'll be using all of you as interviewing officers at some stage or another."

This cheered the detectives up enormously – at least there was something of interest to look forward to. Looking at each other, they exchanged nods and smiles.

"Any questions?" asked Abbie.

The room fell silent.

"Okay then, thank you. The overtime code is DS7 and any more than four hours per person, per day, will require my authority. Understand?"

"Yes, guv."

"Right, let's get busy… let's find this bastard."

FORTY-TWO

Heavy traffic on the M6 had badly delayed their journey north, so it was a tired Jill Turner and Colin Coston who strode into the divisional intelligence unit at Burnley Police Station late on Monday afternoon.

The first thing they noticed about the place was how small the unit was. There were just four civilians sitting at computer terminals on desks in a square in the centre of the room, and a uniformed police sergeant sat at a separate desk in one corner. Their own DIU at Smethwick Police Station had at least a dozen staff, four of whom were uniformed officers.

The man in charge of this DIU was Police Sergeant Leighton Coates, a chubby, moon-faced man, who carried an extra layer all over his body. His hanging jowls and barrel chest were complemented by flabby arms protruding from his short-sleeved white shirt. He looked the archetypal, office-based police officer – the type who hasn't seen active service for a very long time and is hoping he won't have to see it throughout the remainder of his service.

Despite his appearance, he had a pleasant demeanour and warmly welcomed them, taking them up one floor to the canteen, where he paid for their drinks. "A police officer named Leighton Coates living around these parts? Your dad was rather keen on Burnley, eh?" asked Colin, grinning from ear to ear.

The sergeant sighed heavily. "Everyone asks that. Listen, this town is mad about their football, and I'm convinced that people around here have claret and blue blood running through their veins. But to answer your questions, yes, that is my real name, and no, I don't follow Burnley. I'm not the slightest bit interested in football."

Jill rolled her eyes in disbelief that her colleague could have made such a stupid cock-up.

"I... I'm so sorry... I didn't..." stammered Colin.

Leighton held up a hand. "Please, it's not a problem. It happens all the time, believe me. Let's get back to the matter in hand."

Jill nodded her agreement, and Colin blew out a sigh of relief.

Removing a small file he'd been carrying under his arm, Leighton brought them up to speed. "I've been briefed by your DI and received the images from the chippy; my team have been working on it all morning."

"We're very grateful," said Jill. "Any luck so far?"

Leighton's face split into a beaming smile, the stretched skin on his cheeks shining.

"Indeed we have."

He opened the small brown file and removed a copy of one of the images, placing it on the table facing Jill and Colin.

"That is John Horsfall; he lives a few miles out of town in a small village called Barley. He was a right scrote when he was younger, but he's not been in trouble for the past thirty years to my knowledge."

Colin expressed surprise. "That must have been a good spot by someone."

"How do you mean?"

"Well, if he hasn't been in trouble for thirty years, you won't have any recent photos of him. People change a lot in thirty years."

Leighton nodded. "You're right, we don't have any recent photos, but he's very well known by officers at this station." His yellowing teeth were clearly on display, so wide was his smile.

"How come?" asked Jill.

"He's the manager of Munchies." He stared at them, as if they *must* know where Munchies was.

Jill took a sip from her cup and raised one eyebrow enquiringly. "Munchies, what's that?"

"The café next door to the nick."

"Oh, I see."

Clearly warming to his task, Leighton enthused. "He's especially popular with Burnley supporters; he talks endlessly about football with anyone who'll listen, and he never misses a match, home or away. He meets up with a group of friends at away matches, then bores us all to tears with reports of their antics."

Colin pursed his lips and produced a photo from his inside jacket pocket.

"Okay, that's really good, thanks." He slid the photo across the table to Leighton. "Any luck with this man?" He tapped the image of the other suspect wearing Burnley colours in the chippy. "Could this be one of his friends?"

Leighton shrugged. "Possibly, but we haven't managed to ID him yet."

"Well, one out of two is better than nothing," said Jill. "Anything else you've learned which might help?"

He started shaking his head, but then stopped himself. "Oh yes, I nearly forgot. The group he meets up with are called The Claret Pals."

FORTY-THREE

"You're certain that's what the group's called?" The excitement in Abbie Beard's voice was tangible through the earpiece of Jill's mobile.

"That's what the DIU skipper said." Jill had put her mobile on speakerphone, so Colin could join in the conversation.

"Then it's got to be relevant," said Abbie. "The Claret Pals – TCP, it makes perfect sense... and he was one of only seven people who could possibly have placed the poison in that can."

Jill looked uncertain. "Maybe it was two unconnected acts, boss, maybe he was just writing his group's initials, you know, like a graffiti tag?"

Abbie produced a dismissive grunt. "He's a fifty-six-year-old man – he's not likely to be into graffiti, is he? Anyway, matters have developed since you left."

Colin raised one eyebrow in Jill's direction. "How do you mean?"

"One of our civilian station officers at Smethwick has a son in the CID at Rotherham."

"So?"

"He just happens to be working on a murder at a pub in Rotherham when Burnley were in town last month—"

"Could be a coincidence; doesn't mean there's a link," interjected Colin.

"I haven't finished yet!" snapped Abbie. "Her son mentioned a victim having his throat slashed open, and there was a folded Post-it note found on the body… with the letters TCP on it!"

"Oh my God," said Jill. "Why would they do that? I mean, why leave such a big clue about yourself?"

"No idea. Maybe it's a sick bastard who enjoys taunting the police, who knows? The history of murder investigation is littered with killers who liked to leave clues as to their identity. Their deranged minds like to taunt us."

"You're right," said Jill. "But we can't say it's definitely a member of that group; could be someone setting them up."

"No, I'm convinced it's one of that group. I've spoken to the OIC at Rotherham, a DCI called Wilf Marsh, and he's confirmed the letters were written in the same-coloured marker pen."

"What, maroon, like our one?" asked Colin.

"He thought maroon too, but once we discussed the murders, and the link with Burnley Football Club, it became obvious – it's not maroon… it's claret."

"Oh my God," said Jill.

"I'm not finished yet, guys. There's more, much more." Abbie didn't elaborate for several seconds. Jill and Colin could hear papers being sorted, and the silence hung in the air like a cloud.

"Come on, guv, don't leave us hanging!" pleaded Colin.

They heard Abbie sucking in a deep breath.

"I tasked an officer with contacting other police forces where Burnley have played away this season. They were at Bristol City two weeks ago, and guess what happened?"

"Another murder?" asked Colin.

"No, worse than that."

Jill and Colin looked at each other. "What can be worse than a murder?" asked Jill.

They heard Abbie suck in another breath before she spoke. "A double murder. In a tower block close to where The Claret Pals were drinking, a man was thrown from a balcony on the eleventh floor to his death."

"Jesus Christ!" said Colin.

"And if you think that's bad, a disabled man living in the same flat from which the man was thrown, had a carving knife plunged into his neck from behind."

"Oh my God," exclaimed Jill. "That's awful!"

"You're right, it is. But it turns out there's an upside for us."

Jill lifted her eyes to Colin's, asking the question for them both, "How can there be an upside?"

"The poor bastard who did the triple somersault from the eleventh floor had a Burnley Foundation membership card in his back pocket. Guess who it belonged to?"

"A member of The Claret Pals?" asked Colin.

"Correct. And to top it all, in the flat's kitchen the letters TCP had been carved into the chopping board."

For a few seconds silence reigned, then Jill asked, "What was the name on the membership card?"

"Stuart Quigley. He's been nicked, interviewed and bailed by the MIT in Bristol."

"Bailed?" shouted Colin. "How the hell wasn't he charged?"

"Apparently his alibi checked out, so he's in the clear... for now."

Colin stared in disbelief at Jill's mobile on the table. "Sounds like The Claret Pals have got a very clever and very devious killer in their midst. Someone prepared to throw one of their own under the bus."

"I think you're right, and I think we're closing in on him." Abbie had one more directive for them. "I don't want Horsfall to attend voluntarily anymore. The dots are joining up nicely... I want him nicked!"

FORTY-FOUR

The following morning, shortly after 10.00, Jill and Colin were accompanied by two uniformed officers on the short walk to Munchies Café. As they'd been told, it was next door to the police station. A large and bustling café that was busy at any time of day. Popular with both manual workers and office workers, it was especially popular with police officers, and plenty of them were seated at tables enjoying their breakfasts when they entered.

The decision to hold back making an arrest until the morning had been made by Abbie, who couldn't see the benefit in arresting Horsfall in the late afternoon or early evening. By the time he'd been booked in, searched, had his fingerprints, photograph and DNA taken, then spoken to a solicitor, it would be almost time for him to be bedded down for the night. No, he wasn't going anywhere, and he wasn't yet aware of their interest in him, so the best thing was to wait until morning.

In the meantime, late on Monday evening, Abbie had taken part in a conference call with DCIs Wilf Marsh and Stan Jarvis, both of whom were as stunned as her at the obvious link between their investigations. They updated each other on progress and developments in their respective cases and agreed to work closely together in the future. Because the killer's first victim had been in Rotherham, DCI Marsh would assume officer in the case responsibility for the joint investigation, codenamed Operation Stout.

$\overline{\underset{\overline{}}{*}}$

Pushing the door into Munchies open, Jill led the way between tables of customers eagerly tucking into their breakfasts. Through a large serving hatch behind the counter, two members of staff could be seen slaving away over hot stoves, and the smell of cooked bacon wafting out into the café made her wish she'd had more than just cornflakes for breakfast.

Three young female waitresses were busy moving between the counter and tables, taking orders, serving up breakfasts and clearing away. Behind the counter was a rotund middle-aged woman wearing a grimy white apron. A film of sweat beaded across her forehead, showing just how hot it was, or maybe how hard she was working.

Manning the till, which according to Leighton Coates was where he always stood, was John Horsfall, his claret-and-blue Burnley FC apron, covered with Burnley football shirts from past years, looked almost brand new. As one customer finished handing over his money, the next moved up to the till. John seemed happy to chat cheerfully with each person in turn and seemed unwilling to hurry anyone away. The detectives could see he was an excellent host.

Instead of pushing in, Jill, Colin and the two uniformed officers took their place in the short queue, the uniformed officers sharing whispered asides with colleagues enjoying their breakfasts. Two minutes later, Jill stood across the counter from John.

"Hello, love," he said cheerfully. "Not seen you in here before. What did you have?" He hovered his fingers over the till.

Jill and Colin produced their warrant cards. "I'm DC Turner and this is my colleague DC Coston. We're from Smethwick Police Station in Birmingham, investigating the murder of Tommaso Romano."

John's eyes widened in surprise. He replied calmly in his deep Lancashire accent. "I heard about it, terrible business. What's it got to do with me?"

"Could you come around this side of the counter please?" Jill wasn't asking a question; the timbre in her voice made it abundantly clear this was a command.

John turned to the sweaty, rotund woman.

"Jane, take over the till, love." He handed her a bunch of till receipts, before lifting the counter hatch and walking through to stand in front of Jill.

By now, the usual hum of conversation and clinking of cutlery had for the most part abated. John was greatly loved in the café, and everyone was keen to know what all the fuss was about.

Taking a firm hold on John's right arm, Jill said, "John Horsfall, I am arresting you on suspicion of the murder of Tommaso Romero. You do not have to say anything, but it may harm your defence if you fail to mention when questioned something which you later rely on in court. Anything you do say may be given in evidence. Do you understand?"

John blew out hard. "Yes, pet, but you're making a huge mistake. I've done nothing wrong."

"We'll discuss that at the station." Jill walked to the front door leading John by his arm. They passed open-mouthed customers, who'd known and liked John for many years. But there were no problems getting him to the door, flanked as she was by Colin and the two uniformed constables.

Once outside, Jill said, "Who were you with in the chippy?"

"My mate, Ian Calvert."

"Where does he live?"

"Tunbridge Wells. Why?"

Jill remained silent.

John turned to her, concern written all over his face. "Hang on a minute. How long will all this take?"

Colin took hold of his left arm to persuade him to keep moving. "As long as it takes, Mr Horsfall. We've got a number of questions we want answered."

"But Burnley are at home tonight. We've got Preston at the Turf… it's a local derby… I can't miss that!"

FORTY-FIVE

With only ninety minutes remaining before kick-off, the Royal Dyche pub was packed with fans excited about the upcoming match. For a few of The Claret Pals, it was the preferred drinking hole before matches; others preferred the cricket club.

"What do you mean he's been nicked?" Ian stood alongside Fat Joe in the rear garden of the pub. Three other members of the Pals were standing in a huddle with them, all shocked by the news that John had been arrested.

Ian was the only one who didn't live locally; the remainder of the Southern Clarets had given it a miss – they rarely travelled up to night-time home matches from down south.

Joe was known as 'Fat Joe' not because of his size – which was about average – but because he once had a job travelling around restaurants, cafés and chippys collecting used fat for disposal. Answering Ian's question, he leant in conspiratorially, keeping his voice low. "He's been arrested for the murder of that bloke in the chippy at West Brom. A mate of mine said he was frogmarched from the café and taken next door into the nick."

Ian rubbed the back of his neck, an expression of utter bemusement on his face. Out of all the Pals, he was closest to John. They cycled together, visited each other two or three times a year; they even travelled to watch the Tour de France together every year. His arrest had shaken Ian to the core.

"After the game, I spoke to the woman who owns the chippy. She said he'd been poisoned, so we guessed he'd been murdered."

Nobody responded, eyes flicking from person to person, each one waiting for another to make a comment.

Ian, being his usual emotional self, put his head in his hands. "John's done nothing wrong – we've been set up… again!" A dawning realisation slowly crept across his face… "I was with him! They'll be coming for me next!"

"You really think so?" asked Joe.

"Of course they will. I just know they will!" His eyes narrowed. "Why won't any of you listen? We're being set up!"

"Set up? How?"

Ian took a long draught of his beer. "Think about it – you were informed on by someone and then arrested for the murder in Rotherham."

"I wasn't arrested; I went in voluntarily."

Irritated by Joe's remark, Ian snapped, "You're splitting hairs! Look, you were taken in by the police for questioning about a murder close to where we were drinking at an away match. Then two weeks later Stuart is arrested for two murders at our next away match, once again in a location close to where we were drinking. Now John's been arrested for a murder at West Brom on Saturday! And yet again, it happened next door to where we were drinking!"

Joe wrapped a reassuring arm around his friend's shoulder. "I'll admit it's getting difficult to pass it off as a coincidence, but that doesn't mean somebody's trying to fit us up."

"Sorry, mate," Ian said, "you're talking bollocks! I know you're trying to make me feel better, but the finger's being pointed at us, and we all need to get off our arses and find out who's doing it!"

The match turned out to be an uneventful 0-0 draw, played out in pouring rain, and it was a very damp Ian who arrived back at his sister-in-law Alison's house in nearby Colne, where he was staying for a couple of days.

It was only 10.45, but Alison was already asleep, and he was shattered, so he crept as quietly as he could upstairs to bed.

With his head resting on his comfy pillow, he stared up into the inky blackness, his mind racing with images of John being grilled in the police station. His thoughts drifted back to his discussion with Joe in the pub garden earlier that evening. Despite Joe's efforts at persuading him there was nothing unusual going on, he didn't believe that, not for one minute, and he thought that deep down, Joe didn't believe it either.

The image of the woman wearing the Rotherham hoodie swept into his mind. He thought at the time it might have been Gretchen, but Ryan had quickly proved it couldn't have been. Nevertheless, the image persisted. *Whoever the murderer is, they're misleading the police and pointing the finger at us. But who the fuck are they?*

FORTY-SIX

Despite his tiredness and racing thoughts, Ian soon drifted off.

He was awakened a short while later by the sound of the doorbell ringing. Ian pulled himself out of bed as the ringing was followed by three sharp raps on the door.

Wearily pulling on a pair of boxers and a T-shirt, he left his bedroom and bumped into Alison on the landing.

"Who the hell's that at this time of night?" she asked.

He shrugged. "No idea, but we'll soon find out, won't we?" He was already dreading what a wake-up call at this time of night might mean.

Leading the way downstairs, with Alison following closely behind, another loud rapping on the door caused Ian to shout, "Okay, okay, I'm coming!"

Opening the door, Ian and Alison were confronted by four very wet police officers – three in uniform and one in plain clothes, holding up his warrant card.

"Yes?" said Alison, pushing Ian to one side. "Can we help you?"

The officer in plain clothes only had eyes for Ian. "Ian Calvert?"

Rubbing the top of his head and attempting to feign calmness by yawning loudly, Ian said, "That's me."

"My name is Detective Constable Sam McAdam. I'm arresting you on suspicion of the murder of Tommaso Romano. You do not have to say—"

He was interrupted by Ian's wild shouting. "What? Look, I was at the chippy, but I've done nothing wrong! I haven't killed anyone!"

A uniformed officer took hold of Ian's arm, but he resisted strongly, wrenching his arm free and pushing the officer away.

"You don't need to grab me like that; I said I haven't done anything!"

Two more officers quickly subdued Ian, turning him to face the wall, telling him to be quiet and securing him in handcuffs behind his back while Alison begged them not to hurt him.

DC McAdam finished the caution.

"I'm saying nothing – this is shit!" screamed Ian, as he was roughly manhandled out to the waiting police van, his bare feet splashing through cold puddles on the path.

"Please don't hurt him – he's the gentlest man I know," sobbed Alison. "He wouldn't hurt a fly – there must be some mistake."

Ian was roughly pushed inside the van's rear doors wearing just his boxer shorts and T-shirt. The doors closed with a resounding bang and a uniformed officer turned to Alison. "Fetch him a change of clothes please, love. He might be a while."

FORTY-SEVEN

Earlier that evening

The digital clock on the side wall clicked over to 7.33, as the heavy door opened and the officers who had arrested John Horsfall entered the interview room.

John's hand quivered as he wiped away a bead of sweat from his top lip. He had been in custody for over nine hours, but this was his first time out of his cell. He watched nervously as they took their positions at the opposite side of the table, his heart beating fast. Despite listening intently to the evidence they'd given to the custody sergeant, he was still furious that they had brought him here and were accusing him of such a dreadful crime.

The room was cool but not cold, a temperature that perfectly matched the icy atmosphere. The sound of the long buzzer marking the start of the interview finally came to an end, and John looked uneasily at his solicitor Benjamin Walker, who had attended at his request.

Benjamin was a family friend who John had known for twenty years and was, handily, a criminal defence lawyer.

Facing him across the table were detective constables Jill Turner and Colin Coston, both of whom looked calmly professional and determined. Each person identified themselves, before DC Coston posed the first question.

"How long have you been a member of a WhatsApp group known as The Claret Pals?"

"About seven years."

"Are you proud to be a member?"

A confused expression swept John's face and once again he exchanged a glance with his solicitor, before returning his gaze to the detectives.

"We don't have a membership scheme, if that's what you're getting at, and pride doesn't come into it. We're just a group of mates who meet up for a few drinks before matches."

Colin gave a nod. "I understand." He drew in a deep breath. "Let me put it another way – do you like meeting up with the same group of people at *every* away match?"

"I suppose so... yes."

Colin sat back in his seat and Jill leant forward. "Are you reasonably settled in life at the moment, John?"

He shrugged. "I guess so..." One corner of his mouth lifted to give the barest hint of a smile. "Actually yes, I'd say life's pretty good right now."

"So, nothing traumatic has happened to affect you emotionally in the past couple of months?"

John thought for a moment, then shook his head. "Traumatic? No. Nothing."

Jill scrawled something on her notepad, then fixed him with a hard stare. "That's not true, though, is it?"

John was taken aback by the strength of her assertion. "I'm telling the truth – my life is good."

Jill said nothing for several seconds, just stared with an emotionless gaze, her eyes flicking from John to his solicitor, then back again. After what seemed to John like an eternity, she finally spoke. "Tell me about your relationship with Gretchen Grover."

"What's my relationship with Gretchen got to do with anything?"

Not replying, Jill waited for John to answer, allowing the silence to hang uncomfortably.

Realising he wasn't going to get an answer to his question, John blew out a long sigh. Leaning forward, he rested both forearms on the table. "Look, we were together for six years, I thought we were happy, but about six weeks ago she broke up with me."

Jill fabricated a smile. "What was the cause of the break-up?"

A broad smile split John's face. "She couldn't handle my obsession with Burnley Football Club."

"And you find that funny, do you?"

His face cracked into an even wider smile. "A little bit, yes. Don't get me wrong, I was disappointed when we split, but it was her fault for giving me an ultimatum."

"An ultimatum?" asked Colin.

"She told me to choose between going to the match at Rotherham or my relationship with her. I chose the match." He shook his head. "Silly really, after six years, but that's all there was to it."

"And she gave up on a six-year relationship solely because you wanted to go to the Rotherham match?"

John looked down at the table. "It wasn't just that; to be honest, we hadn't been good together for a while. It was becoming stale."

Jill glanced at Colin, who gave a gentle shake of his head. "So, you weren't angry or upset at breaking up?"

John removed his forearms from the table and sat back thoughtfully.

"For a short while, yes. Like I said, I was disappointed." Then he brightened. "But actually, it's been a relief. No more arguments on match days and no more nagging."

Realising Jill was heading down a blind alley with her line of questioning, Colin took over. Removing photographs from a small white envelope, he laid the first one on the table facing John: a photo of him standing at the counter of For Cod's Sake.

"Can you identify this person please?"

Frowning at the question, John sneered. "Of course, it's me."

Five more photos followed, two of men wearing West Brom colours, two of men sporting no team colours and one of a woman wearing a West Brom football shirt and baseball cap. The cap's peak was pulled down low over her face.

To each photograph John shook his head and said he didn't know them. One extra photograph was then slowly, and somewhat theatrically, placed on the table by Colin. "And what about this one?"

John was fully anticipating this, but it still felt strange as he stared down at the photo of his best friend. "That's Ian – we were collecting fish and chips for the rest of the Pals."

"Ian?"

"Yes, Ian Calvert."

"And where does Ian live?"

"Tunbridge Wells, in Kent, but he's staying at his sister-in-law's house in Colne for a couple of days."

"What address in Colne?"

"44 Crown Mead."

"Thank you, and who exactly are 'the Pals'?"

"The group you asked me about earlier, The Claret Pals. They were next door in the pub garden."

Colin wrote down Ian's name and address, slid the paper across to Jill and tapped it gently. She gave a small nod.

"Are you sure the two without team colours are not members of The Claret Pals?"

"Absolutely certain."

Over the next twenty minutes, John was shown CCTV recordings of customers being served inside For Cod's Sake. It was pointed out by DC Coston that he and Ian were two of only seven customers who leant across the counter with an arm tucked underneath their body, thereby obscuring the victim's can of Vimto. This meant it had to be one of the seven of them who poisoned the drink.

The seriousness of his predicament suddenly hit home like a sledgehammer. "Hang on a minute. I know what it looks like, but I didn't kill that poor sod! Why would I want to hurt someone I'd never met before?"

"I've no idea," said Colin. "You tell me?"

"Why on earth would you suspect me or Ian? We're not even from the area; it's probably a local he's upset or something."

Jill fixed John with an expressionless face. "In that case, why did the killer leave the letters TCP written in claret marker pen at the scene?"

"TCP?" John knew exactly what they were getting at but played dumb.

"Yes, John," said Colin. "The initials of The Claret Pals."

John snorted. "Don't be ridiculous – those letters could stand for anything!"

Colin smiled and sat back in his seat. "You're right, they could, but right now it looks the most likely thing they stand for is The Claret Pals."

His supremely confident manner left John feeling decidedly uneasy.

Jill was drumming her fingers on the table, attracting John's attention. He turned to face her.

"Thing is, John, those same letters were found at a murder scene in the Hammer and Sickle pub in Rotherham, and at the scene of a double murder in Bristol. On both occasions it was when Burnley were in town, and each offence took place close to where The Claret Pals were drinking."

John felt the colour drain from his face.

"And it happened again last Saturday," Jill added. "Doesn't look good for you and your mates, does it?"

Unsettled by this, John nevertheless held Jill's gaze. He relaxed back in his chair, trying hard to appear he wasn't bothered by her pressing. "I agree things don't look good, and I can see why you're pouring all your efforts into our group, but like I said, those letters could stand for any number of other things."

"Don't be bloody ridiculous!" snapped Colin. "Four murders, committed in towns hundreds of miles apart, all with the letters TCP at the scenes, and all of them occurring only metres from where a group called The Claret Pals were meeting? Give me a break!"

Solicitor Benjamin Walker intervened. "Your job is not to make statements, Officer, your job is to ask questions. Do you have a question for my client to answer?"

Jill glared at Colin for his outburst. Turning back to John, she produced a photograph of the letters written under a lip on the side of the counter display; she turned it around so the photo faced John. Pushing it towards him, she tapped the letters with the end of her pen, forcing John to look at them.

"You're right, they could stand for something else, but I put it to you that as they appeared precisely when two members of The Claret Pals were visiting the shop, it was one of you who wrote them."

John was getting exasperated. "You're barking up the wrong tree. I didn't kill him, and neither did Ian!"

Colin had been looking more and more irritated as the interview proceeded and, despite being warned by Jill to button it, he angrily jabbed a finger at John's face. "Officers are searching your house as we speak – if they find poison of any kind, or a claret marker pen, then you're looking at being charged with murder, sunshine."

John was incensed by his tone and leant forward to snap back, but at the last second, he realised that was exactly the response the detective was hoping for. Controlling himself with difficulty, he sat back in his seat, holding Colin's angry stare but saying nothing.

Colin raised his voice even more. "I put it to you that you were devastated at being dumped by your girlfriend, and since then you've gone on a spree of violence!"

Staring open-mouthed at the detective's ridiculous allegation, John's mouth moved to speak, but no words came out.

"That's shaken you, hasn't it, nothing to say all of a sudden?"

Regaining his composure, John calmly scratched his right eyebrow and, latching on to the comment made by his solicitor, calmly said, "I'm sorry, I thought I was here to answer questions. I didn't hear any question during your rant about poison, marker pens and charging me with murder, so I decided to keep quiet."

Colin flared angrily, his face reddening as he once more jabbed his finger across the table. "Think you're clever? Think you're funny? Well, you'll be laughing on the other side of your face when…"

Colin's tirade was cut short by the hand of his colleague gripping his shoulder and easing him back in his seat. The strength of her grip, and the urgency in how she moved him back, caught the words in his throat and brought him swiftly to his senses.

Jill took over the questioning once more. "Apart from yourself and Ian Calvert, who else from The Claret Pals purchased food from the chippy?"

Turning over his bottom lip, John gave the merest of shrugs. "Nobody as far as I know. Just the two of us."

"So, you're certain nobody else entered For Cod's Sake?"

"Whoa, hold up a minute. Of course I'm not certain. I said nobody 'as far as I know'."

"Okay, but as far as you're aware, just you and Ian?"

John nodded.

"Out loud please."

"Sorry. Yes, I presume it was just me and Ian, but like I say…"

"Yes, I understand, you're not certain." She tapped Colin gently on the arm; their exchange of looks needed no words.

Jill searched through her paperwork, lifting a new sheet of paper to the top of the pile and holding it in both hands. "Do you have a home computer, John?"

"Yes, a small laptop."

She lifted her eyes to his. "That laptop will be examined, and your search history gone through. Have you ever researched different methods of killing someone on your laptop?"

"No, of course not."

"How about looking up poisons?"

John snorted, coughing. "Don't be daft."

"Have you carried out searches on either of those subjects on your mobile phone?"

"No, you're welcome to check if you want."

"Oh, we will, John. We will."

Suddenly looking and feeling more relaxed, John sat back in his seat and smiled.

"Good luck with that. You won't find anything of interest, apart from a decent amount of porn." He chuckled to himself.

"I'm glad you find it so funny, because if there's anything that incriminates you, John, anything at all, they'll find it. It doesn't matter if you've deleted it; they'll still find it."

John grinned. "Like I said, good luck."

---

*

Four hours later, as he was being released on bail by the custody sergeant, John glanced up at the digital wall clock, which was displaying the time 12.17. He sighed heavily.

"First Burnley match I've missed in almost five years." He cast a gaze around the custody suite. "Anybody know the score?"

A young PC sitting on a bench waiting to book in his drunk prisoner looked up. "0-0. Apparently it was a pile of shite."

"Thanks, pal," said John. "Are you a Claret?"

The constable nodded. "Season ticket holder in the Cricket Field Stand, but I miss quite a few games because of shifts."

John lifted a thumbs up in thanks.

"Pop into Munchies when you get a chance. We'll have a good chat."

The custody officer was not impressed with one of his PCs fraternising with a prisoner, let alone about to be bailed on suspicion of murder. "That's enough thank you, PC Barton, keep an eye on your prisoner; he's sliding off the bench!"

John was released on bail, with a return date set for Tuesday, 4 October at 7.00. On the station steps, Jill Turner said, "Don't bother trying to warn Ian." She pointed at a police van entering the gates to the rear yard.

FORTY-EIGHT

"Hello, boss. Wasn't expecting to hear from you this late!" said Jill. Her mobile phone had sounded at 12.30, at the very moment Ian was being booked in by the custody officer. "I'll have to call you back, just booking Ian Calvert in."

"Let Colin take care of that. You need to hear this right now. I think we've hit the jackpot!"

As Jill took the call, the custody sergeant continued processing Ian.

Jill walked a few metres down the cell passage, where she could take Abbie's call away from the tumult in the main custody area.

"Okay, boss, it's mad busy here but I'm alone now. Fire away."

Abbie had an element of glee in her voice as she imparted her news. "I've just been told that Ian Calvert was arrested when Burnley were in town last year."

Before she could continue, Jill interjected, "That's great news, boss."

The excited tone in Abbie's voice rose an octave. "He was arrested for causing a disturbance in For Cod's Sake."

"Oh my God, what are the chances of that?"

"You haven't heard the best bit yet... he threatened Tommaso Romero as he was being dragged away."

This was dynamite news, and Jill knew it. The link was devastating. "What was it about?"

"They were arguing about money – Calvert said he'd been short-changed by thirty pounds, and Romero refused to refund him. Then he told Romero he'd get even with him if it was the last thing he ever did!"

A shudder of excitement travelled down Jill's spine. *This is it! We've got the bastard; we've fucking got him!*

"Thanks for the call, boss, that's just what I wanted to hear. We'll get him booked in and bed him down for the night."

"No problem. Oh, and Jill."

"Yes?"

"Update me as soon as the interview is finished – the bosses are on my back, and this just might shut them up."

FORTY-NINE

Ian had not endeared himself to the custody suite staff, or indeed the officers investigating his case. He'd been deliberately obstructive when having his fingerprints, photograph and DNA taken, banged on his cell door most of the night, which had infuriated his fellow inmates who were unable to sleep because of the noise, then refused all offers of food and drink at breakfast.

He demanded to be allowed to order his own refreshments, which he wanted brought in from outside the police station – a request that was begrudgingly agreed to in an attempt to keep him sweet.

His behaviour meant that when Jill and Colin booked him out for interview, their relationship was already strained close to breaking point.

Ian refused the offer of a solicitor, figuring that having one appointed might delay him getting out of there even longer. He was confident in his own ability to deal with whatever questions a couple of thick coppers wanted to throw at him. They wouldn't be able to pin anything on him – he'd done nothing wrong.

"Thought you'd taken me by surprise, didn't you?" Ian cockily leant back with his fingers locked behind his head, glaring contemptuously at the detectives across the table, his chair balancing precariously on the rear two legs.

"Sorry?" asked Jill, looking up from a final check of her interview notes.

"I knew you'd be coming for me after John was arrested. It's ridiculous, just because we'd visited that chippy."

"Can you wait until I've turned the tape on, please." Colin's tone of voice indicated it wasn't a question.

Seeing that his behaviour was only delaying matters, Ian rocked his chair back onto all four legs and rested his forearms on the table, staring down at his clasped hands and shaking his head.

"Come on then, Dipstick and Makeshift, get on with it."

The customary opening necessities of a police interview were completed in short order, before Jill, twiddling a black Biro between her middle and index finger, posed the first question. "Please take a look at these images." She laid out the same photographs shown to John the previous day. Like John, Ian confirmed their presence in the chippy but denied any involvement in the poisoning of Tommaso Romero.

Jill collected up the photos and returned them to a white A4 envelope and pushed them to one side, opening a small blue file. "Have you visited For Cod's Sake prior to last Saturday, Mr Calvert?"

"Yeah, loads, about half a dozen times over the years."

Her eyes bore into his and she pursed her lips. "What about last year?"

"Yep, why?"

"Do you recall anything in particular regarding that visit?"

Ian could see where this was going and decided to take control; suddenly becoming serious, he said determinedly, "I do."

Jill pressed him. "Go on."

"It was pissing down with rain and the match was shite – we lost 3-1."

Colin, who was becoming riled by Ian's arrogant and dismissive demeanour, smacked the palm of his hand down hard on the table.

Jill placed her hand on his and shook her head at him. Red faced, Colin removed his hand, sat back and said nothing. Turning back to Ian, Jill came directly to the point. "You were arrested in For Cod's Sake on Saturday, 17 November last year. Do you recall what for?"

"I do."

Jill raised her eyes to the heavens in exasperation. "And what was that?"

"The twat behind the counter served my food; I got out my wallet and handed over a fifty-pound note, but he only gave me change for a twenty."

"Yes, the 'twat' – as you call him – was Tommaso Romero. And you got aggressive towards him, didn't you?"

"Was that his name?"

"It was."

Ian said dismissively, "In that case, yes, I did." He jutted his chin forward. "You seem keen to ignore the fact that he'd fiddled me out of thirty quid!"

Jill tapped her middle finger on the tabletop. "Police officers who were patrolling nearby were called in to calm things down, yet you continued to make threats towards him."

Once again, Ian could see where her questioning was leading, and his expression became more sombre. "Yes, I know, we'd been in the pub, and it was probably the drink talking. After what has happened to him, I regret my behaviour now."

"Do you remember what you shouted after you'd been arrested, as you were being escorted from the premises?"

Ian looked blankly at Jill but made no reply. Jill sat back

and stared at Ian, the same tactic she'd used against John. The silence stretched for over a minute, until he could stand it no longer.

"Okay, okay. I threatened him. I said I'd get even. There, happy now?"

"That's not the whole truth, is it? According to witnesses, you said you'd get even with him 'if it was the last thing you ever did'." She said nothing for a few seconds. "Do you remember saying that?"

He nodded, slowly. "Yes, but it was in the heat of the moment. We've all said stupid things we didn't mean. It was probably the drink talking."

Jill formed a sarcastic smile. "There, that wasn't so difficult, was it?"

Sensing that this wasn't going as well as he'd anticipated, Ian went on the attack. "So, I said a few stupid words a year ago, what does that prove? I made a drunken threat after I'd been done out of thirty quid." He held his arms out. "Do you truly believe I've held a grudge all this time, poisoned a man I don't even know at the risk of ruining the remainder of my life, all because of an argument over change at a chippy?" He started laughing. "Have you tried listening to yourselves? You're being ridiculous."

Ian's words hit home with Jill, who realised after listening to his viewpoint that it did sound ridiculous. But his previous confrontation with Tommaso, together with the specific threats he'd made, meant he had motive (albeit a weak one) and opportunity to poison him, but they still needed to show he had the means.

"Are we really? Well, we'll see, won't we?"

*

The interview continued for another twenty minutes, with the detectives stressing the fact that TCP, the initials of The Claret Pals, had been found at each murder scene. He was asked why that might be over and over, but Ian had shut up shop, refusing to be drawn, and answered 'no comment' to every other question. At lunchtime he was returned to his cell, where he was offered a meal, which this time he accepted.

Lying on his blue plastic mattress in his spartan cell, Ian made plans for when he finally got out of there. If the police couldn't do their job properly, he would have to find the killer himself.

In the late afternoon, he was taken back to the interview room, where he was bombarded with questions for a further hour. On top of that, he was informed they had searched his room in his sister's house and seized his laptop, which he took everywhere with him. They had also obtained a warrant to search his flat in Tunbridge Wells.

Unable to elicit a confession, they released Ian on bail, with an undertaking to return to Burnley Police Station on 4 October, the same date as John.

FIFTY

Back in the CID office, Jill updated Abbie with the current situation, with Colin listening in. "We need more evidence before we can prosecute either of them. I think we're done here for now, boss."

Abbie wasn't best pleased on hearing this. "Bollocks, I was hoping one of them would crack or squeal on the other."

"Nope. Like I say, we've got nothing like enough to charge either of them just yet. They're both bailed until 4 October."

Jill heard Abbie blow out hard. "Oh well, if we're right, and one of them is the killer, at least we've made life more difficult for them."

Jill and Colin shared a glance. "Boss?"

"Their bail conditions… I sent you a text."

Jill hurriedly searched through her text messages. "Sorry, boss, I haven't received a…" Her heart sank as she saw the message she'd missed. It had arrived while they were interviewing Ian. *Impose conditions for Ian Calvert not to attend any Burnley football match and not to contact John Horsfall!*

"Fuck! Sorry, boss, I completely missed that."

FIFTY-ONE

Returning to his sister's house after his arrest, Ian seethed with anger. One of the first things he did was to phone John, who persuaded him to pop over to Barley and spend the rest of the week with him. Ian had been due to travel back to Kent on the Wednesday afternoon, ready to return to work on Thursday, but events had shaken him to the core, so he called in sick with a 'viral infection'.

Three hours later, Ian arrived at John's small, terraced house, close to the Barley Mow pub in the beautiful hillside village of Barley, six miles north of Burnley town centre.

Ian embraced his best friend with a crushing hug, which was returned in kind. Their arrests had affected them both deeply, and the simple fact that they were free men after such an intimidating ordeal was overwhelming.

Releasing Ian's grip and pushing him back slightly, John smiled as they faced each other just inside the door. "Come on, I'll make a brew."

Ian nodded and watched John cross the tiny lounge and enter the kitchen. He dropped his holdall and sat down on the settee. His eyes had moistened, but unusually for Ian, no actual tears had appeared just yet. He raised his voice a little so that John could hear him from the kitchen. "They grilled me for ages because I'd argued with that bloke last year."

The kettle was coming loudly to life, so John also lifted his voice. "I thought they might. Did they ask you about the ones with no colours on?"

"Yes, I told them they're probably Albion fans."

John laughed. "Yeah, me too."

Ian stood up and walked to the kitchen door, leaning heavily with his left shoulder on the door jamb. "Who's doing this, John? Four murders, all close to where we were drinking, and all with the letters TCP written at the scene!"

Pouring the boiling water slowly and carefully, John filled the two cups, added milk and stirred. Since his interview, he had slowly come around to Ian's point of view that somebody was setting them up. "Beats me, but it's got to be someone who travels to Burnley's away matches and someone who knows our movements."

Frowning, Ian took the cup offered by John and returned to the settee. "Exactly. The killer obviously knows where we're going to be drinking and chooses their targets accordingly."

"Which can mean only one thing…"

"It must be one of the Pals?"

John slowly lowered himself into an armchair, taking care not to spill his brew as he did so. He nodded his head. "That's what I'm thinking – we're a tight-knit group and we're rarely in the company of outsiders. Whoever is doing this knows where we'll be drinking in advance of every match."

Blowing the surface of his tea to cool it down, Ian pondered John's comment for a few seconds. "Maybe it's a past member?"

Leaning back and crossing his legs at the ankles, John placed his cup onto the chair's arm. "Like who? I can't think of anyone."

Ian knew his next words would hit John hard, but he needed to hear them. "What about Gretchen, Steve or Graham? They've all stopped coming to matches in the past year – that's three just off the top of my head."

"Steve's been diagnosed with Parkinsons, he's too ill to travel to games, and Graham has emigrated to Australia!"

"That only leaves one then."

"Gretchen?" John guffawed. "You're not on that again, are you? You're talking daft!" John stopped laughing and his expression darkened. Anger momentarily flashed in his eyes. "Why would you think my girlfriend is capable of killing?"

Ian ran a finger around the rim of his cup. "She's not your girlfriend anymore though, is she? And remember, she was my girlfriend too once."

"Not for very long. I was with her for years. So, I think I probably know her a bit better than you!"

They glared at each other for a few seconds, then John's face softened, and Ian repeated his point.

"She's not your girlfriend, mate. In fact, she's pissed off at you… and pissed off with the group which took you away from her."

Listening to his friend's words, John suddenly saw that they made sense. She was bound to be pissed off with him, but could she really have killed four men, just to get revenge on him? Gretchen? "Well, you can't just go to the police and say: 'It wasn't me; it was Gretchen Grover.' They'd laugh at you."

Ian repeated what he'd first said at the cricket club. "And I thought I saw her at the Rotherham game."

"No, mate, you saw a woman who looked like her."

"Alright, a woman who looked like her, but just think about it for a moment. Making herself look like a Rotherham fan would be the perfect disguise, and by pointing the police towards the Pals, it would deflect attention away from her."

John shook his head in disbelief. "You've really got it in for her, haven't you? You never showed any dislike for her while we went out together. What's changed?"

"Nothing, mate. I like Gretchen, I've always liked her, I've just got alarm bells sounding in my head, and I'm worried that I'll ignore them at my peril."

John stared at his best friend over the rim of his teacup, gently sipping on the piping hot brew.

"Okay, so you think you saw her at Rotherham. That still doesn't make her a killer. Unless you've got anything else?"

Leaning forward to rest his cup on the coffee table, Ian entwined his fingers. "Remember what Ryan told us at the cricket club?"

"About what?"

"He says he took a call from Gretchen in the pub garden at Rotherham – shortly after the murder – she claimed to be at home."

"So?"

"He also took a call from her before the Bristol game, both times just happened to be shortly after the murders."

Ian could see by John's face that he was now recalling the conversation. "Yeah, I remember. But what does that prove?"

Ian wasn't finished. "Nothing, but she also called him when we were on the way back to our cars after the West Brom match. Which was shortly after that murder. Ryan declined the call and messaged her to say he'd call later."

"Alright, she keeps calling him. I'm not bothered anymore; he can have her."

Rolling his eyes and blowing out hard, Ian made an exasperated face. "Are you deliberately missing the point? She phones him after each killing so that someone other than herself can alibi her not being anywhere near the murders!"

Squeezing his nose between forefinger and thumb, John screwed his face up. "Alright. That does seem strange. It could still just be coincidence though."

"Coincidence! It would have to be a fucking huge one for

her to just happen to call him immediately after murders have been committed on three separate occasions!"

"I still can't see it."

Ian sat back, exasperated. "Well, we've nothing else to go on, so I'll be watching out for her like a hawk at future matches."

John finally conceded. "Okay, so will I. But it's almost certainly not her, so we'll need to keep an eye on the others too."

"What, all of them? That won't be easy."

"No, it won't. Hopefully, the killings are over and done with, but if there's another, we need to keep an eye on everyone's movements. We must discover who just happens to be missing at the relevant time."

"That's a great idea."

The friends spent two days walking in the beautiful Lancashire hills, discussing their arrests, pondering why The Claret Pals were being targeted, discussing the personalities of other members of the group, trying to recall where they all were at the time of each murder and concluding that none of them could have possibly committed all four.

Whoever the killer was, they were superb at covering their tracks.

FIFTY-TWO

Saturday, 17 September dawned cold and dreary, as Ian and John made their way towards Burnley for the home match against Coventry City. The Claret Pals had once again arranged to meet at the Royal Dyche.

Entering the pub, the TV screens were filled with live coverage of Blackburn's lunchtime kick-off away at Huddersfield Town. Every touch of the ball by a Blackburn player being greeted with booing and whistling, followed by an ear-splitting cheer when Huddersfield scored.

The two friends grinned at each other and pushed their way to the bar to order drinks.

Today's game was an important one: Coventry were sitting fourth in the table, three points off top, two places and three points above Burnley, in sixth. As Ian and John stepped outside after collecting their pints at the bar, a group of lads belted out John's favourite song.

"In our Lancashire homes! In our Lancashire homes! We speak with an accent exceedingly rare, the Longside at Burnley will always be there! In our Lancashire homes!" This was quickly followed by a short burst of, "We are Burnley, we are Burnley, super Burnley, from the north!"

Half a dozen Pals had already assembled in the rear garden,

meaning Ian and John were greeted with a huge cheer when they made an appearance. The previous week had been alive with WhatsApp messaging, facetime conversations and even conference group discussions about their arrests.

"Fucking hell!" said Val. "It's Bonnie and Clyde!"

Laughter filled the air.

"Very funny," said John. "It might be one of you next!"

"Which one of you is John Reginald Christie?" asked Simon, referring to the famous poisoner. Once again, the comment produced a great deal of merriment.

"That'll be John," said Ian. "He's the ugly fucker who wears glasses!"

John laughed at his friend's joke and slapped him on the back. "Good one, but remember, if I'm Clyde, you're Bonnie!"

Joking over, they chinked glasses with their friends and gratefully accepted the warm welcome back into the fold. Two of the Pals managed to purloin a table at the bottom of the garden, around which they all gathered, earnestly going over the apparent attack on their group.

Ian and John said nothing about Ian's suspicion of Gretchen, or their plan to watch every other member of the group closely at future matches. They simply went along with the flow of the discussion, which followed the lines of everyone agreeing to keep their eyes peeled for anyone behaving suspiciously at future games. Their next trip was on Tuesday, when Burnley were away at Premier League Brighton in the Carabao Cup third round.

Out of those at the Royal Dyche that afternoon, only Ian, John, Joe and Val would be at the Amex Stadium (Brighton's home ground) the following Tuesday. Simon and three others declaring it was too far for a night-time fixture in a 'tinpot' cup game. Their numbers would likely be swelled by a few of the Southern-based Pals.

Burnley romped to a 3-0 victory, sending the home fans into raptures. They drew level with Coventry on points but went above them into fourth place by virtue of goal difference.

---

*

Back at John's house, Ian chose to head home straight away. "I've got a few things to sort out before work."

The friends shook hands, as Ian stressed the urgency of their situation. "We've got to find the killer before our bail date. The police will be under pressure to charge someone by then… and it mustn't be one of us."

John agreed. "You're right, but it's not just the police I'm worried about. The CPS are next to fucking useless. If the police want to charge us, they're just as likely to go along with it, even though there's only circumstantial evidence!"

Climbing into his car, Ian threw his holdall onto the front passenger seat, raised a hand and waved goodbye to John. "See you on Tuesday!"

He drove away past a group of people enjoying an evening drink outside the Barley Mow. He had plenty to occupy his mind on the 285-mile journey back to Tunbridge Wells.

FIFTY-THREE

Jack and Ginny held hands as they snuggled up on the sofa watching an episode of *The Crown* on Netflix. As the closing titles scrolled up the screen, Ginny looked at the digital clock on their lounge wall. It was 10.18. "Let's watch the last few minutes of the news before bed."

Jack leant to one side to reach for the remote control, farting loudly as he did so.

"That's disgusting!" complained Ginny.

"You're just jealous you didn't do it!" Jack laughed, as he selected the *BBC News at Ten*. A government minister was promising urgent action to combat the number of migrants crossing the channel in small boats.

"What a load of shit!" said Jack loudly. "They've been promising to stop the boats for years now. There's nothing they can do, and they know it!"

"Stop being miserable," said Ginny. "You're always moaning about something." She reached for Jack's hand and squeezed it playfully.

Newscaster Peter Mount filled the screen. "And now a special report from our senior crime correspondent, Jayne Howard." The picture cut away to Jayne standing alongside a huge screen showing a picture of a smiling Mario Spiteri.

"Police have today confirmed they are hunting a serial killer." The image on the screen changed to one of Burnley's ground, Turf Moor. "A killer who appears to be using Burnley Football Club's away fixtures to target their victims."

The picture changed back again, and she held an arm out to the image. "This is the killer's first victim, Mario Spiteri, a Maltese national working as a waiter at the Hammer and Sickle public house in Rotherham." The image flicked to a picture of the pub for a couple of seconds.

Jack and Ginny stared open-mouthed at their TV, their grip on each other's hands loosening.

Turf Moor filled the screen again. "That was the first of four murders, all of which took place when Burnley were playing an away fixture." The image changed to one of Roberts House. "Two more victims were killed in Bristol – Gavin Stoneham, a local taxi driver, was thrown from an eleventh-floor balcony, and Keith Clarkson, a wheelchair-bound disabled man, was stabbed with a kitchen knife in the back of the neck. They were both killed shortly before Bristol City's home game against Burnley."

The image changed to one of For Cod's Sake chippy. "Finally, Tommaso Romero, an employee of a local fish and chip shop, was poisoned just before West Bromwich Albion's home game against Burnley." An image of a grinning Tommaso filled the screen.

Moving away from the giant screen, Jayne took a seat opposite a woman dressed smartly in a blue trouser suit, black shoes and a white blouse. "This is Detective Inspector Abigail Beard, the senior officer in charge of the investigation into the murder of Tomasso Romero. Good evening, Inspector."

"Good evening."

"Why have police waited until now to reveal to the public that there's a serial killer on the loose?" Jayne's tone was both abrasive and confrontational.

Abbie crossed her legs in an unconscious act that body language experts would have classed 'defensive'.

"The link didn't become obvious until after Mr Romero's murder. As soon as the link was discovered, we carried out extensive investigations to confirm our suspicions before releasing it to the public, which is what I'm doing here now."

"Are you looking at a Burnley fan being the killer?"

"At the moment we're keeping an open mind."

"An open mind you say?"

"Yes."

"Okay." Jayne tidied the papers she was holding by tapping them on her knee. "What can you tell me about certain letters being scrawled at each of these crime scenes?"

Looking shaken, Abbie's face reddened. "How do you know about that?"

Jayne ignored the question and leant forward. "Isn't it right that the letters TCP were found written close to the bodies at every scene?"

"Yes, that's true, but—"

Jayne quickly interrupted. "What do these letters signify, do the police have any idea yet?"

"As I say, it is true that the letters were written close to each murder, but at the moment—"

"It sounds to me, Inspector, that you know what the letters stand for, but you're unwilling to say, why is that? This is a serial killer who might strike again soon. Don't the public have a right to know?"

Feeling Ginny squeezing his hand tighter, Jack stared open-mouthed at the TV screen.

"Christ! She's really going for her. It's only a matter of time before the identity of every member of the Pals becomes public knowledge."

Ginny looked at her husband. "This is terrible; thank heavens the police haven't released details yet."

Jack rolled his eyes and shook his head. "It's just a matter of time. The investigating teams know what TCP stands for, and come to that, so do we, not to mention the rest of the Pals; there will be a leak to the press soon enough."

Jack and Ginny watched the report with growing trepidation. Abbie confirmed that this was now a joint investigation and that three separate forces were co-operating. She stressed it might not be a Burnley fan carrying out the killings, but rather someone cleverly using the games as a vehicle for their sick killing spree, purposely sending police in the wrong direction.

Each murder had been gone over in detail, but other than that, nothing significant had been revealed.

"Currently, investigations are continuing," said Abbie, desperately trying to wrestle back the initiative. "From here on in we will be keeping both the press and public fully updated as things develop."

"Is there anything you wish to ask of the public, Inspector? People out there are worried and desperate to help."

Abbie sat upright. "Yes. If anyone has information about any of these killings, no matter how small or insignificant it seems, please contact the incident room at Operation Stout. We have a team of trained detectives waiting to take your call."

"Detective Inspector, thank you for your time." Jayne Howard turned to face the camera. "Officers will be keeping an eagle eye out at future Burnley away matches, and everyone is wondering the same thing – will the killer strike again? Burnley will be playing away again this Tuesday at Brighton in the Carabao Cup, so we'll know soon enough. This is Jayne Howard, Sky News."

The screen was once again filled with newscaster Peter Mount. "And finally, something a little cheerier…"

Ginny muted the sound, sat back and looked up at the ceiling, blowing out hard.

Jack stared blankly into space. "Well, that's fucked it!"

FIFTY-FOUR

"Three of Burnley Football Club's away games this season have resulted in the brutal murders of four innocent men, men who had nothing to do with Burnley Football Club or their opponents. It appears that they just happened to be in the wrong place at the wrong time."

DCI Wilf Marsh faced his laptop computer with a grim expression, as he led the conference call between himself, DCI Stan Jarvis, DI Abbie Beard and Superintendent Anna Swanston, the gold commander in charge of policing Burnley's upcoming match, away at Brighton.

Wilf, Stan and Abbie had been in regular contact since the murders were linked, and all three agreed the murderer was probably not finished yet and likely to strike again. However, Anna Swanston wasn't convinced by their arguments, remaining impassive and unmoved as she listened to what they had to say. When they'd finished, she cited her budget restraints as being the reason she wouldn't be able to swamp a city like Brighton with officers before and after the game.

"It's not Brighton you should be worried about," said Abbie. "We've put feelers out and it seems likely The Claret Pals will be meeting up at a pub called the John Harvey Tavern, close to the river in Lewes town centre."

Anna's expression softened and she gave a small nod of the head, her expression indicating she was weighing things up in her mind. "Okay, that makes things a little easier. I'll redeploy one of our regular PSUs from Brighton town centre and see if I can scrape the money together from somewhere to provide another."

"That's great. Thank you, Anna," said Wilf, speaking for everyone.

Stan Jarvis piped in, "You're doing the right thing, Anna. Until we catch this bastard, we've got to do our utmost to prevent them killing again."

Abbie moved her face closer to the screen. "Hopefully, if the killer is intending to strike in Lewes, they'll see an increased police presence and think twice."

Nodding her understanding, Anna said, "I'll do my best. Like I said, we'll deploy two extra PSU serials to Lewes town centre. It sounds like overkill to me though – the town will be swimming with bobbies!"

FIFTY-FIVE

Walking through the small town of Lewes in East Sussex, Gretchen was enjoying the warm, late September sunshine. It was just after 3.30 in the afternoon, and for the past couple of hours, she had positioned herself inside a wonderfully quaint café in the market hall. She'd spent her time messaging Cindy and making final plans for the day, her warped view on reality convincing her that what she had planned was the right way to achieve the revenge she so badly craved.

For thirty minutes after leaving the café, she explored the town, confident that none of the Pals would arrive until around 5.00; they never did for a night match. But all the same, she kept an eye out, just in case someone arrived unexpectedly early. They would have been unlikely to recognise her anyway, dressed as she was in a purple knee-length dress and white trainers. To top everything off, she was sporting a strawberry-blonde bobbed wig, which curled around the sides of her face like a 1960s pop star, and a white baseball cap.

Glancing at her reflection in shop windows, Gretchen smiled; never mind the Pals not being able to recognise her, she hardly recognised herself!

The size of the police presence in the town centre had taken her by surprise, with uniformed officers in twos and threes on almost every street corner. She'd been to Brighton away twice before, and the Pals had always based themselves in the sleepy town of Lewes, only a seven-minute train journey from the stadium. At past games, the policing in Lewes had been low, almost understated; she had certainly never seen anything like this. *So, they're expecting something to happen, are they? Well, I don't like to disappoint!*

Using a narrow alleyway, Gretchen found her way down to the banks of the beautiful River Ouse. Slowly ambling along the riverside path, she began to leave the houses of the town behind her.

The further she walked, the greater the density of reeds adjoining the footpath, and the fewer the number of walkers. It was attractive to look at, of that there was no doubt, but solitude and pretty scenery wasn't what she was there for. Nearer the town there had been several anglers trying their best to land a catch, but now there was only one every fifty metres or so.

On the footpath, the only person in sight was a woman around the same age as Gretchen. She was using a long-lens camera and seemed to be happy in her own world taking pictures of wild birds along the riverbank. Seeing someone with a camera made her uneasy, but she convinced herself that she was just being paranoid and carried on. A hundred metres further on, Gretchen spotted a narrow track leading off the main path into the head-high reeds. Having had no luck finding what she sought so far, she decided to investigate.

The track wound for forty metres into the reeds, until it was well out of sight of the main path. Turning yet another bend, Gretchen came across an elderly man sitting on the grass bank close to the river's edge. He was painfully thin, sitting on the steep riverbank with his forearms resting on his thighs, which were bent at ninety degrees to his scrawny shins. His legs, jutting out under his light-blue, knee-length shorts, were glaringly white. His thinning, wispy, grey hair was dishevelled and wind-blown, and his painfully thin arms, almost hairless and covered with age spots, sneaked out from a matching light-blue T-shirt. She approached him from behind and looked at him pitifully as he gazed at the outgoing tide, appearing to be lost in his thoughts.

"Hello," she said. "Are you alright?"

He started on hearing her voice and looked over his left shoulder to see who was there. "Oh, hello, sweetheart. You made me jump. I didn't hear you coming."

"I'm sorry, I didn't mean to startle you. I just wanted to make sure you were okay."

Returning his gaze to the river, the old man said wistfully, "My dad used to bring me here fishing when I was a boy; he died twenty years ago today, but I feel close to him here."

Gretchen could feel her eyes moistening as she heard the love for his father in the old man's voice.

"I thought I'd spend some time revisiting the place where we used to sit, you know, spend a few moments remembering him."

Gretchen was genuinely touched by the old man's words. "That's so sweet. What's your name?"

He replied without turning to look at her. "Albert."

"It's lovely to meet you, Albert."

"You too, love, what's your name?"

Removing the heavy metal bar from her handbag, she said, "Gretchen, my name's Gretchen."

As she said her name for the second time, she brought the bar crashing down on the right side of Albert's head, causing him to slump to his left side, his head resting on the grassy bank close to the water's edge. Aware the blow would have only rendered him temporarily unconscious, she knew she needed to work quickly and replaced the bar into her handbag.

Using her feet, she turned him onto his front, then slid him half a metre down the steep bank, until his face was immersed under the water's surface. Pressing her left foot onto the back of Albert's head, she shook with excitement as she watched the air bubbles coming from his nose and mouth, seeing them burst on the surface.

Suddenly, she saw Albert's right hand clench, then open, and she felt resistance through her foot. He was coming to and beginning to push back against her foot, desperate to lift his head from the water and suck in a lifesaving lungful of air. But the fight in him was pitifully weak, and she simply pushed her foot down harder. Within seconds, the struggling stopped, and the bubbles gradually reduced, before finally stopping altogether. Albert was dead.

Gretchen's heart was beating fast, and her breathing had become ragged. She was loving the thrill and excitement pulsing through her veins. Pulling Albert's light-blue T-shirt down on one side, so that it hugged tightly to the bony frame of his body, she removed the claret marker pen from her bag and scrawled the letters TCP across a dry part of the fabric covering his lower back.

*

Twenty minutes later, after keeping well away from the town centre, Gretchen had circumnavigated the north side of the town using only footpaths. When she arrived back at the quiet residential road where she'd parked, she unlocked her car, climbed into the driver's seat and sat there quaking uncontrollably, as the surge of adrenalin coursing through her searched for an outlet. For the first time in her killing spree, tears flowed freely, and her shoulders juddered as she sobbed uncontrollably. Her tears were not for Albert and not for the loss of her relationship with John; they were for herself.

It was a full fifteen minutes later that Gretchen had calmed down enough to drive safely. Before turning the key in the ignition, she moved the rear-view mirror to look at herself and was pleased to see a reflection which was practically unrecognisable. Pulling the wig from her head and releasing her long, brunette hair, she brushed and brushed until she was satisfied it was neat and tidy.

With the tears now finished, she allowed herself a cruel smile at a job well done. Returning the mirror to its correct position, she turned the engine on and started out on the long drive back to Lancashire.

*

Sitting on her own outside a small café in the heart of Lewes, Emily flicked through the images she'd taken of Gretchen walking alongside the riverbank of the River Ouse. Her favourite being the one she'd taken from long distance, showing her walking off the footpath and onto the track between the reeds. Enlarging the image, she examined it closely and said quietly to herself, "Perfect."

FIFTY-SIX

The Burnley fans packed into the John Harvey Tavern in Lewes were in full voice as they belted out another of their favourite songs. "Bertie Mee said to Bill Shankley have you heard of the North Bank, Highbury? Shanks said no, I don't think so, but I've heard of the Longside, Burnley! We are the Longside, Burnley! We are the Longside, Burnley! We are the…"

"We're so happy to see you both," shouted Ginny to Ian and John, fighting to be heard above the din of singing. "It must have been awful, what you've been through."

The singing subsided, allowing normal levels of conversation to resume. The Claret Pals had gathered earlier than usual, meeting at 4.30 in the pub, close to the famous Harvey's Brewery. They had pushed two tables together alongside the windows in the upstairs room, with a view overlooking a small car park area and the river slicing through the town. The view wasn't amazing, but pleasant enough. Val, Stuart, Ryan, Joe and Becki occupied one table, while John and Ian sat opposite Jack and Ginny on the other.

"It wasn't great," said John, his usual ready smile nowhere to be seen. "But we keep reminding ourselves that they've got nothing on us."

Jack's police experience had taught him to never fully

believe a suspect accused of a serious offence, but in John and Ian's cases, he found himself making an exception. He believed absolutely that his friends were telling the truth; there was no way either of them could be such a brutal murderer.

"Come on, Jack," said Ian, leaning back and holding his hands behind his head, fingers interlocked. "You were a copper. What's going on here?"

Downing a large gulp of his Diet Coke, Jack slowly returned his glass to its coaster. "It seems to me that it's unlikely the killer is a member of our group."

Without looking up, Joe said dryly, "That's what we all hope, but let's face it, it's probably one of the Pals."

"I agree," said Becki.

"You're both wrong – the killer isn't one of the Pals," said Jack, a degree of certainty in his voice.

John shook his head vigorously. "Then why are the killings only happening when we're close by, with clues pointing the filth towards us every time?" A distinct tone of irritation and annoyance was obvious in his voice.

Jack was about to answer, but he was distracted as a noisy crowd came up the stairs. They joined in with the singing coming up the staircase from down below. "…He asked me to play, I answered him nay, said rubbish like yours I could beat any day…" Everyone joined in with the chorus, "…And it's no, nay, never, no nay never no more, 'til we play bastard Rovers, no never, no more! We hate bastards. We hate bastards. We hate bastards…"

The singing subsided to the extent that Jack was free to speak once more, and the giggling group quietened down as they found a table at the opposite end of the upstairs room. "You would have to be stupid to continually leave clues pointing towards the group you belong to. No, I'm convinced it's an outsider who, somehow, knows our plans each week."

Ian held his hands out. "Why? Why would someone who's nothing to do with our group do that?"

Jack raised his eyebrows. "I didn't say they were nothing to do with the group."

John and Ian's eyes locked. John giving him a hard stare, accompanied by a small shake of his head. His suspicions should remain unspoken – for now.

"Go on, Ian, were you going to say something?" Ginny encouraged.

Ian thought quickly. "I was just going to ask Jack what he meant."

All heads turned to Jack, who leant forward and patted the tabletop with the palm of his hand. "The killer might not be a member of the Pals, but they might be seriously pissed off with one of us, pissed off enough that they're trying to destroy not only that person, but the whole group."

Val looked amazed, her mouth falling open, her distinct West Country twang sounding much stronger than usual. "That's bollocks! Are you seriously suggesting they're prepared to kill people because one of us has pissed them off?"

"That's exactly what I'm saying."

"Nah, I'm not having that," she said, taking a sip of her Coke.

"Listen," said Jack, leaning in conspiratorially. "You have no idea the mad shit people will do to gain revenge for the smallest of wrongs."

"That sounds twisted!" said Becki.

"The human brain can make you do mighty strange things when it goes wrong!" added Ginny.

John and Ian had been exchanging knowing looks throughout Jack's assessment of the situation, and John wanted to know more. "So, you're saying it's someone fucked up enough in the head to kill people in order to punish one of us?"

Jack pursed his lips. "No, I'm saying that's a possibility."

"Anyone got any ideas?" asked Val. "I can't think of anyone I've pissed off enough for them to behave like that."

"Me neither," chimed Stuart and Becki in unison.

"Nor me," said Ryan.

Joe said nothing but firmly shook his head.

"It's neither of us," said Ginny.

All eyes moved to John and Ian, seated side by side facing the window. "The only person we've upset is Gretchen," said John. "But she wouldn't kill someone, and anyway, Ryan says he can prove she was somewhere else for two of the murders."

Ryan nodded. "That's right – she was at home when we were in Rotherham and out shopping with mates when we were at Bristol."

"Well, whoever it is," said Ian, "we've got to find them. And soon. The police are looking to charge someone sooner rather than later, and currently it's either me or John in the frame!"

"Are any of the others coming down tonight?" asked Ginny, an idea developing in her mind.

"No," said Becki, swinging a finger around the group. "This is everyone."

"Can't blame them – it's a long way from Burnley on a Tuesday night. Well done for making the effort." Stuart's compliment was aimed at John and Joe, the only ones to have travelled down from Lancashire.

"You know me," smiled John. "Never miss a game."

"Right," said Ginny, her voice raised, commanding the group's attention. "We stay together from now until we reach the stadium. If one person needs to go shopping, someone goes with them. If one person goes to get a round of drinks or needs the toilet, another goes with them."

"Why?" asked Val, her brow furrowed.

"Because that way, we can all alibi each other if there's another murder today."

"That's brilliant!" said Becki. "Ginny's right – if there is another killing, her plan removes all of us from suspicion at a stroke!"

"One thing though," said Joe. "They've struck at every away league game, but nothing happened at the cup game at Millwall, so it might be all quiet tonight anyway."

Despite Joe's observation, there was general agreement that Ginny's idea had merit.

"Right, let's have a round of shots to celebrate!" said Becki.

FIFTY-SEVEN

One hour earlier

Jim and Sally Bower smiled warmly at the pretty lady in her purple dress, as she passed them on a footpath close to the River Ouse. She responded by smiling back and offering a cheerful, "Hello. Isn't it a beautiful day?"

"Yes, it's lovely," said Sally.

They both noticed how happy and carefree the woman seemed, leading Jim to comment, "No wonder your dad loves it down here so much – it's beautiful, and the people are so friendly."

Sally pulled him to her, and they stopped walking. "Thank you for being here with me today. Dad's been talking about the anniversary for weeks. It means an awful lot to him." They kissed and hugged.

"You're certain he'll be where you think?"

She nodded. "Yep, absolutely. He tried taking me fishing there a few times when I was small, but I was never really interested." Pulling Jim along once more, she said, "Come on, it's not far now."

Twenty metres from reaching the narrow track through the reeds to Sally's father's favourite spot, they passed two police officers in uniform.

"Good afternoon," said one of them cheerily.

They both smiled, and Jim replied with, "Lovely day." Moments later, they deviated from the main tarmacked path and headed off down a track through the reeds. Seconds later, they stumbled across the dead body of her father, his head partially submerged in the mud. Sally released an ear-piercing scream, which brought the officers they'd just passed running back.

The two young constables, like every officer on duty for the Brighton v Burnley game, had been fully briefed that the killer might strike again, but the horror of what confronted them still rocked them to the core. They were staring down at yet another victim of a murderer who the police had nicknamed 'the TCP killer'.

FIFTY-EIGHT

Back at the John Harvey Tavern, the ongoing concerns about who the hell the murderer might be were all talked out. Subjects as diverse as the Tour de France, work, family problems and football, were now the matters being discussed. As usual, copious amounts of alcohol were being consumed, with the usual suspects – Becki, Joe and John – particularly jolly as a result.

Suddenly, the wailing of sirens was accompanied by a wave of customers entering the pub. They spoke of hurried police activity in the nearby streets, and the Pals' conversations came to an abrupt stop.

"Oh no, it can't be happening again." Becki looked around the table, but the others were equally as dumbfounded. Ryan placed an arm around her shoulder and gave a reassuring squeeze.

Jack leant forward earnestly, one forearm on the table. "One of us needs to find out what's going on."

"No," said Ginny, forcefully. "It must be at least two. Until the killer is caught, nobody goes anywhere alone."

Standing up determinedly and pulling at Ian's arm, John said, "We're the ones in the frame right now. It's best if we go."

Ian pulled himself to his feet to follow his friend, and without another word, they quickly walked down the stairs and out into the warm autumn afternoon.

Ten minutes later, they returned with grim faces and retook their seats.

"Well, what's going on?" Val almost shrieked.

John took a long draught from his pint. "There's been a major incident somewhere along the riverbank. Police are up and down it in both directions."

"Oh my God!" exclaimed Ginny.

"They were a long way off, the far side of the Harvey's Brewery buildings, it looked like a stream of yellow ants on the riverbank; there's dozens of them. They're putting up scene tape, you know, that blue-and-white 'police – do not cross' type of stuff," said Ian. "You could still see along the riverbank when we got there, but within a couple of minutes they cleared us off that side of the bridge. They're restricting pedestrians to the opposite side only now."

Stuart chimed in with a question. "Did you find out what's going on before they moved you?"

John turned his bottom lip over and shook his head. "No." He paused. "Hang on a minute though, I do remember one thing. I saw two men in suits – they went right up to the cordon tape, spoke to an officer with a flat cap for about a minute, then the tape was lifted, and they walked off along the riverbank."

"Did you see where they went?" asked Jack.

"No, the river passes under a huge road bridge, then it bends around to the left and out of sight."

"And none of the officers gave a clue what the incident was?"

John shook his head.

"It's the killer. They've murdered some poor bastard, I just know it," Ian said.

Jack's policeman brain was kicking into overdrive, and Ian's words made perfect sense. He knew that level of police activity could only mean something extremely serious, possibly a rape or a firearms incident, but far more likely a murder.

FIFTY-NINE

The train journey from Lewes to Falmer, to reach Brighton and Hove Albion's Amex Stadium, takes just seven minutes, which meant The Claret Pals could stay in the pub until 6.15, walk to the train station and still reach the stadium by 7.00. Moving off as a group, they pondered whether yet another murder had occurred, and if it had, whether the finger would inevitably be pointed at them again. Their worries were already ruining their enjoyment of the day.

The platform was packed with an even mixture of fans from both clubs, the royal blue and white colours sported by Brighton fans appearing to mix well with the claret and sky blue worn by Burnley supporters. The train pulled into the platform to a chorus of friendly rival chanting. "Burnley! Brighton! Burnley! Brighton! Burnley! Brighton!"

Crammed into a carriage with both Brighton and Burnley fans, the banter continued, with the Burnley contingent singing, "Where were you at Turf Moor? Where were you at Turf Moor?"

The Brighton fans replied with, "Is this all you take away? Is this all you take away?" Both sets of fans seemed to be enjoying the baiting, and for a few minutes the Pals forgot their troubles and enjoyed the moment, laughing out loud as the chanting continued.

Arriving at Falmer, the fans poured from the train, walking up the ramps leading to the wide and spacious areas around the modern bowl-shaped stadium. Heading up a flight of steps fifty metres short of the away supporters' turnstiles, Ian spotted a group of four Burnley fans he knew in a tight huddle. They were in deep discussion and crowded around one of their number holding up his mobile phone; they were so engrossed in what was on the screen, that they were oblivious to Ian's presence.

"Hiya, guys!" he shouted. "What's the big secret?"

They turned as one to face him, their faces only breaking into half smiles. The tallest of them was a man with angular, sharp features. "Alright, Ian? It's a rum do this killing, in't it?"

Ian's mouth dropped open. "What killing?"

"In Lewes. An old boy on the riverbank apparently. It's all over Twitter."

Becki and Val linked arms for support, too stunned to speak. A couple of the Pals pulled out their own phones and searched Twitter.

"How was he killed?" asked Stuart.

"Nobody knows yet. The police aren't saying anything."

John nudged Ian gently in the back, moving him in the direction of the away fans' turnstiles.

"Come on, mate, let's get inside."

Once inside the stadium, the Pals purchased their food and drink, then gathered in a tight huddle close to an exit gate, as far away from prying ears as they could manage.

"Oh well," said Ryan, casually. "Here we go again."

"For fuck's sake, Ryan, you're the master of the understatement!" John's face flashed with a mixture of irritation and anger.

"Right, everyone, calm down," said Ginny, firmly. "We've got enough problems without falling out with each other."

"Ginny's right," said Val. "We're stronger together."

Ian had nothing to say and pulled himself away from the huddle. He needed time to himself, pacing through the throng of supporters, his plastic beer glass held in one hand.

"We've got to face facts," said Jack, his face set with a grim expression. "It looks like the killer has struck again…"

"Well, obviously!" said Becki. "You're hardly Sherlock Holmes!"

"Let me finish!" snapped Jack.

"Sorry!"

"If the killer has struck again, the upside is that it rules each and every one of us out as a suspect." He downed a mouthful of Diet Coke. "The downside is that if they follow the pattern, they've likely left the letters TCP at the scene. It's a matter of time before…"

The trilling of Ryan's phone interrupted Jack's flow, and he paused to let him answer. Looking at the screen, his face flared red. "Oh. Hi, Gretchen… yes, I'm at Brighton with the Pals; we're having a drink in the stadium…" Ryan's voice faded as he moved away from the group to speak more privately.

John and Ian exchanged knowing looks, and Ian whispered in his best friend's ear. "See! I told you. I fucking told you!"

SIXTY

The game ended in a disappointing exit from the Carabao Cup for Burnley, losing a penalty shoot-out after extra time. It had been 1-1 at full time and there had been no extra time.

The terrible events of the day had once again hugely affected the Pals. Unsurprisingly, none of them had truly enjoyed the game. They were only too aware that the connection between the murders and their group would probably become public knowledge quite soon.

Immediately after the game, they returned to Lewes, then went together to Brighton Police Station, which was a hive of activity with officers in both plain clothes and uniform coming and going in large numbers. They explained their link to the recent murders (Operation Stout) and made voluntary statements confirming their whereabouts throughout the afternoon and evening.

It meant that the last of them didn't leave the police station until after 2.00, but it had been a necessary sacrifice. By making the statements, they had effectively alibied not only themselves but also each other. Proving to both the Brighton Major Investigation Team and the bosses of Operation Stout that none of them could possibly be the killer.

Luckily, everyone had travelled to the game by car, so

leaving the police station in the early hours wasn't too much of a problem. Statements submitted, every member of the Pals felt like a weight had been lifted from their shoulders, especially John and Ian.

SIXTY-ONE

The following day, in the late afternoon, Joe and John arrived at Joe's parents' home in Rochdale. He hadn't seen them for a while and thought they'd enjoy sharing an evening meal with him and John before dropping John off in Barley and then heading home to Clitheroe. Opening the front door, he invited John inside, and they walked through the hallway to join his mum and dad in the kitchen. After greeting them both with a hug, he introduced John, and they both helped with preparing the evening meal.

Conversation flowed freely, and apart from asking a couple of questions about their trip and the result of the match, Joe's parents seemed oblivious to the fact that another murder had occurred. Breathing a heavy sigh of relief, Joe looked at John and held a finger to his lips. They would leave them in blissful ignorance.

Settling down with their meals on lap trays in the comfortable lounge, they were just in time to catch the start of *North West Tonight*, the local BBC news programme. Presenter Gus McDonald smiled into the camera. "Good evening. Yet another murder was committed close to Burnley's away fixture in the Carabao Cup at Brighton last night. The victim was the fifth by a murderer dubbed the TCP killer.

We now go to Brighton, where we have a special report from Hayley Downes."

"Bloody hell, Joe!" said his mother, fixing him with a disbelieving stare. "Another murder! Why the hell didn't you say something?"

Joe finished a mouthful of potato and shrugged. "I didn't want to worry you."

His mum was about to speak again, but his father cut her off with a loud, "Shh!", pointing towards the screen with his knife.

A grim-faced Hayley Downes filled the screen, standing outside the main entrance to Brighton Police Station. "A murderer now dubbed the TCP killer struck again last night, choosing yet again to commit murder close to a Burnley FC away fixture." The screen image changed to a head-and-shoulders photo of an elderly man smiling broadly. "The victim was eighty-two-year-old Albert Hayward, from Crowborough in Sussex. He leaves behind a wife, two daughters and five grandchildren. He was brutally struck over the head with a blunt instrument, before being drowned.

"Police have revealed that they're reconsidering one line of inquiry they've so far been actively investigating – that the letters left at each crime scene might refer to a group of Burnley fans known as The Claret Pals. Detective Inspector Abbie Beard from Smethwick Police Station in Birmingham, where the fourth killing took place, said: 'Statements taken late last evening in Brighton have eliminated nine Burnley supporters known to belong to a WhatsApp group called The Claret Pals.' However, DI Beard didn't elaborate as to whether they have any other ideas what the letters might mean."

Joe's dad swallowed a mouthful of chicken. "Whoever it is, they're a raving lunatic!" He turned to his son. "I take it you provided a statement last night?"

"I did, yeah."

"Then why didn't you say something, Joe?" His mother looked hurt.

"I'm sorry. I just I didn't want you worrying about me."

"Worrying? You and your mates are suspects for murder."

"I know, and I'm sorry." For a moment, Joe looked genuinely contrite, then a small smile cracked his face. "But every one of us who went to last night's game has been eliminated now, so it's all good!"

"It's better than good," beamed John. "It's bloody brilliant!"

SIXTY-TWO

"Hi, Gretchen, how are you?" Ryan was relaxing at home as he called her on his mobile phone. He was sprawled out on the settee wearing only his boxer shorts, his left leg hung lazily over one of the arms, while his right foot was planted on the floor. They'd last spoken for five minutes on Tuesday evening, when she called as he stood with the Pals on the concourse, just before the Brighton game, and he'd promised to call her before the weekend. The fact that she'd called him again so soon after yet another murder had certainly made Ryan think, but he still couldn't believe she could harm anyone. His love for her was blinding him.

"Good thanks. How was Brighton?"

He grunted. "Hmm, not great."

"I saw the news report about the murder. How awful!" A deceitful and wicked smile spread across her face.

"Yeah, it's not good. Sorry I didn't mention it on Tuesday; we'd only just heard ourselves. Until I knew more, I couldn't see the point in burdening you with it."

"That's okay."

"And sorry I couldn't talk for long. You know what it's like when the Pals get together."

"Don't worry about it. Do you mind if we don't talk about horrible things like that; it makes me feel uncomfortable."

"Of course, sorry." He deliberately made himself sound as cheerful as possible. "What would you like to talk about?"

"Us," she said in a sultry voice.

Ryan's face broke into a smile; he'd been hoping he was getting somewhere with her, and she'd just confirmed it. They chatted for twenty minutes about the difficulty of starting a long-distance relationship, and how they could wangle seeing more of each other. Ryan confessed how he'd felt about her since they'd first met, and Gretchen asked for a little while longer, before she would be ready to fully commit to a relationship. The thought of being romantically involved with him made her skin crawl, but she'd string him along while he remained of value to her.

The subject moved back to football. She knew that Queens Park Rangers' stadium was called Loftus Road. She also knew that it was only a few miles from Ryan's flat in Kew, so Burnley's game there next Saturday wasn't one he'd be likely to miss. But she asked the question anyway, as innocently as she could. "Will you be going to a game this weekend?"

"Yes, we're away at QPR."

"Oh wow, that's handy for you!" She tried to sound as though she'd no idea where they were playing. "Are the Pals meeting somewhere near the ground?"

"Not really. All the pubs around Shepherd's Bush are home fans only, so we're heading down to Hammersmith."

"I don't know Hammersmith. What's it like?"

"It's okay, like most places in London – some nice parts, some shit parts."

She laughed. "What's the pub called?"

"The William Morris. It's a 'Spoons so the beer should be cheap."

Gretchen was playing a clever game, behaving exactly as she had done previously and asking the same kind of questions.

But for the first time since the Millwall match, she'd made the decision not to bother attending. The Claret Pals were now being spoken about openly on news programmes and their match days were being ruined; their cosy little gatherings would soon be a thing of the past. She began to feel that her work was done.

"You take care on Saturday, Ryan, that nutter is still out there somewhere. I know they're your friends, but do you think it might one of the Pals?"

"Oh, I forgot to tell you. They've eliminated most of us from their inquiries."

Gretchen's heart sank. This was staggering news and she had to work hard to force a happy timbre into her voice. "That's great news. How did that happen?"

"Ginny came up with the idea of staying together while we were in Lewes."

"What, all of you?"

"Yes. If any of us needed to go somewhere, another of the Pals went with them. We never went anywhere alone until well after the match."

She felt her heart lurch. This was a disaster. *Ginny? That skinny, ginger-haired bitch?* Remaining calm and keeping her voice measured, Gretchen replied quickly, "That's good. So, who has been eliminated?"

Ryan listed their names. "Hopefully, they'll concentrate on finding the real killer now," he said.

Ending the call promising to call him back on Sunday, Gretchen slumped down at the kitchen worktop where she'd been preparing a meal for herself. After all her efforts and all the risks she'd taken, it looked like Ian and John could be getting off scot-free! *No, there's no way that's going to happen. You bastards are going to pay!*

SIXTY-THREE

Frantic messaging between the Pals was the order of business for the next couple of days. Every member of the group had a ticket for Saturday's match at Queens Park Rangers, and John had come up with a radical plan, posting his idea on the group's WhatsApp group. *Only those who were at Brighton should go to the game. Everyone else should stay away, and make certain you're with someone who can alibi you all day.*

The post was not well received, with several members expressing their displeasure at the thought of missing another game. Simon, who lived in the Scottish borders, left John in no doubt about his feelings, posting his WhatsApp reply. *I've booked return train tickets and a hotel in Euston for my son and me – there's no way I'm not going!*

John pushed his point. *All of you who weren't at Brighton will still be regarded as suspects! By staying away and in company with someone throughout the day, you'll have the perfect alibi if the killer strikes again!*

Ollie, who lived in Wolverhampton, echoed Simon's sentiments. *I've booked the train too, and I haven't missed a match in London for two years!*

Desperate to make them see sense, Ryan posted his thoughts in capital letters. *COME ON, GUYS! MISSING*

ONE GAME MIGHT FREE YOU FROM BEING A MURDER SUSPECT!

Ryan's ploy made an impact, as one by one, the remaining Pals agreed to forgo the game. Simon was the last to concede the idea. *Okay, I'll find something else to do with my son all day, but he's not going to be happy!*

You're all doing the right thing, posted Jack. *The killer has struck at every away game except one, so they'll probably strike again this Saturday.*

Simon made one last post. *He'd better do, or you lot will owe me for train tickets, hotel room, match tickets and about ten pints!*

SIXTY-FOUR

As it turned out, Saturday's match at Queens Park Rangers proved to be a damp squib for almost everyone involved.

The Pals who had been to Brighton met up at the William Morris, a Wetherspoons pub in Hammersmith, close to the underground station. In the pouring rain, it was going to be an unpleasant thirty-minute walk to the Loftus Road Stadium. In previous seasons they had struggled to find a pub that accepted away fans anywhere near the ground, so although it wasn't perfect, this was the best option. Luckily, several other Burnley fans had chosen the same pub for a pre-match bevvy, and they'd enjoyed a great atmosphere, with a few singsongs thrown in.

John and Ian were noticeably chipper, having apparently been given a reprieve. Once the group had settled around a long table, John explained to everyone why they were so happy. "The old bill has cancelled our bail to return dates!"

"Really? How did they inform you?" asked Jack.

"By letter."

Jack's policeman head sprang into action. "Did the letter say there would be no further action?"

Ian and John looked at each other and shook their heads. "No."

"Hmmm, that's interesting." Seeing his comment had brought concerned expressions to their faces, he sought to reassure them. "They'll probably send an NFA letter in the next few days."

"I assumed we were in the clear?" asked Ian.

Realising he'd spoiled the moment, Jack said, "I'm sure you are; it's probably an admin mistake."

The walk to the stadium proved to be a miserable affair, and they arrived at Loftus Road thoroughly drenched.

Match commander Graham Maxwell had increased police numbers by just over double, giving a very heavy presence in all the streets close to the stadium, including nearby Shepherd's Bush Green. But as it turned out, there were to be no murders at this fixture, with the killer failing to appear. Was it because of the extra policing Graham had put in place? That was undoubtedly how he would frame it to his bosses, but in truth, he would never know.

As it turned out, the Pals who had given up their match tickets, train fares and hotel bookings needn't have bothered. They had missed the game for nothing!

Those who did attend were soaked to the skin both before and after the match, thanks to the relentless heavy drizzle.

The game was a dreadfully dull affair, with two well-matched teams fighting out an utterly forgettable stalemate. Players were struggling to play any kind of passing football in the wet conditions, and the game looked like it might be abandoned at any moment because of a waterlogged pitch.

*

Walking through the beautiful woodland alongside Skipton Castle, Gretchen smiled to herself, imagining the consternation she had caused for both the police and The Claret Pals. She was enjoying having time to herself and drank in her beautiful surroundings. Still seething about what Ryan had told her, she quietly pondered her next move. The following Saturday was an international break weekend, meaning Burnley had no game, and the weekend after they were at home, giving her an extra couple of weeks to decide what to do next.

SIXTY-FIVE

John and Ian hated international breaks, as indeed did every right-minded football fan, so Ian invited himself up to John's place again. His job as a marketing consultant allowed him to work compressed hours, Monday to Thursday one week, then Tuesday to Friday the following week. Luckily for him, his three-day weekend coincided with the international break.

Leaving home on the first train out of Tunbridge Wells on Friday morning, Ian was collected by John from Burnley Manchester Road station. The journey to John's house in Barley took just twenty minutes, and after a quick cup of tea and a slice of coffee and walnut cake each, they set out to climb Pendle Hill.

"That is a wonderful view," said Ian, as he fought to remain upright in the ferocious wind buffeting both him and John at the summit.

"What?" screamed John, who could hear that Ian had said something but was unable to decipher a word.

Ian moved closer, pointed down into the valley and shouted directly into his friend's ear, "Wonderful view!"

John didn't bother attempting a reply. Remaining on their feet was proving a difficult enough task, so trying to hold a meaningful conversation at the same time would be practically impossible. He pointed towards the leeward side of the hill, where they could find at least a smidgen of respite from the howling wind.

Nodding his understanding, Ian led the way, leaving the small cairn and triangulation point registering the highest area of Pendle Hill behind them. Two minutes later, sheltering behind a small outcrop of rocks in a shallow depression, the friends were finally able to draw breath without it being sucked back from their lungs by the strength of the wind.

"How the fuck can the weather be so gorgeous, yet so windy?" asked Ian, pointing to the cloudless blue sky and dazzling sun.

John shrugged. "No idea, but it manages it quite often in Lancashire!"

Reaching into his small rucksack, Ian pulled out two bananas and handed one to John, who accepted it gratefully. The climb up Pendle Hill requires a decent amount of effort whenever you attempt it, but the requirement was doubled when the wind was this ferocious. Making themselves as comfortable as possible on the rocky ground, they tucked into their fruity sustenance.

Their position allowed them extensive views across the town of Burnley to the horizon.

"You're right," said John. "That view's a belter."

"Huh?" Ian clearly hadn't been listening.

John pointed. "The view, it's a cracker."

"Oh, yeah, it is." Ian propped himself up on one elbow. "Isn't life great sometimes?"

John rolled onto one side. "That's a bit deep."

Ian reclined flat on his back again and stared up at the sky. "One minute we're both suspects for a string of murders, the next we're climbing Pendle Hill together on a beautiful sunny day. Free men, completely exonerated."

"Fucking hell, you turning soft on me? Come on, I need to get you to the Pendle Inn as soon as possible – you need some beer inside you. A spot of lunch and a few pints in your belly will soon have you back to normal."

Their late lunch at the Pendle Inn, nestling at the foot of Pendle Hill, had been more liquid than solid, so it was a very merry pair of friends who arrived back at John's house shortly after 4.00 in the afternoon. Opening the front door, John bent down to collect two items of post lying on the doormat. The first was an official-looking envelope, the second a piece of plain white paper which had been folded in two and posted through the letter box. Nothing was written on the outside, but when unfolded, it revealed an intriguing note: *John and Ian. Please meet me at the Boot Inn in Burnley at 7.30 this evening. I have information you will both find beneficial. A friend.*

John read the note, then passed it to Ian. "What's this about?"

"No idea," said Ian, shaking his head. "Should we go?"

Throwing his eyes to the heavens, John said. "Have you forgotten already?"

"Forgotten what?"

"We've been invited to my son's house for a meal tonight. His wife's a great cook and she'll be preparing something special."

Ian sighed heavily. "Oh shit, I'd completely forgotten, sorry." Kicking off his boots, he slumped into an armchair, still holding the note. "It looks like a woman's handwriting – why would someone need to speak with us so urgently?"

Perching on an arm of the settee, John shrugged, then rubbed his eyes vigorously with a finger and thumb. "No idea." He regarded his friend and could see he had the same questions racing through his mind. "I'm as intrigued as you are, but I haven't seen James and Laura for ages, and they've taken the trouble to invite us, so we can't disappoint them."

Ian gave a small nod, folded the note and placed it on the coffee table. He was intrigued and wanted to make the meeting but understood John's standpoint.

Standing up and moving a couple of paces to stand alongside him, John reached down and placed a hand on Ian's shoulder. "I'll tell you what, I'll make up an excuse for you not being there. You go and meet whoever it is on behalf of us both."

"Thanks, mate."

John placed the official-looking envelope on a sideboard to be read later, but something made him pick it up again and open it. What he read shook him to the core.

"Shit!" he said loudly.

"What's up?"

"It's from Operation Stout."

"What does it say?" said Ian, sitting bolt upright.

"The time of death for Albert Hayward has now been reassessed as between 3.30 and 4.10. Therefore, the voluntary statements made at Brighton Police Station no longer eliminate you or your friends from our enquiries."

Ian's face fell and he slumped heavily in the chair. "That means the rest of us will have received the same letter. Smethwick Police will want us back on bail again. For fuck's sake, just when we thought it was over."

SIXTY-SIX

Alighting from the taxi at shortly before 7.30 in the evening, Ian made his way the short distance to the Boot Inn, a Wetherspoons pub on St James's Street, in the centre of Burnley. Ian wasn't keen on 'Spoons pubs, but this was the designated meeting point, and right now he badly needed a drink. He had no idea who might be the originator of the unsigned note and no idea what he might be walking into. Nervously, he pushed the front door and strode up to the bar. "Pint of Doom Bar, please, pal."

The tall young man with a neatly trimmed hipster-style beard looked totally disinterested but replied cheerfully enough. "Coming right up, sir."

Ian looked around the half-full tables but failed to recognise anyone he knew. His heart sank a little; he'd been hoping to spot a passing acquaintance, or at least a face he recognised, anyone who might have penned the letter. But he saw nobody he knew, so it looked like he would be waiting until the mystery person approached him.

The young barman pushed the pint across the counter. "Everything okay? You look like you've got the troubles of the world on your shoulders," he asked.

Ian was about to reply, when he heard a gentle cough

alongside him. He turned to see an elderly man holding two empty pint glasses, waiting patiently to be served.

"Sorry, fella," said Ian, picking up his pint and moving aside to allow the elderly gent access to the barman. He offered a resigned shrug; he would not be telling his story anytime soon. The hipster threw a short nod in return and began serving the old man.

Casting his gaze around the bar, Ian selected a table towards the rear, alongside the large plate-glass windows overlooking the rear courtyard. He slumped down on a chair at a table for four people, choosing a seat facing the courtyard. In the circumstances, he preferred not to have eye contact with other customers. He only wanted contact with whoever had written the letter; he simply wasn't in the mood for smiling or exchanging pleasantries with anyone else.

His brain provided him with a plethora of images he would rather forget. Being in Burnley town centre brought back memories of the interrogation he'd endured just up the road in the police station. They had pounded him with difficult questions, attempting to trip him up at every turn. They'd suggested he must have been involved in murdering Tommaso Romero, but they were lacking the vital piece of evidence they required to conclusively prove his guilt.

Gulping down half of the pint in one go, he watched three men standing in the courtyard. Their carefree banter and hoots of laughter made him smile. That pleasant state had returned to his life once more for a short time, then been snatched away again. And the letter... who on earth could have written it? It must have been someone who knew where John lived. But what did they want, and why didn't they simply wait for John and him to return after their climb?

Resting an elbow on the table, he placed his chin on an upturned hand and his other arm on the table, casting the perfect 'thinker' pose.

Feeling a gentle touch on his elbow, he lifted his left arm from the table and turned his head. A tall woman with angular features and short-bobbed mousey hair towered over him, smiling down with a kindly face. Her slim figure was clad in blue jeans and a long-sleeved blue sweatshirt with a large yellow arrow and the words 'Buen Camino' on the front. She was holding an almost empty glass of something in her left hand.

"Hello, Ian, do you mind if I join you?"

Her accent was local, but he failed to recognise her. "Sorry, love, do I know you?"

"No, not yet." Her eyes burned into his. "But I'm the person with the answers to all your problems." She pointed at one of the seats on the opposite side of the table and raised her eyebrows enquiringly.

Curious who this woman might be, and what the fuck she might be talking about, Ian held out an arm to indicate a vacant chair.

Placing her small blue handbag down, the woman squeezed her long legs between the table and chair, sitting directly across from him. The long, slim fingers of her right hand slowly swept back the hair from the right side of her face and tucked it behind her ear. She spoke in a husky voice. "You're probably wondering who I am and how I know you and John?"

Downing the rest of his pint, whilst never taking his eyes off her, Ian placed his glass carefully onto a coaster. He wiped his lips with the back of his hand.

"You're right, I am." He nodded towards her glass. "Can I get you another?"

She ran the index finger of her right hand around the top of her glass before raising it to her lips and downing the contents. "Bacardi and Coke please." She slid the glass towards him and smiled warmly. "Where's John?"

"He had an appointment he couldn't get out of."

She nodded. "Doesn't matter, you'll do."

Lifting her glass from the table, he climbed to his feet and headed for the bar, glancing back at her as he did so.

"Back in a minute."

While ordering the drinks, he kept glancing back to the woman, all the time wondering who on earth she could be. Returning with their drinks, Ian settled back into his chair. "Go on then, surprise me. Who are you, and why are you so interested in John and me?"

She sat up straight in her seat. "My name is Emily Spicer and I know that neither of you had anything to do with killing all those people."

Sensing a trap, Ian looked behind him, then cast his gaze around the bar. "You're police, aren't you? You're hoping I'll say something while I'm off guard."

Emily laughed. "I can assure you, I'm not."

"Then how come you know so much about the murders?"

"Because I was there for two of them."

"What?"

"Well, let's just say I was in the vicinity."

Ian couldn't quite believe what he was hearing; he could feel his chest tightening.

"Sorry, are you a Burnley fan, because I've never seen you before?"

"No, I'm not." She sipped her Bacardi. "I was there keeping an eye on someone." The corner of her mouth curled up.

Shaking his head in disbelief, Ian asked confusedly, "I've no idea what you're talking about, keeping an eye on who?"

Lifting the glass to her mouth and taking a sip, her mouth broke into a broad smile. "The murderer."

SIXTY-SEVEN

He could feel his mouth rapidly drying up. *Is this woman telling the truth, or is she a nutter?* Drumming the fingers of his right hand on the tabletop, Ian studied her carefully as he considered his response, his features a grim mask. "You're not winding me up, are you? Because if you are, it's not very funny."

Emily leant across the table, ignoring a patch of spilled beer soaking into her sleeve. She covered one of Ian's hands with her own. "I promise you I'm not lying. I know who the killer is, and I know why she's trying to point the blame at The Claret Pals."

His mouth dropped open in surprise. "How do you know about the Pals, and—"

Interrupting, she squeezed his hand to stop him speaking. "I know everything, Ian… everything."

"Hang on a minute, you said *she's* trying to destroy the Pals? You mean it's a woman?"

Emily released his hand, her sharp features lighting up with a beaming smile, suddenly making her far more attractive. "Isn't that what 'she' usually means?"

His doubts about her were rapidly diminishing, her confident smile and calm manner slowly convincing him she was telling the truth. "Well go on then, you've captured my interest. Don't leave me hanging. Who is it?"

Suddenly looking nervous and unsettled, she scanned the tables closest to them, ensuring nobody was within earshot. Lowering her voice to a whisper, she said, "It's Gretchen, Gretchen Grover."

"Fucking hell, you're serious, aren't you?"

Emily nodded, but as he studied her, Ian could see her previously confident persona evaporating before his eyes.

"I am." She shuffled uneasily, suddenly seeming nervous. "She's been targeting the Pals ever since he chose following Burnley over being with her."

Running his right hand back over his hair, Ian opened his mouth to speak. "Did she—"

Holding a finger to her lips, Emily cut him off. "Not here, it's not safe. I promise I'll tell you everything, but can we please go somewhere else?"

Ian registered the worried look spreading across her features. "Why, what's wrong with telling me in here?"

She shifted. "I know you dated her, but believe me, you've got no idea what she's capable of. She's dangerously unhinged, and I've a horrible feeling she could be watching us right now."

He laughed. "Don't be daft, of course she's not."

Once again, she took his hand in hers, her voice fracturing. "Trust me, Ian. You might think you know her. John may have thought he knew her. But neither of you could possibly understand what she's really like."

He could feel her hand trembling and cupped it inside both of his. "Okay, okay. Calm down. Let's walk down to The Bridge, it's a great pub, and it won't be too busy this early."

"I'd be happier at a pub nearer where I live; I don't feel safe hanging around Burnley." She looked pleadingly at him, and Ian knew the next drink wouldn't be downed anywhere around here.

Draining his drink, Ian stared at her. "Alright then, where do you live?"

"Skipton."

"Skipton!" He gawped at her. "That's twenty miles away."

She held his gaze and stood up. "Come on, I've done a little pre-planning."

His brow furrowed. "What do you mean?"

"I've booked a cab." She pointed towards an Asian man approaching the bar. "I'm guessing that's the driver now. Once we're safely in Skipton, I'll tell you everything."

Lifting himself to his feet, Ian followed her towards the door. "Taxi for Spicer!" called the barman.

SIXTY-EIGHT

The taxi journey to Skipton gave little chance for further discussion, their talkative driver constantly gabbling made sure of that. He dropped them off just over the canal bridge and Ian gallantly insisted on paying the fare.

Shortly after 8.45, Emily and Ian sat alongside each other on a dark-red leather settee in a canalside wine bar called Phoenix. Once again, Emily ordered a Bacardi and Coke, while Ian, once he'd been told they didn't sell beer or lager, settled for a whisky and ginger ale.

Ian forced a smile and searched Emily's features, desperately trying to read her thoughts. "Right then, young lady, I've thoroughly enjoyed your company, but it's time for you to start talking."

A broad grin split her features. "Young lady? I haven't been called that for a while. I'm thirty-nine, you know?"

Feeling himself warming to this charming woman, Ian nevertheless needed to press her for more details. He raised his voice just a little to emphasise the urgency of the situation. "I don't want to be rude... please just tell me what you know."

Emily sucked in a long breath, then blew out hard. "I was friends with Gretchen in primary school. When I was six, I saw that bitch stab my pet rabbit in the eye with a pencil." Her voice fractured with emotion at the memory. "It was the most horrible sight I've ever seen... after that, I went from being a normal, cheerful girl, into a snivelling wreck. I just couldn't shift the image from my mind; I still can't. I've suffered with mental health problems ever since, and it's all been because of her."

Ian touched her knee softly. "I'm so sorry; it must have been awful."

She pushed her hair back behind one ear. "It was – I've had years of therapists, but every one of them has failed to rid me of my torment and desire for revenge."

He nodded. "Revenge is a powerful emotion."

"Recently, I decided I'd had enough. If I couldn't get rid of those feelings, I'd deal with them another way, so I traced her on Facebook and made contact."

Ian shook his head. "That sounds like a crazy decision."

"I wanted to get revenge for Lucy, and to make her pay for ruining my life."

"Lucy?"

"My rabbit."

Sitting back, Ian blew out slowly and gently shook his head.

"Christ, stabbing a rabbit in the eye, what an evil bitch! How was she when you made contact, wasn't she surprised to hear from you after all these years?"

Emily raised her eyebrows. "For Christ's sake, Ian, don't be stupid! I used a fake identity; she thinks I'm a woman called Cindy from Arizona!"

He nodded appreciatively. "Clever. Very clever!"

Beginning with when Gretchen was small, Emily told Ian everything she'd learned about her younger life, including how she'd poured boiling water on the legs of her boyfriend's six-year-old sisters.

She then told him how she'd deliberately befriended her in the guise of Cindy, and how Gretchen had told her she wanted to make them all pay for hurting her.

"Oh my God, if she was prepared to stab a rabbit in the eye and pour boiling water over children, what the fuck did she have planned for John and me?"

"She's totally deranged. She thinks she'll see one of you imprisoned for murder and the Pals get-togethers ruined forever."

He sat back and screwed his face up. "What, just because we like going to watch Burnley?"

Even all these years later, just talking about what happened to Lucy caused tears to well in Emily's eyes. "She hurt me, Ian, just like she's hurt so many others, and now she's gone one step further – she's a killer. She deserves to be locked up for the rest of her life." She wiped away a tear with the back of her hand. "You see, Gretchen doesn't directly attack those who have hurt her. She prefers to hurt someone, or something, they care deeply about."

Ian was listening intently. The more he listened to Emily, the more it was beginning to make sense. "So, by pointing the finger at the Pals, she believes she's getting revenge on me and John?"

"That's part of it."

"When did she start planning all this?"

"Not long after she'd split up with John. She said a member of the Pals told her the meeting place in Rotherham was the Hammer and Sickle. Within a week, she'd lured a member of the pub's staff into going out with her, a foreign guy named Mario."

Ian nodded. "That's right, he had his throat sliced open. The poor bastard." He sat forward, his head in his hands. "I'm still struggling with the idea of Gretchen doing something like that."

Emily lifted her glass to her lips, then placed it down again without taking a drink. "We were in regular contact from just before the West Brom game onwards. She messaged me a couple of days before the match, and we discussed the disguise she was planning to wear." She opened the gallery on her phone to show Ian a video of Gretchen entering For Cod's Sake, then another of her hiding between merchandise stalls.

He viewed it eagerly, only just recognising the image as the woman he'd once dated. "So, you followed her?"

"No. I travelled there before her and waited across the road from the chippy. We'd planned this one together, so I knew exactly where she would be. I videoed her at Lewes too."

"But what was the point of videoing her? Why get yourself involved? Why not just go to the police with what you knew?"

She shrugged. "I guess that's my own mental health condition kicking in. I feel like she's had the better of me my whole life, and I thought without hard evidence it would be my word against hers. I desperately needed something to give me a hold over her, something to punish her with when the time is right, and I think that time is now. You and your friends could use the evidence on my phone to prove that she's guilty, and you are innocent."

Looking into Emily's face, Ian understood that his salvation was almost certainly inside her mobile phone.

"You're right." He placed a hand on hers. "You are the answer to our prayers." He became thoughtful for a moment, his head still hurting with processing the information that Gretchen was a killer. "You know, I thought I'd seen her heading away from the pub just after she'd murdered that poor sod in Rotherham, and my friends tried to convince me I was mistaken."

Emily frowned. "If you thought it was Gretchen, why didn't you challenge her?"

"Because I wasn't one hundred per cent sure it *was* her; I certainly hadn't expected to see her in Rotherham colours! I suppose once she'd passed me, I convinced myself it couldn't possibly have been her, just someone who looked like her." He lifted his gaze to the ceiling. "She's got such a sweet manner; I can see how Mario was taken in."

Emily sipped her drink and swilled it around her mouth before swallowing. "I know what you mean – she can be very convincing. She told me that, after just a couple of dates, Mario fell for her in a big way. She said he wasn't working on the day of the match, so they arranged to meet up at the pub. She convinced him she wanted to shag him, and he fell for it like a stone." She paused for a few seconds, staring down at her hands. "You know what happened next."

Ian could suddenly feel a cold finger running down his spine. Emily knew Gretchen's plans from West Brom onwards and was therefore complicit in two murders. "Hang on a minute, if the two of you were discussing things on Facebook, that means you were…" His voice trailed away.

"Aware she was going to kill again? Yes, I was, and believe me I feel terrible about it, but it's been a necessary evil to ensure I manage to destroy her."

A wave of horror swept over him. "I've only known you for an hour, but you seem so normal. It's hard to believe you would condone murder!"

She stared at him, genuine sadness and remorse etched on her face. "Condone it? I did more than that – I helped her plan two murders stage by stage. I know that makes me an evil cow, and I know I'll end up in prison for what I've done." She ran a finger around the rim of her glass. "But my life's ruined anyway, and it will be worth it to see that bitch locked up."

"Why not just make copies of the videos and send them to the police with Gretchen's details? You could get off scot-free."

"You don't see it, do you? I don't want to get off scot-free; I deserve to be punished. I didn't want to see you and John suffer because of my crusade against Gretchen. Once the murders were linked, it looked like a matter of time before either of you was charged, and that wouldn't have been fair. I knew I had to contact you and come clean."

Ian downed a mouthful of his drink. "And here we are."

She pushed her tongue into her cheek. "That's right, here we are. It would have been better if John was here too, but I've enjoyed chatting with you."

Ian could sense his eyes moistening. "I can't believe this is happening to me! I'm having a drink with a woman involved in two murders."

She giggled nervously, but her eyes weren't laughing. "Don't worry, you're quite safe. I'm not the actual killer." She sat back and tapped her hand on the back of an adjoining chair. "I'll hand you all the evidence I have, our Facebook conversations and the videos, enough to help prove that she committed each murder. It's enough for even the most useless of cops to convict her."

He slid his chair backwards, preparing to stand up. "Okay, I've heard enough. Come on, let's go to the cops right now."

Emily stayed rooted in her seat, casually swirling the Bacardi and Coke around her glass. "Not now, I'll meet you outside Burnley Police Station at 10.00 tomorrow morning. I promise. I just need some time to put my affairs in order. I live with my parents, and it's only fair I explain everything to them – they're going to be devastated."

Despite his longing to have the matter sorted tonight, Ian was confident she was being sincere; it was only a few more hours. So, despite the sense of urgency nagging at him, and not really wanting to wait, he agreed to her plan. "Okay then." He pursed his lips. "Since we won't see each other again after tomorrow, why don't you tell me everything in more detail?"

"Okay, but you can buy me another one of these first." She held up her glass and wobbled it until Ian took it from her hand.

Two minutes later, he rejoined her at the table and handed her a fresh Bacardi and Coke. Sitting down and gulping a mouthful of his whisky and ginger ale, Ian sat back, crossed one leg over the other and held out both arms enquiringly.

"Come on then, I'm listening."

SIXTY-NINE

Walking from the wine bar, Ian was still reeling. It concerned him that Emily had been a part of such dreadful crimes, but he was sure she would keep her end of the bargain and meet him as arranged. After all, why would she have approached him in the first place? They'd swapped mobile numbers, and she'd promised to meet him outside Burnley Police Station at 10.00 in the morning.

He'd gallantly offered to walk her home, and they strolled together from the wine bar along the canal towpath, heading away from Skipton town centre. After only a few short steps, a discarded white plastic carrier bag blew along the towpath and landed at Ian's feet. Litter was a pet hate of his, so he bent down to pick it up. "Why can't people use the bins provided?" he moaned. Screwing the bag up, he pushed it into his front pocket. They chatted quietly about the situation they found themselves in and swapped stories about Gretchen.

Five minutes later, with only the dim light from the town for visibility, Emily stopped and turned to face him. "Right, this is me."

Ian could just about see the lights from two rows of terraced houses stretching away in the distance, as they twinkled through the branches on the opposite side of a small area of parkland.

A new metal gate set in what looked like a brand-new staked fence was swinging open on its hinges, creaking eerily in the near darkness. The gate showed the way into the darkness of the park. "I'll walk you to your door if you'd like?"

Emily smiled warmly. "Thanks, but no thanks."

Removing the carrier bag from his pocket, Ian placed it into an overflowing rubbish bin and pushed it securely down. Turning his bottom lip over playfully, he said, "It looks dark and scary inside the park; I could help you get home safely. Don't you trust me?"

Emily reached out and gave his hand a squeeze. "Don't be silly, of course I trust you, please don't feel offended. I just need to be alone." She turned to walk through the gate, then looked back over her shoulder. "I'll see you outside the police station, okay?"

He nodded. "Okay, see you then. I'd better get back anyway – my taxi will be here soon."

*

Returning to John's house, Ian found his friend making himself a cup of tea. John had not been in long and had waited up to see who the mystery letter writer might be.

Listening to Ian's tale and hearing that Gretchen was the killer hit him hard.

"Right, let's go to the police right now," John said determinedly.

"No, I've promised Emily I'll give her until the morning to put her affairs in order."

"You're fucking mad – you can't trust her, Ian!"

"Well, I do trust her, and I'm not prepared to break our agreement."

"Okay then, but on your head be it, if it goes wrong."

For John, it was tough to hear Gretchen's evil plans. He could barely believe his ears, but, strangely, it all made sense. They talked well into the early hours, finally climbing the steep, narrow staircase to their bedrooms around 3.00.

SEVENTY

A chance look at a group chat on Facebook had alerted Gretchen to Emily's devious plans. An ex-pupil from her primary school had posted then-and-now pictures of their year two class, when pupils were aged six or seven. Seeing herself in the school photo, she clicked her name underneath the picture, which brought up a recent Facebook image of herself.

Crossing out of her own image, she looked once more at the school photo and homed in on the tall girl standing alongside her on the back row. Her mind drifted back to her wonderful friend Emily – they had been inseparable for three years when they were small, and she recalled their parents joking that they were joined at the hip. They'd made a 'pinky promise' to be best friends forever. Then her face darkened, remembering only too clearly how Emily had dropped her like a stone, because she wanted to be best friends with another girl. *I wonder what she looks like now?*

Clicking on the name Emily Spicer, a recent Facebook image appeared, filling the screen. She was smiling happily into the camera while posing on a low wall – it looked like she was somewhere at the seaside. Her mousey, bobbed, wind-blown hair was a bit messy, which meant she didn't look much like the small girl in the class photo, but it was undoubtedly her. In the photo she was pointing proudly with both hands at the words written in blue on the front of her white T-shirt: 'Freedom for Skipton!'.

Staring incredulously at the image, Gretchen shuddered as she remembered that she'd seen that T-shirt somewhere before, and it was recently. But where? Then it came to her… it was being worn by a woman in the queue for programmes at West Brom. The woman had been directly opposite her, wearing that exact same T-shirt. She couldn't remember what the woman's face looked like, which wasn't surprising considering she'd just murdered somebody, and she wasn't really paying attention, but she certainly remembered that T-shirt!

And there was something else she recalled – the woman was holding her phone up, as though she might be taking a video or a photo.

Could that have been Emily? She'd never seen another T-shirt like it before or since, and she guessed Emily still lived in the Burnley area, so why wouldn't she go to a game?

Parking the thought at the back of her mind, Gretchen felt so grateful she wasn't alone in her efforts, with her wonderful online friend Cindy still providing reassurance and support.

As the Brighton game approached, she once more linked up with Cindy on Facebook. After telling her how the operation in West Bromwich had gone, they began to make plans, and it was both before and after the Brighton game where Emily made her mistakes. Had it been overconfidence on her part? Was it because everything had gone like clockwork so far? Who knows, but for Emily, they turned out to be fatal errors.

Her first mistake was positioning herself out in the open taking photographs of riverside scenes, so confident was she that Gretchen wouldn't suspect her. But unknown to Emily,

Gretchen had been getting more and more jumpy about being identified, and this time she had drifted far too close for comfort. Gretchen thought she looked familiar, and the alarm bells in her head, which had been sounding louder and louder for a few days, had now become deafening.

Emily's second mistake had been during their latest conversation on Facebook. With each killing, Gretchen's mental health condition meant that she was unconsciously becoming more and more paranoid. On the face of it she felt confident enough that everything was going to plan, but subconsciously, she'd begun to question everything and everyone. One of her doubts now centred around Cindy's identity, and this was reinforced during an exchange of messages.

I felt exposed walking along that riverbank, I could easily have been recognised.

Nah, you've nothing to worry about, looking like that people wouldn't have considered you might be the killer for a second.

Gretchen stiffened; she'd been about to say how she'd disguised herself but, up until that point, hadn't mentioned it. *How could she have possibly known what I looked like?* Then it dawned on her... Cindy's knowledge of her attire could mean only one thing – she had been there! Suddenly, all the pieces slotted into place, and it all made stark, heartbreaking sense. *The woman I saw wearing that T-shirt at West Brom, and the woman with the camera in Lewes, it was Cindy – she's been there both times, filming me!*

Taking a couple of minutes to compose herself before replying, Gretchen gave nothing away throughout the remainder of their messaging. After signing off, she poured herself an extra-large glass of red wine and settled down to consider her next move. This would need very careful consideration.

Later that evening, while checking through her Facebook posts, she stumbled once more across the then-and-now photos of her year two class at school. In some of Emily's recent posts, she spoke freely of her mental health issues and even said that she'd recently had to give up her flat and move back in with her parents in Skipton. And for Gretchen, everything became clear.

SEVENTY-ONE

Emily walked quickly along the canal towpath, then cut up through a small park towards her small, terraced house. She pushed up the gradual incline through the trees, heading away from the canal towpath, a contented smile on her face. She was satisfied that everything had gone entirely to plan so far. Once her evidence was presented to detectives, it would be only a matter of hours before Gretchen was arrested. She would probably never see the light of day again.

Knowing her actions would ensure she would also be imprisoned didn't bother her in the slightest; it would be well worth a few years' incarceration to destroy Gretchen's life, just like she had destroyed hers.

The gate in the fence at the higher side of the park was now in view, just twenty metres ahead. Through the branches of a small cherry tree, she could see the welcoming glows of both the single lamp she'd left in the window of her lounge and the porch light above her front door.

Without warning, a crunching blow to the back of her head sent Emily plunging face first onto the ground. White light and stars exploded in her head, accompanied by indescribable pain. Before she could regain her senses enough to cry out, she felt a heavy weight pinning her to the ground, then something warm and dry was forced into her mouth and a plastic bag drawn down over her head and pulled tight to her face. Breathing became instantly difficult, and overwhelming terror surged through her. She began struggling, trying to scream for help, but whatever her attacker had forced into her mouth meant just a muted, garbled sound came out.

Her fight to remove the bag and draw a breath was gaining urgency, but attempts to move her hands to the bag were proving futile – a heavy weight was pinning her upper arms to the ground, and she was simply unable to move them. Her head was lying to one side and the assailant was pulling the bag tighter and tighter, preventing her from spitting out whatever had been forced into her mouth. In a very short time, there was no more oxygen available inside the bag and full-blown panic set in.

Realising the assailant was sitting on her back, with their knees pinning her upper arms to the ground, she only had seconds to move them off her before she would lose consciousness. With a superhuman effort, Emily managed to draw first one knee up, then the other, forcing her hips and bottom up from the ground. She was about to lunge her bodyweight forward and to one side to throw her assailant off, when a crunching blow to her right kidney collapsed her knees and sent her torso crashing back to the ground.

Whoever was attacking her repositioned themselves. She could sense the bag being held even tighter, and now she could feel the fight leaving her. The extreme pain in her lungs and throat had swiftly surged to unbearable levels, but those levels were now diminishing, as she started to lose consciousness.

Her time was running out – she was dying, and she knew it. With one last desperate effort, Emily twisted her body as hard as she could, but despite her attempt, her assailant remained in place. Blind fear was slowly replaced by acceptance, as Emily slipped into the void.

SEVENTY-TWO

Three hours earlier, Gretchen had seen Emily climb into a taxi outside the family home in Skipton, where she'd stabbed Emily's rabbit in the eye all those years ago. She'd followed the cab to Burnley and seen Ian and Emily enter the Boot Inn separately. She knew this wasn't a chance encounter and had correctly guessed what Emily had planned.

She'd had an uneasy feeling that someone was onto her for a couple of weeks but hadn't made the link with that person not only being Emily, but that Emily was also Cindy. Now she was fully up to speed and stopping her passing on what she knew had become a priority.

Creeping up to one of the pub's ornate windows, she peered in to see Emily standing over Ian at a table towards the rear of the pub. He looked unsure who she was, so in Gretchen's mind she correctly deduced that Emily had probably made contact and was in the act of introducing herself. A chill ran down her spine. *What if she tells him everything she knows? They could walk out of the pub and be at Burnley Police Station in a couple of minutes; she would show detectives our Facebook discussions; plus she might have photos and recordings on her phone.* Her life would effectively be over, and right now, there was nothing she could do about it!

Returning to her car, she opened a can of Red Bull to keep her alert and watched the pub's front door through the windscreen. Her car was parked in a line of vehicles, so they would be unlikely to spot her when they left. As it turned out, she didn't have to wait long. A taxi pulled up right outside the pub, and an Asian man with a very long beard stepped out, pushing the pub's front entrance door open. When he reappeared, he was accompanied by Emily and Ian.

Gretchen's heart sank as she watched them climb into a taxi together. *Fuck, shit and bollocks! What the fuck am I supposed to do now?* Switching on her engine, she pulled out from her parking space and followed the taxi at a sensible distance. Three quarters of an hour later, she watched them walking through the doors of Phoenix wine bar, in Skipton.

I don't understand. What are they up to? Why didn't they go straight to the police station?

If they weren't going directly to the police, she had to work on the assumption they would split up at some point and go their separate ways, which left her with a decision to make. Did she wait near the wine bar, or did she stroll over to the small park near Emily's parents' house and wait there?

The obvious route to the house was much shorter than walking the road route – it was a short walk along the towpath and up through the park, so that's where she waited. Suddenly, she could hear a man and woman approaching but could only make out the occasional glimpse through the foliage. She hadn't imagined for a second that Emily would have Ian in tow, yet, if it was them, here they were coming towards her together. This was a hugely dangerous moment. Were they thinking about spending the night together? If that was the case, she was in a lot more trouble than she'd previously imagined!

Their voices gradually increased in volume as they approached, and soon enough she was able to make them out through the branches. She was unable to decipher what they were talking about, but she knew Ian's booming voice only too well. She assumed the other voice, which was rather deep and husky for a woman, belonged to Emily. It seemed strange to finally hear the voice of someone she'd been in contact with so regularly on Facebook. Moments later, they were at the gate from the towpath that led into the small park, and now she could hear every word.

She heard Emily first. "Right, this is me."

Ian's voice was loud, strong, and he sounded scarily close with his reply. "I'll walk you to your door if you'd like?"

Fuck, don't, please don't!

"Thanks, but no thanks."

Phew, thank God!

"It looks dark and scary inside the park; I could help you get home safely, don't you trust me?"

She knew that tone in Ian's voice well. *He's trying to pull her; he fucking fancies her!*

"Don't be silly, of course I trust you, please don't feel offended. I just need to be alone. I'll see you outside the police station, okay?"

Gretchen could feel herself shaking with a mixture of fear and anticipation. *The police station? Sorry, guys, I can't let that happen.*

"Okay, see you then." There was a moment of uncomfortable silence, then, "I'd better get back anyway – my taxi will be here soon."

Pulling a white carrier bag from her pocket, Gretchen bent down and picked up a thick broken fence stake, which had been carelessly discarded when the fence was built and not cleared away. She gratefully heard the last of Ian's swiftly departing footsteps disappearing into the distance and, for the first time, saw the silhouette of Emily at close quarters, as she strode up the incline towards the twinkling lights of the houses.

Stepping out from her hiding place between two thick bushes, she quickly and silently closed the gap between herself and her prey. Raising the stake high above her head, she brought it crashing down on the back of Emily's head, moving swiftly to pin her to the ground once she collapsed.

When she was certain Emily was dead, Gretchen reached down with a gloved hand and pulled the mobile phone from her jeans pocket. She would dispose of it a long way away from here, somewhere it would never be found.

SEVENTY-THREE

At 10.00 on Saturday morning, the police investigation sprang into action. A hastily assembled team had been gathered following the discovery of a body at 6.00 by a man walking his dog.

"Settle down please, everyone." Detective Inspector Amanda Scott didn't have the loudest voice, or the most commanding manner, but she was getting royally pissed off by the blatant disregard of her requests for silence. She had asked the four detectives and two uniformed officers gathered in the Skipton Police Station CID office to be quiet three times, yet two grizzled old detective constables were still muttering to each other, flashing disparaging looks in Amanda's direction between fits of giggling.

She flared with fury and shouted at the top of her voice, making the assembled officers jump in alarm, "I said shut up!" She glared at the two older detectives. "Is that too difficult for some here to understand?"

Rising from her chair and moving to a corner of the room, she picked up a remote control from a window ledge and pressed a button, which illuminated a large screen displaying an image of a female lying face down in the grass, with a plastic carrier bag lying alongside her head. Her purple face was set in a mask of screaming terror, her mouth still open as she gasped for air. "Our victim has been identified as Emily Spicer, thirty-nine years old. She lived in Mynn Crescent, only forty metres from where her body was found."

Amanda turned to face her audience, then used a laser pointer to indicate the plastic bag. "When the first officers arrived on scene, that bag was still loosely wrapped around her head. The dog walker who found the body said it had been tightly wrapped around her face, and he'd loosened it to check if she was still alive." She paused and took a deep breath. "The bag had been used by whoever knocked her to the ground to asphyxiate her."

She clicked the remote, changing the image to a close-up of the back of Emily's head, showing where it had been split open from a severe blow. "She was hit hard from behind with a wooden fence post that was found discarded nearby. After knocking her to the ground, the assailant stuffed her mouth with an old cloth, pulled a white carrier bag tightly around her face, straddled her back and pinned her arms down. A fresh bruise above her right kidney suggests she must have fought for her life, but she was battling a very determined killer. She didn't stand a chance."

SEVENTY-FOUR

Four hours later, the door to Amanda's office received three hard raps.

"Come in," she shouted.

The door was opened by two detectives.

"You really need to see this, boss – it's dynamite!"

Two minutes later, Amanda was being shown CCTV from above the door of Phoenix wine bar. It showed Emily and an unknown man leaving. They appeared to be comfortable in each other's company but weren't holding hands. They certainly didn't look like they were romantically involved. The film showed them taking an exit from the bar leading onto the canal towpath, then a separate camera showed them slowly walking away from the town centre. Only a few seconds after leaving, a white carrier bag blew down the towpath and was stopped by the man, who bent down to collect it.

Amanda glanced at her colleagues. "Fucking hell, whoever that is, we've got him!" Her eyes burned into the final minutes of Emily Spicer playing out in front of her. She tapped the screen with the index finger of her right hand. "That's the murder weapon right there, that bag!"

The man could be seen saying something to Emily, who

didn't appear to respond, as she watched him push the bag into his jeans pocket.

As they continued along the towpath, their images became smaller and smaller, until the canal's path followed a shallow bend, and they disappeared off the right-hand side of the screen.

Amanda looked up at the detectives. "Great work, guys, we need to get this sent to surrounding stations as soon as possible."

"I'm on it, boss." One detective showed Amanda a still photo taken from inside the wine bar, showing a side view of Emily and an excellent face-on image of Ian. "I've already had this image enhanced."

Taking the photo in her left hand, Amanda took a close look at the face of her suspect.

*

Just before 6.00, Amanda received a call at home. "Boss, we've identified the suspect in the wine bar."

"Who is he?"

"Ian Calvert, lives in Tunbridge Wells, Kent."

"Tunbridge Wells! What's he doing up here?"

"He was born in Burnley but moved down south years ago. Apparently, he's a mad Burnley supporter, and listen to this, he was arrested recently and taken into Burnley nick… on suspicion of being the TCP killer!"

"Fucking hell!" She considered what would be the best move. "He'll have almost certainly run for home. Contact Kent Police and arrange a spin of his address."

"On it, boss."

"Once you've done that, find out what contacts he's still got in this area, just in case he's still up here and gone to ground somewhere."

SEVENTY-FIVE

A sleepy Ian barely registered the gentle humming sound, as his mobile phone vibrated on the lounge coffee table. Ignoring it, he rolled over on the settee and sighed with relief when the humming stopped. John had popped out to visit an elderly neighbour, and Ian took the chance to take a nap, having not had much sleep the previous night.

It was a very annoyed Ian who responded seconds later, when the humming started again. Propping himself up on one elbow, he fought to focus his eyes on the wall clock. 8.10. Flopping back down, he buried his head under a cushion. The humming stopped but restarted again seconds later. "For fuck's sake!" he mouthed angrily, reaching for his phone. Sliding the image of a green telephone across the screen, he answered the call sleepily.

"Hello?"

"Ian, it's Sandy, where are you?"

Sandy was Ian's next-door neighbour in Tunbridge Wells and a great friend. Fighting to clear his head and wake himself up, Ian's response was slow and uncertain.

"Um, I'm staying in Lancashire for the weekend. Why? What's up?"

"The police are at your house, loads of them. They

hammered on your front door, shouted for you, then smashed the door in."

The surge of adrenalin coursing through Ian's body meant he was instantly fully awake. "But… why would… they don't… what the fuck are they playing at?" His mind raced as he stared out through the lounge window, a thin sheen of sweat forming above his top lip, as he struggled to find the right words.

"They said you were wanted for murder."

"I don't understand. I've already been arrested for that, but they bailed me. What's going on?"

Sandy spoke with what Ian perceived to be doubt in his voice. "I don't know, mate, but they're here, and right now, they're carrying out door-to-door enquiries. They're knocking the whole street up!"

Fighting to reassure Sandy of his innocence, Ian said, "I promise you I'm not the TCP killer, Sandy, but I've recently learned who is. Why the hell would they break into my house? I'm returning on bail next week – why couldn't they wait? They just…"

"They're not here about the football killings," interrupted Sandy loudly. "It's about the murder of a woman called Emily Spicer, last night – in Skipton."

SEVENTY-SIX

Standing in the doorway, John watched as Ian hurriedly packed his bag.

"Why don't you just hand yourself in to the police and tell them everything Emily said?"

Ian rounded angrily on him, incensed his best friend could be so thick. "Don't be stupid – can't you see what's happening here? Gretchen's got me all ends up!"

John shrugged. "Not completely, what about the Facebook messages?"

"She'll have deleted them by now. And why would the police believe me anyway? Even if they did believe me, they'd have to obtain a court order for Facebook to release them, which could take days!"

Holding his friend's gaze, John nodded his understanding.

"Emily was right – Gretchen was watching us the whole time. Once I left her in Skipton, Gretchen must have been nearby somewhere, and now she's shut her up for good. Once she'd done that, she'd have taken her mobile, thereby removing every shred of evidence pointing at her and pointing all the evidence relating to Emily's killing directly at me."

"So, you're saying…"

"The police will have no knowledge of Gretchen's involvement because she'll have destroyed all the evidence.

Which means they'll come after the person who was with Emily just before she was murdered… me!"

John looked incredulously at Ian before rubbing both eyes with the heels of his hands. He knew his mate's words made sense, but it all seemed too unbelievable to be true. "Okay, I get that, but what's the sudden rush to leave?"

"For fuck's sake, John, wake up and smell the coffee! The police know I'm not at home, so they'll assume I'm still up north somewhere. They'll be hoping someone can tell them where I am. They'll try Alison's house, then it's only a matter of time before they work out I might be staying with you."

Drawing in a deep breath, John puffed out his cheeks, then slowly blew out. "What are you going to do?"

Ian threw the last of his clothes into his holdall. "I just need to keep my head down until we can prove that Gretchen is the killer."

John rubbed his hands, before intertwining his fingers and pushing the pads of his thumbs together.

"What do you want me to do?"

"Don't call me. At some stage they'll get permission to monitor our phones, so I'll quickly make a note of a few numbers, then turn mine off."

John handed him a scrap of paper, and he scribbled a few numbers down.

"I'll call Joe or Becki from payphones and tell them to pass messages to you in person. Secondly, try talking some sense into Ryan – he's fallen for Gretchen hook line and sinker, which means he could be in real danger."

"Anything else?"

"Yes, let Becki know what's going on, and ask her to give Gretchen a friendly call – she might just let something slip."

John nodded. "Good idea – they were always quite close." Looking thoughtful, he asked, "Where will you go?"

"Sorry, mate, I think it's best you don't know."

John shrugged. "Fair enough."

Two minutes later, the friends shook hands and hugged, before Ian stepped out into the late evening darkness. He knew the area well and moved quickly off the roads and onto nearby footpaths, only using the torch on his mobile phone sparingly when he absolutely had to. Before long, he was striding out in the direction of a nearby village called Newchurch in Pendle.

Newchurch was directly due south of Barley, and close to the village was a place where Ian knew he could hide up for the night, somewhere he would be safe, warm and dry. He'd packed enough food and drink for a couple of days, but after that? He had no idea.

Taking a circuitous route and making certain he kept well away from any roads, Ian covered the one and a half miles in thirty-five minutes. Inside a small strand of woodland close to the village's outskirts, he went straight to the tiny wooden cabin where he'd once sheltered from the midday sun with a local farmer.

Walking off the footpath at a right angle, Ian strode out towards the area of thick pine woods, irregular in shape but roughly triangular and no more than eighty metres in length on the longest side.

Three minutes later, he was safely ensconced in what can only be described as a Heath Robinson construction. The cabin was around eight feet by six, but it contained a small, brown leather armchair, a low table and a white plastic patio chair. Ian had passed this way on various footpaths many times before, but until the farmer had showed him the way, he had no idea the cabin existed, so well hidden was it by the thickness of the surrounding trees.

This would be his base, and when he felt an urgent need to contact someone, he knew that Gladys would help him. Gladys was the owner of Witches Galore, a shop and tea room less than half a mile away in Newchurch. He'd popped in for a chat several times with John over the years. Mobile phone signal was practically non-existent in Newchurch, but Gladys would happily allow any customer to use the shop phone for a small fee. The police would be monitoring the area, so he would need to make use of this sparingly.

Blowing out heavily, he closed his eyes, wondering how long he could possibly remain free, while trying to somehow convince the police of his own innocence and Gretchen's guilt.

SEVENTY-SEVEN

The harsh rapping on John's front door at 9.45 on a Saturday evening sent his stomach lurching. Not because he was wondering who it might be, but because he knew precisely who it would be.

Pulling the door wide, he eyed the short, stout detective with a neatly trimmed goatee beard holding up a warrant card for his perusal. The detective was accompanied by two uniformed officers. Painting on a smile, John drew in a breath.

"Good evening, officers, how can I help?"

The detective held up a sheet of white A4 paper. "I am Detective Sergeant Roy West, and this is a warrant to search these premises for Ian Calvert. Is he here?"

John shook his head. "No, he was, but he left earlier this evening – he'd arranged a lift to the train station; he's heading home to Kent."

"Don't lie to us, Mr Horsfall. His mobile phone was traced to this village, but it's now been switched off. This isn't a minor matter. He's wanted for the murder of a woman last night."

"He's done what? I don't believe it," said John, sounding incredulous.

"I'm afraid it's true. Now where is he?"

"I told you, he isn't here."

"Who picked him up?"

"No idea – he walked to meet them near the Pendle Inn; he's got plenty of friends and relatives in the area."

Easing John out of the way, the detective stepped inside, instructing one of the officers to accompany him and the other to guard the front door.

"Then you won't mind if we look around, will you? Oh, and he needn't try getting out through the kitchen; I've got an officer guarding the back door."

"That's fine, do what you want." John moved out of their way and flopped down on the settee.

Satisfied that Ian was not in the house, the officers climbed back into the police van, but not before the detective issued a stern warning.

"If you're stupid enough to be helping him, Mr Horsfall, you'll be guilty of harbouring a fugitive, which could mean a prison sentence."

John shrugged. "I've no idea where he is or what his intentions are. He just left suddenly this evening."

"Did he explain why there was a sudden rush?"

"No."

"Didn't you think it was odd?"

"I did, but I've been his mate for years, and one thing I've learned is that Ian's extremely odd."

"I can agree with that, seeing what he did to that poor woman."

John shook his head. "You couldn't be more wrong about that – Ian's not a killer."

Closing the front door, John stepped through to the kitchen and flicked the switch on the kettle. Spooning himself four teaspoons of Ovaltine into a cup, he leant his shoulder on the door jamb as the kettle slowly gurgled into life.

Fucking hell, Ian. We've been in a few scrapes, but I can't see a resolution to this one.

SEVENTY-EIGHT

The following morning, John sat down on his favourite armchair with a steaming cup of tea and lifted his mobile phone from the coffee table. *I wonder if the police are monitoring my mobile yet?* He decided to take a chance and called Becki, but played it cool, just in case they were being overheard.

"Hi, Becks, how's life in sunny Wimbledon?"

Puzzlement swept his face as he heard her chuckling at the other end.

"I'm not at home. Ryan and I travelled up to Burnley by train yesterday; we booked a couple of rooms at the Premier Inn."

Thinking hard, John closed his eyes, trying to figure out what was best to say next without letting the cat out of the bag. "What are you doing up here?"

"Ryan's been desperate to see more of Gretchen. They're sort of going out together now – are you okay with that?"

For fuck's sake, she's a killer! "I'm fine with it. I presume they've arranged to meet up?"

"No, he's going to surprise her by turning up at her house with flowers. How romantic is that?"

John's heart sank. "That's lovely. I would never have thought he had it in him."

She laughed. "Me neither."

Forcing a fake laugh, John struggled against the overwhelming sense of foreboding crushing his senses. "Can I have a quick word with him?"

"No, he's walked down into town to buy some flowers, before getting a taxi to Gretchen's. He's meeting me outside Burnley Manchester Road station at 7.00 this evening, then we're back to London."

Jesus! You idiot, Ryan.

"Okay, what are you doing while the love story is being played out?"

"I'm meeting Joe for brunch at Barden Lane at 10.30. You and Ian can join us if you want?"

"Whereabouts on Barden Lane?"

"Reedley Marina. There's a smashing little café there."

"Yep, I know it. I'll be there to join you if that's alright, but Ian's gone home."

"Sounds great. See you later."

SEVENTY-NINE

The late autumn sunshine sparkled on the water between rows of colourful narrowboats. John, Joe and Becki had selected their food and chosen to sit out on the decking, high above the boats in the marina. Reedley Marina café was a favourite haunt of locals, and on this late autumn morning, it was buzzing with activity.

"Wasn't expecting to see you here." Joe's comment was directed at John, as he worked his words around a mouthful of cheese toastie.

John's face was set grimly, as he stirred the teabag in its pot.

"You guys need to know something." He paused as he filled his cup messily from the shiny steel teapot. Fixing them both with a steady gaze, allowing his eyes to settle on each person for a couple of seconds, he drew in a breath. "Ian was right – Gretchen is the killer."

Becki and Joe exchanged disbelieving glances, and for a moment, it looked like neither of them could find words.

"Why would you think that?" Becki asked.

Over the following few minutes, John told them about the letter arriving at his house. Then described in detail Ian's meeting with Emily in the Boot Inn. How she'd introduced herself, how she knew about them and how she knew Ian couldn't possibly be the killer. How she'd pretended to be someone else on Facebook, wormed her way into Gretchen's confidence and become embroiled in her plans. Once she had convinced Gretchen she was on her side, she conspired together with her, not because she wanted to help her commit murder but purely to gain revenge.

Joe and Becki stared with wide-eyed astonishment as John relayed each new detail, all the way up to Emily's death and the police searching for Ian.

Joe pointed at John with his fork, which just happened to be holding a sizeable piece of ham.

"If that Emily was telling the truth, Gretchen sounds like a total nutter, a complete fruit-loop. How could you not know, mate? You were with her for years."

John held his hand up. "Apparently, she only has meltdowns when people leave her, some kind of mental health problem when dealing with abandonment."

Joe screwed his face up. "So, is that why she left the letters TCP after each killing, to implicate the Pals?"

"I think so. She was purposely trying to direct the police at the group, but more specifically at me."

Becki's brunch lay on the table going cold, her usual bright-red cheeks and happy persona replaced with a grey pallor and a mouth downturned in each corner. "Fucking hell, hearing that makes me really worried."

"Why?" asked Joe, who appeared totally unconcerned, as he shovelled in mouthful after mouthful.

Becki rested her elbows on the table, head in her hands. "Ryan is convinced she had nothing to do with the killings; he talked about nothing else but her being innocent all the way up here. And now he's going to visit her!"

John stopped eating. "Becki's right; Ryan could be in real trouble – she's a nutcase!"

Becki started to sob.

John shared a look with Joe, who inclined his head towards Becki. John slid his chair next to hers and wrapped an arm round her. "If she did murder that woman last night, she'll be on edge; she'll be covering her tracks."

Becki sat back and huffed, wiping her eyes with her sleeve. "What about those Facebook messages?"

"They're all we've got, and they don't provide any evidence that actually places her at any of the murder scenes."

"At least it's something. Why don't we just go to the police anyway?" asked Joe.

"We might well have to, but it won't change anything for Ian; they'll still think he murdered Emily on Friday." He paused for a moment, deep in thought. "We've got to find something that proves Gretchen is the killer, and we haven't got long."

"Come on," said Becki. "Ian and Ryan need our help."

John nodded. "Ryan won't be safe dropping in on her unannounced. Not right now – she's just killed again, and she'll be dangerously unstable. If he pressurises her, you never know what she might do!"

Picking up her mobile from the tabletop, Becki pressed a couple of buttons.

"What are you doing?" asked Joe.

"I'm calling Ryan. I'll tell him the truth about her. Hopefully he'll see sense."

Ryan didn't pick up, and after seven rings, the answerphone kicked in.

"Ryan, it's Becks. Keep away from Gretchen – she's the killer, and she killed again on Friday night. Call me back when you get this."

"Fuck, what are we going to do?" John asked.

Tears formed in Becki's eyes, as the horrific possibility dawned that Ryan, lovely Ryan, her very best friend, could be in mortal danger. They weren't just friends; they were like brother and sister – everybody knew that. They were practically joined at the hip, and they loved travelling to games together. She was the first to leap to her feet, her food remaining uneaten.

"I can't just sit here and do nothing. I've got to warn him!"

EIGHTY

Armed with a small bouquet of lilies just coming into flower, Ryan stepped from the taxi and paid the driver. He'd asked to be dropped at the end of Cryern Avenue, a short walk from Gretchen's house. His feelings for her had grown stronger and stronger in recent weeks, despite the doubts some of the Pals harboured about her. She wasn't the killer, of that he was certain, and speaking to her today, he'd find something to prove it.

Quaking with excitement and anticipation, Ryan walked along the road until he was standing outside the olive-green door of number 23, Gretchen's house. There was no doorbell, so he rapped hard on the shiny metal knocker and waited. Moments later, the door was swung open to leave him facing a startled Gretchen.

"Ryan! What on earth are you doing here?"

"I thought I'd surprise you!" He smiled, theatrically producing the bouquet of flowers from behind his back.

Gretchen stared at him, wide-eyed. "But I thought we'd agreed to meet up next weekend, after the Stoke game?" She looked and sounded annoyed.

He desperately attempted to rescue the situation. "I'm sorry, I just wanted to see you. I wanted to talk to you." He lowered his head, trying to hide his disappointment.

Gretchen was furious, but she couldn't afford to lose a potential asset like Ryan, however irritating she found him. She had to play the game. Softening her pose, she stepped forward and wrapped her arms around his broad shoulders, squeezing him tightly and kissing him on the side of his cheek.

"I'm sorry, I was just shocked to open the door and find you standing there. It's lovely to see you. Come in; I'll make a brew."

She could feel him watching her as she filled a vase with water for the lilies.

"What's so important that you felt you needed to come up this weekend?" she said, without turning to face him.

"I... uh... it's just that..."

God, just spit it out! "What?" she insisted, trying to hide her growing annoyance.

"It's just that some of the Pals have been saying that you... well. That you might be... you know..."

"What?"

"It's ridiculous, but somehow involved in the killings?"

Gretchen felt a shudder course through her whole body, starting at the back of her neck, then spreading down through her torso all the way to her legs, which seemed on the verge of buckling. Hoping Ryan hadn't noticed, she swiftly conjured a chuckle and dropped teabags into the cups.

"Me? I wouldn't even swat a fly. How on earth could I be a killer?" She forced another laugh.

Moving behind her, Ryan felt emboldened and wrapped his arms gently around her waist. "Don't worry, I've told them they're being stupid."

She stiffened on first contact and fought off her natural reaction to push him away. *Come on, Gretchen, stick with it; he might not be your type but he's gullible, and he's on your side.* She folded her forearms over his and rested her head backwards on his chest.

"Thank you. You've always been a true friend." She turned without releasing herself from his arms, holding him close around his broad chest with her own. "Let me guess, it's John and Ian that are saying it, isn't it?"

Ryan's face clouded briefly. "Does it matter? They're both in your past, aren't they?"

She fixed him with a steely look. "Of course they are, but it matters to me if they think I'm capable of being involved in murder."

He drew in a breath and blew out slowly. "Okay, yes, they both have doubts about you. It was mainly Ian at first, but now John is leaning that way too."

Fuck! This is not good! Pretending to sob, she pushed her face into his chest, her shoulders juddering. "How could they be so horrible?" She lifted her face to his, showing the fake tears she had fabricated. "What happens if they go to the police? I'll be arrested and I haven't done anything wrong!"

Steering her back into the lounge, Ryan sat down on the settee, pulling her down alongside him and holding her close. Once she had calmed down, he patted her leg. "Wait here. I'll go and make the tea."

Two minutes later he returned to the lounge.

"Thank you." She snivelled, taking the cup he handed to her and placing it onto the coffee table. "Why would anyone think I could be capable of being so evil?"

Sitting alongside her, Ryan scratched his right eyebrow with the back of his finger. Seeing the woman he loved in distress hurt him. But, over the past couple of weeks, he knew that no matter how much he cared for her, she had questions to answer. Once he'd heard those answers, he would spend his time convincing the Pals of her innocence.

Resting his hand on the settee's cushion, the tip of his fingers gently stroked hers. "Alright, I'll tell you." He lifted her chin to face him, then sat up straight. "Ian thought he recognised you wearing Rotherham colours outside the pub in Rotherham. He said you wore a hoodie and were walking quickly away from the pub where that barman was killed."

He paused, expecting Gretchen to say something, but she just sat there, looking blankly at him.

"They also think it's more than just coincidence that every time a murder occurs, you call me shortly afterwards." Once again, he waited for a response, but there was none. "And you're the only one of the former Pals who has a grievance against the group."

This time her eyes filled with genuine tears. "What, you mean because I'd split up with John? That's ridiculous! I don't hold a grievance against anyone. He didn't dump me, I dumped him, so why would I be the one holding a grievance?"

He nodded; her words made absolute sense. He shifted uncomfortably. "John and Ian are two of my best mates, and they genuinely believe they might be right. I know they're confused just now, but they're both decent blokes. Please don't think too badly of them. Some bastard is trying to point the finger at the Pals, and it's driving everyone crazy. I'm sure they'll realise their mistake in time."

Strange sensations were sweeping Gretchen's mind. It suddenly felt like she was in a tiny room all alone, and the walls had started closing in around her. If the police were contacted by John and Ian in an attempt to convince them of her involvement, it would be only a matter of time before they started checking her movements on match days. ANPR checks would show her car in the area at some matches, and CCTV would show her arriving at train stations on other match days.

Her paranoia began spiralling out of control – *they're coming for me! Everyone hates me! They're all against me! I'm in trouble! There's no way out!* Only one thing helped her to remain calm – she hadn't yet reached her goal of making John and Ian pay, and it was in that moment that a way of achieving it sprang into Gretchen's head. *So, they think they're going to win, do they? I'll give them more pain than they've ever imagined!*

"I can't explain why I called you when I did, Ryan; I had no idea it was near the time murders had taken place. I suppose subconsciously I missed being with everyone on match days, and that's why I called when I did. As for Ian saying he saw me at Rotherham, that's completely nuts! He sounds obsessed!"

"Thank you, that's what I was hoping to hear." Ryan beamed with delight.

Gretchen took a deep breath, as though clearing her head of dark thoughts, and then smiled. "I don't want to stay indoors anymore. Can we go out somewhere?"

Ryan looked delighted. "Of course, let's go for a walk around the town centre. Do you know a decent pub? I'll buy lunch."

She shook her head. "No, I need to get out into the countryside, somewhere up in the hills. I need to stretch my legs and get some fresh air."

"Okay," he said hesitantly. "Where would you like to go?"

She pretended to think for a moment, but she knew exactly where she wanted to go. "How about The Singing Ringing Tree?"

Puzzlement swept his face. "That's miles away."

"I know, but it's my favourite place. I feel happy whenever I'm there." She prodded him playfully. "Come on, we can take my car."

Ryan shrugged. "But I'm getting peckish, what about lunch?"

Lifting herself from the settee, she painted on a smile.

"We'll be fine; I'll make a packed lunch." So saying, she strode into the kitchen and set to work.

Walking down the front path to her car, Gretchen carried a clear carrier bag containing two Tupperware boxes stacked with food, together with bottles and cans of drink. The next-door neighbour, a small woman in a hijab, was kneeling on the path weeding her front garden. She smiled warmly on seeing her neighbour, but eyed Ryan up and down warily.

"Hi, Gretchen, are you going somewhere nice?"

Gretchen smiled back. "Yes, my favourite place. I'll tell you all about it when I get back."

EIGHTY-ONE

The sound of birdsong filling the trees surrounding the cabin contrasted starkly with the feelings of isolation and injustice sweeping through Ian's mind. *This isn't fair. I've done nothing wrong. I've never hurt a soul in my life. That bitch has stitched me up and there's nothing I can do!*

The night he'd spent quaking with anger and unable to sleep in the cabin had seemed more like three days, so heavy was time hanging on his shoulders. Stepping outside, he pulled in a huge lungful of the sweet, clean, morning air, greedily sucking in the pine scent. Tiny patches of dappled sunlight managed to find their way through the dense canopy, dancing amazing patterns on the bare ground. At any other time in his life, this would have been a wonderful, almost magical moment, but not right now. Not while Gretchen Grover was wandering around as free as a bird, while he was cowering like a frightened rat, hiding away from the life and people he loved.

Although he'd only been there a few hours, his situation brought him to a stark realisation. *I can't do this. I'm not going to hide away and let her have the upper hand. Cowering from the world isn't an option – I've got to start fighting back!*

Stepping back inside the cabin, he fumbled inside his holdall and lifted out his wallet, pushing it into the rear pocket of his jeans. Hoisting up the holdall, he carried it outside and hid it in the centre of a small group of short and dense bushes. Visitors to the cabin were extremely unlikely, but he wasn't about to take any chances by leaving his possessions inside.

Fifteen minutes later, he ducked down behind a drystone wall on the outskirts of Newchurch in Pendle. The shiny, new, metal kissing gate led the way out from the relative safety of the footpath, onto the short stretch of roadway that separated him from Witches Galore – the only shop in the village.

Witches Galore existed mainly thanks to the Pendle witch trials of 1612, when ten women and two men from the local area were charged with the murders of ten people – using witchcraft. One of the accused died in prison, but the other eleven were tried, with ten being found guilty and one acquitted. Those found guilty were hanged. This made the souvenir shop and tea room a magnet for those wanting to know more, or just those who wanted a witch doll on a broomstick hanging on a thread of cotton from their ceiling, a witch trials tea towel, a black cat and witch salt and pepper set or some other witch-themed souvenir of their visit to the area.

Looking up and down the steep, winding hill to check the coast was clear, Ian was pleased to see the village looked completely deserted. Exiting through the kissing gate, he walked quickly down the narrow road and opened the door into Witches Galore, heaving a sigh of relief as he closed the door behind him. There were a couple of customers in the shop, but none so much as looked up at him.

Smiling warmly at him from behind the counter was Gladys. Although she looked every bit of her seventy-four years, with her blue-rinse hair and dark-green old-lady dress, she was still very much a force of nature.

Ian walked up to the counter. "Hi, Gladys, long time no see."

She nodded and raised her eyebrows. "Yes, quite a while. You were last here in April, just before the Rovers match."

Grinning and shaking his head, he marvelled at her incredible memory; she always knew precisely when he'd last been in, and whenever he checked, she was always right. *I wonder if she can do that for every customer?*

"How have you been?"

"Not too bad. Business isn't as good as it was, but I'm surviving."

She'd said the same thing each time he'd visited over the past ten years, but it still made him smile.

"Well, I'm glad you're surviving. I'd miss this place."

Gladys stopped tidying the counter, fixed Ian with a questioning gaze and lowered her voice so the other customers couldn't hear. "You're in trouble, aren't you?"

Shaken by her confident assertion, Ian steadied himself. Had the police already visited the shop and asked questions? "Why would you think that?"

"Because you look scared."

Forcing a smile, he leant in conspiratorially. "I'm fine, honestly, but my mobile's got no signal around here. Could I possibly use the shop phone?"

Gladys studied him without changing expression. He guessed she knew he was lying. Nevertheless, she reached down and opened a flap in the counter and gestured for Ian to come through. "Of course you can, and in the circumstances, there's no charge."

He didn't bother questioning 'in the circumstances' and moved to the side wall, where the phone's cradle balanced precariously on a narrow shelf. Checking Becki's number on the piece of paper he'd listed the numbers on, he lifted the phone's receiver and started to dial.

EIGHTY-TWO

"Becks, it's Ian, I need your help."

Becki, who was sitting in the front passenger seat of the taxi, span round excitedly to John and Joe, mouthing the word 'Ian' and pointing at her mobile phone.

"Where are you?"

"Newchurch, in the shop. I've found a place nearby to hole up in for a while."

"Newchurch? Okay, what do you need?"

"You've got to contact John for me."

"I'm with John and Joe now; we've just left Reedley Marina in a taxi. We're on our way around to Gretchen's house."

"What for?" he asked incredulously.

"Ryan's in love with her and he's on his way to surprise her by turning up unannounced. He's also going to ask her about people thinking she might be the killer."

"Call him and stop him! If he puts pressure on her she could do anything!"

"I know, I've tried, but he's not answering."

"That's not good, not good at all. The poor lad, he's not thinking straight. Look, Becks, come and pick me up and take me with you. I'll make that bitch confess!"

"No. Sorry, Ian, if it goes wrong, you'll be arrested. You'll end up being charged with that girl's murder in Skipton."

John tapped Becki on the shoulder. "Don't be stupid, Becki, tell him we'll come and get him."

She covered the mouthpiece on her phone and replied in a stern whisper. "No, it will delay us getting to Ryan."

John wasn't in the mood for backing down. "For fuck's sake, Ian's only three miles away. We'll only be delayed seven or eight minutes at the most... please, Becki."

Rolling her eyes and blowing out hard, she released her hand from the mouthpiece. "Stay there, Ian, we'll pick you up in five minutes."

Ian's heart soared. "Thanks, Becks, see you in a minute." He ended the call and replaced the receiver in its cradle. Heaving a sigh of relief, he turned to see Gladys standing at the counter, placing a selection of postcards into a small white paper bag and thanking an elderly couple for their custom.

Pulling a five-pound note from his wallet, he touched Gladys on the shoulder. As she turned to face him, he gripped her wrist lightly and placed it firmly in her hand.

"Here you go, a little something for helping me out."

She looked down at the note and shook her head. "I told you there was no charge."

He shrugged. "Sorry. I like to pay my way, always have."

She gave the merest of nods and her face cracked into a broad and thankful smile, seven decades of lines and creases evident around her eyes. "Thank you."

He reached forward to hold both her hands in his. "You were right, Gladys, you're always right."

Gladys lowered her eyebrows and tilted her head to one side.

"What do you mean?"

Ian lowered his eyes and stared down at their joined hands, temporarily unable to meet her gaze. "I am in trouble... big trouble."

EIGHTY-THREE

The tiny frame of Gladys seemed to fill the doorway of Witches Galore as she bid Ian goodbye. Her face was set in a wry smile, which widened even further on seeing John, who lived nearby and popped in for a chat on an almost weekly basis. He waved and smiled at her through the taxi's rear window.

Moving quickly around the back of the vehicle, Ian opened the rear driver's side door and leant in. "Morning, guys. Come on, Joe, budge up."

"Why should I budge up? I hate sitting in the middle; I get car sick. Why can't John budge up?"

"Because you're the smallest!" said John, pulling Joe into the centre as Ian pushed him across using his hip. Safely inside, Ian pulled the door closed alongside a still grumbling Joe.

"For fuck's sake, I hate always having to go in the middle; I'm no smaller than John."

"This time we definitely want to go to Cryern Avenue, Darwen, please," Becki said to the taxi driver.

"No problem." The heavily overweight driver, with his dyed black hair, Elvis-style quiff and enormous black sideburns smiled warmly, as he completed a three-point turn and drove off down the hill.

"Right," said Ian, "have you heard back from Ryan yet?"

Becki turned in her seat to face him. "No. I've left a voice message, two WhatsApp messages and a text. He hasn't responded to any of them."

Ian leant forward and looked at John, his face a mask of concern. "If she's hurt Ryan, I'll fucking swing for her."

EIGHTY-FOUR

As Gretchen's blue Skoda Kamiq turned the corner at one end of Cryern Avenue, a scruffy white Audi A3 taxi pulled into the opposite end of the road.

During the thirty-minute journey from Newchurch, Becki had become increasingly concerned, continually asking the driver to hurry. Ian, John and Joe sought to reassure her throughout the journey, but by the time they pulled up outside number 23, she was frantic with worry. She turned to the driver and handed him fifty pounds in cash.

"Wait here, please?"

The driver nodded.

Gretchen's neighbour looked surprised as John, two other men and a shouting woman poured from the taxi. They moved quickly to the front door, totally ignoring her as they did so.

It was John who reached the front door first, pressing the doorbell and banging the knocker as hard as he could. When that elicited no response, he hammered his fist on the wood.

The neighbour lifted herself to her feet and rested a soil-covered hand on the metre-high wall dividing the front gardens. "Hello, John. Haven't seen you for a while. I was so sorry about you and Gretchen."

"Hi, Renu, sorry. I should have said hello. We've got a big problem; we urgently need to speak to Gretchen."

"She's gone out. You literally just missed her."

"What?" Becki was shaking her head quickly, worry on her face.

The woman looked sympathetically at John. "She had a young man in tow; it looked like they were going for a picnic."

Ian moved to face the woman over the wall. "What did this man look like?"

She pushed her tongue into a cheek and drew in a breath. "He was a chunky monkey, you know, heavy set, stocky."

The four Pals exchanged nods, but Ian wanted more. "What else?"

She seemed to ponder her reply. "Short, dark-brown hair, tall, quite good-looking really."

"That's him," muttered Becki. "That's Ryan!"

Joe poked her playfully. "It can't be him – she said good-looking."

She rounded on him. "For fuck's sake, Joe, not now!"

The woman looked shocked by Becki's expletive and stepped back from the wall.

"I'm sorry, I..." Becki began, but Ian held both hands up to stop further conversation.

"We're wasting time," he said. "Do you have any idea where they were going, Renu?"

She shook her head. "No, I'm sorry, I don't."

Becki began crying, leaning her head into Joe's chest as he held her tightly.

The neighbour moved back to the wall, visibly touched by Becki's distress. "What's happened, is one of them in trouble?"

"No," said Ian. "They both are."

"Think hard, Renu." John was pleading now. "Did Gretchen say anything at all which might indicate where they went?"

"Hang on a minute, she did say something." Renu's words instantly gripped their attention.

Becki pulled away from Joe. "What? *What?*" she half-shouted.

"She said they were going to her favourite place." Renu held her arms out and shrugged. "But I've no idea where that is."

"I do!" shouted John, turning back to the cab. "Come on, let's go!"

As they clambered back into the waiting taxi, John called out, "Thank you, Renu, you might have just saved someone's life."

Taking his seat in the taxi, John gave the driver a destination. "The Singing Ringing Tree please. As quick as you can!"

EIGHTY-FIVE

It was shortly after noon by the time Gretchen and Ryan had parked up and walked the short distance to The Singing Ringing Tree, a clever artwork of pipes of varying lengths which 'sang' as the wind blew through them. The clever thing was that when the wind changed direction, the 'song' did too, meaning that regular visitors never had the same audible experience twice.

A popular landmark with the locals, it stood high on windswept open moorland, high above the town of Burnley. As a bonus for many Burnley supporters on match days, The Singing Ringing Tree was sometimes visible on a clear day to supporters sitting in the upper tier of the north stand.

When they arrived, the only other car in the small parking area was in the process of being filled by a young couple with their small toddler. Which meant that as they walked over to the artwork, they found themselves alone.

For the first week in October, the weather could best be described as average. It was cool but not cold, and although the sky was overcast, the day was bright, not dismal. Luckily, there was no hint of rain in the air. However, unusually for a month renowned for gales, very little wind was blowing across the high moorland where the artwork sat, meaning very little 'singing' was coming through the pipes.

Walking for a few minutes, they found a patch of grass on the leeward side of the hill, well away from The Singing Ringing Tree. The grass was clear of droppings, even though it had been mown almost bare by the mouths of innumerable sheep. They settled down on the ground facing a wonderful view across the town to the flat-topped expanse of Pendle Hill in the far distance.

"Have you ever climbed Pendle Hill?" asked Ryan.

"Loads of times; it's John's favourite place. You?"

"Doesn't interest me at all. I'm not into all that healthy living and exercise stuff."

She glanced at his well-layered physique. *Yes, I can see that.*

"What do you like then?"

"Eating good food, drinking good beer, spending time in a nice pub, staying in and watching a good movie."

She smiled. "Sounds wonderful."

He glanced at the bag. "Are you hungry yet?" he asked.

Reaching into the carrier bag, Gretchen pulled out the larger Tupperware box. Smiling happily, she handed it to him.

"Here you go, cheese and pickle, I know they're your favourite. Oh, and there's a bag of salt and vinegar crisps too."

Ryan gratefully accepted, opening the box and heartily tucking in. "Thanks, I'm starving."

Cuddling up closely next to him, she bit into her own ham and tomato sandwich. "I'm so happy you're here, Ryan, I'd have been on my own all weekend."

He shifted slightly, and she turned her head to his and gently kissed him on the corner of his mouth. "What would you like to drink? I've got a can of Pepsi, two cans of Fosters and a couple of bottles of Budweiser."

Ryan grinned. "I'd love a Bud, thanks."

She turned away from him and reached over to her right, removing a bottle of Budweiser from the carrier bag and opening it with the bottle opener she'd pulled from the kitchen drawer. Glancing to her left, she saw him paying close attention to what she was doing. She pointed down across the valley. "Great view of the Turf from here!"

Removing his gaze from her to glance at the view she was pointing at was all the time she needed, as she deftly slipped the cyanide tablet into the top of the bottle and handed it to him.

EIGHTY-SIX

"Look, there's Gretchen's car!" The urgency in John's voiced was palpable as the taxi rounded a corner and crested the hill. The Singing Ringing Tree had been visible for the past two hundred metres, but the car park only came into view once they'd gained the extra height.

They pulled up alongside the blue Skoda. "That'll be—" the taxi driver began.

"Here," said Becki, shoving another fifty pounds into his hands. "Will that cover it?"

The driver looked astonished. "Yes, that's very generous."

Becki opened her door and looked at the driver. "Would you mind waiting again?"

He shook his head. "Sorry, I've got a pickup in Colne at 1.15."

"Oh well, thanks for your help."

The men had vacated the rear seats and joined Becki on the uneven, rocky path leading away from the parking area.

"Come on," said Ian. "Let's find them." His words were growled through gritted teeth. "That bitch is going to admit what she's done!"

He strode off at a fast pace along the two-metre-wide stony path.

Reaching The Singing Ringing Tree in less than a minute, they were dismayed to find Gretchen and Ryan nowhere to be seen. Four pairs of eyes scanned the hillside in all directions, but try as they might, they couldn't locate them. The bright, but cloud-covered, sky added a brooding dimension to their search, perfectly matching how they felt.

"Did you two come here often?" asked Joe.

John nodded. "At least once a month, she absolutely loves the place."

"Then where are they?"

"Come on, mate," said Ian, urging John to remember anything that might help. "Does she have a favourite spot or a favourite view?"

John's eyes suddenly widened. "Yes, she loves the view over to Pendle!"

All eyes turned towards Pendle Hill, looming large in the far distance, a whisper of cloud kissing its flat summit.

"Come on, let's go!" Becki led the charge, the men hurrying behind her.

Fifty metres down the hillside, heading away from the artwork in the direction of Pendle Hill, Ian suddenly spotted Gretchen and Ryan leaning back against rocks in a small, sheltered hollow. Their backs were towards the hunters, who they clearly hadn't heard approaching. He lifted a finger to his lips, urging everyone to remain as quiet as possible.

Creeping closer, they watched as Gretchen sipped from a can of Coke, while Ryan drank from a bottle of beer. Placing the bottle by his side, they faintly heard him say, "Just what the doctor ordered."

In a flash, Ian sprinted the last few metres and launched himself over the rocks to land in front of the startled pair.

Ryan leapt to his feet, spinning around to see that Ian wasn't alone. "What the fuck are you all doing here?"

As they'd approached, Joe had surreptitiously turned on the video on his mobile phone, holding it close to him, recording everything that happened and everything being said.

Ian pointed at Gretchen, standing right in front of her. "She's a murderer, Ryan! She's the TCP killer and she's also killed a woman called Emily Spicer in Skipton!"

Gretchen laughed hard and shook her head. She glared barely disguised hatred at Ian but didn't deny his claim.

Thinking quickly, John stepped forward to stand alongside his friend. "Ian's right, Ryan, he's shown me copies of videos Emily showed him when they met on Friday evening! Videos that show Gretchen at every one of the murder locations. We've sent them to the police and they're out to arrest her."

The laughter swiftly left Gretchen's mouth, and suddenly she looked frightened. Then, suddenly, a cruel smile turned up the corners of her mouth. "You're right, I am the killer." She casually took a sip from her can. "And, yes, I killed that bitch on Friday too… she had it coming." Placing the can on the grass, she lifted herself to sit upright. "But today I've gone one better. This might just be my greatest achievement."

Becki, who had been staring open-mouthed listening to Gretchen's admissions, finally found her voice. "You evil bitch!"

Gretchen smirked dismissively.

"What do you mean today is your greatest achievement?" Joe asked.

The crow's feet around Gretchen's eyes deepened as she smiled cruelly at Joe. "You may think you've won. But today's the day I've finally destroyed the Pals. None of you will ever get over this."

"What do you mean?" asked Joe. "Never get over what?"

She pointed to Ryan, her features emotionless. "Ryan's just swallowed the same amount of cyanide that killed that pratt at

West Brom. Once he's dead, your precious Pals will never be the same again."

The blood drained from Ryan's face, his heart beating fast. He stared back at the woman he'd thought he loved so much.

"No, no, no… why would you… I thought we were…"

Gretchen sneered nastily. "Then you're more stupid than you look. *We* were never going to be anything."

Pushing Ian aside, Becki pulled her arm back and punched Gretchen hard in the nose, bursting it open and causing a torrent of blood to pour down her face. At the same time, her head whipped backwards from the blow and the back of her head hit the rock hard. She cried out in pain and lifted her arms to protect herself from further blows. Becki screamed in her face.

"You're lying. You're fucking lying!"

Lowering her forearms to reveal a mixture of blood, snot and mucus smeared across her features, Gretchen spat blood from her mouth at Becki's feet. "He's going to die the most horribly painful death, and he deserves it. You all do."

"I don't feel great, Becks," Ryan muttered suddenly, his chest heaving as he breathed in. "I feel dizzy."

"Sit down here, mate," said John. "I'll call an ambulance."

"Call the police, too," said Becki. She turned to Ryan. "When did she give you the bottle?"

"About a minute before you arrived."

Becki crouched down in front of him, her face close to his. "Ryan, you're going to be fine!" she said firmly.

Rummaging in her handbag, she pulled out her customary bottle of water, then dived into the front pouch, where she kept various items purloined from cafés and restaurants: small sachets of ketchup, sugar, HP sauce, pepper and several of the one she required at that moment – salt.

"Ryan, get on your knees!"

"What for?"

"Do you want to live or not? Get on your fucking knees!"

Ryan did as he was told. John called the emergency services, while Ian secured the bottle which contained the poison.

"This will put you away for the rest of your life," he said, holding up the bottle as he stood guard over her. "Why, Gretchen? All those innocent people are dead, and for what?"

Leaning back on the rock, she spat out another globule of bloody spit. "To see you all suffer, that's what." She nodded at Ryan. "And when he's dead, the job will be complete."

As she said this, Ryan groaned in agony as his stomach cramped hard, folding him almost double as he clutched his abdomen.

Having separated the sachets, Becki opened her bottle of water and poured the salt in, before screwing the top back on and shaking it vigorously.

Suddenly, the distant sound of approaching sirens could be heard. Joe knelt next to Ryan, an arm around his shoulder. "The ambulance will be here soon, mate. Hang on in there!"

Kneeling on the ground in front of Ryan, Becki lifted his chin to look him directly in the eyes.

"I'm sorry, Ryan, this is going to be horrible, but you need to drink the whole bottle in one go, and you're not going to find it easy." She removed the bottle cap.

"What for?"

"You need to be sick as quickly as possible, before more of the poison gets into your system. It's the only way we can flush it out of you. You haven't drunk more than about half of the bottle, and the poison hasn't had much time to work yet."

He nodded and took the bottle from her.

"Come on, Ryan," said John. "Imagine you're in the Dyche, down in one!"

Lifting the bottle to his mouth, Ryan poured the contents

down his throat, his face screwing up in disgust at the foul taste of heavily salted water.

"For fuck's sake, that's awful." He reached out a pleading arm to his friends. "Give me something to wash it down with!"

"No!" shouted Becki, before any of the men had the chance to react. "We don't want to dilute the mixture. His body will want it out soon enough."

The sirens were now very close by.

"I'll run to the car park and guide them in," said Ian.

John looked down at the bloody face of his ex-girlfriend. "How could you be this evil?"

She raised her eyes to meet his. She spoke softly. "All I wanted was you to love me more than Burnley." A tear ran slowly down her cheek. "Was that too much to ask?"

"I did love you."

Gretchen's face contorted with anger, and now her words were full of vitriol. "Well, it wasn't enough to top your love for fucking Burnley, was it?"

John couldn't hold her gaze, staring instead at the wild moorland above her head. "I'm sorry, Gretchen."

Ryan had started to heave, but nothing was coming out. Becki pulled him forwards onto his hands and knees.

"Open your mouth as wide as you can!"

Ryan did as he was told, and Becki pulled an emery board from her handbag.

"I'm going to tickle your gag reflex; that should help." Ryan nodded. She bent to look into his mouth and carefully slid the emery board deep into his throat. Almost immediately, Becki's hand was covered with a deluge of Ryan's stomach contents, soaking the cuff of her sleeve as he heaved and heaved.

Moments later, they were joined by two uniformed police officers and two paramedics. One of the paramedics quickly took control of Ryan, as Becki relayed his condition to them.

They injected him with something, then helped him to his feet and guided him back up the hill towards the ambulance.

"I'll go with him," Becki said to Ian, John and Joe. "I'll call you later." Ian gave her a quick hug, then she jogged up the hill and disappeared from view.

The police officers listened to what everyone had to say, then viewed the video Joe had taken on his mobile and seized the bottle of Budweiser as evidence. Moments later, they arrested and cautioned Gretchen for murder, who had a sneering smile playing on her lips throughout. As she was led away, she shouted, "Don't get your hopes up, Ryan's dead. Do you hear me? Dead!"

Becki, John and Ian were asked to attend the police station, where comprehensive statements were taken from them. Once they'd finished, they headed over to Burnley General Hospital, desperate to know how Ryan was.

EIGHTY-SEVEN

Ten weeks later

"We love you, Burnley, we do! Oh, Burnley, we love you!" As the cold early December rain battered on the pub's windowsills, The Claret Pals were in good voice, gathered around a large table inside the Coach and Horses, a fifteen-minute walk from Carrow Road, the home of Norwich City Football Club.

Burnley had been on a great run since the shocking events at The Singing Ringing Tree, winning five games and drawing four, leaving them second in the table, only two points below leaders Coventry City. The away allocation of 1,600 tickets for the match was sold out, and Burnley fans were hopeful of a swift return to the Premier League.

Stuart returned to the group struggling with a large tray laden with drinks.

"Here, let me help," said Simon, lifting two pints of beer from the tray and lightening the load. He handed one of the pints to Joe, who chinked glasses with Simon.

"Cheers, mate."

Jack, Ginny, John, Ian, Val, Ollie and Becki lifted their drinks from the tray, thanking Stuart as they did so.

"I've heard a whisper that Gretchen is up for sentencing at the Old Bailey sometime in the new year – is that right?" Becki's question was directed at John, who was sitting alongside her at one end of the table.

"It is," said John. "She finally decided to plead guilty to all charges, after fucking about for weeks."

"What's she likely to get?" asked Simon.

"The detectives who took my statement reckon a life sentence with a minimum thirty-year recommendation."

"I reckon she might get a full life sentence," said Ian.

"That would be wonderful," said Becki.

Ian prodded his left ear with a finger. "It would be, but it doesn't help Ryan, does it? We haven't seen him for weeks."

"That's true," said Val. She turned to Becki. "By the way, how's he getting on?"

Becki looked straight past Val and smiled. "Why don't you ask him yourself?"

All eyes turned to where Becki was looking and the Pals were astounded to see Ryan walking into the pub, a beaming smile on his face.

"He was declared fit to travel by his consultant earlier this week," said Becki. "We came up together last night and stayed in a little bed and breakfast. We thought we'd surprise you all!"

Engulfed by hugs, kisses and handshakes, Ryan lapped up the attention. Ian wrapped an arm around him and shook his hand vigorously.

"It's great to see you, big fella! We thought you'd not make a game until at least the new year."

"So did I, but my consultant called me in the week and said my scans have shown a massive improvement. He now thinks I'll make a full recovery."

"Brilliant news!" said Stuart. "Now you're back, the Pals are up to full strength again."

Joe decided the group should celebrate with a song. Raising his voice to the roof, he leant back and sang. "I went to an alehouse I used to frequent, I saw Kenny bastard, his money was spent."

The Pals wrapped arms around each other and raised their glasses as they joined in. "He asked me to play, I answered him nay, said rubbish like yours I could beat any day! And it's no nay never, no nay never no more, till we play bastard Rovers, no never no more! We hate bastards! We hate bastards! We hate…"

John leant to shout in Ian's ear. "I fucking love this group, don't you?"

Ian laughed and they chinked glasses as the singing came to an end.

"Burnley fans, best fans in England by a country mile!"

"Hey, Ryan," said Joe.

"What?"

"See that girl over by the doorway, the one with the long, dark hair?"

"Yeah."

"I think she fancies you. Why don't you ask her out?"

A wide smile creased Ryan's face. "Fuck off, Joe!"